VILLA MIRABELLA

FICTION   Pezzelli, Peter.
Pezzelli
P.   Villa Mirabella

JUN´ - 2010 $15.00

DATE DUE

(6+1) 2/19/11

Books by Peter Pezzelli

HOME TO ITALY

EVERY SUNDAY

FRANCESCA'S KITCHEN

ITALIAN LESSONS

VILLA MIRABELLA

Published by Kensington Publishing Corporation

VILLA MIRABELLA

PETER PEZZELLI

KENSINGTON BOOKS
www.kensingtonbooks.com

KENSINGTON BOOKS are published by

Kensington Publishing Corp.
119 West 40th Street
New York, NY 10018

All Kensington titles, imprints, and distributed lines are available at special quantity discounts for bulk purchases for sales promotion, premiums, fundraising, educational, or institutional use.

Special book excerpts or customized printings can also be created to fit specific needs. For details, write or phone the office of the Kensington Special Sales Manager: Kensington Publishing Corp., 119 West 40th Street, New York, NY 10018. Attn. Special Sales Department. Phone: 1-800-221-2647.

Kensington and the K logo Reg. U.S. Pat. & TM Off.

ISBN-13: 978-0-7582-2051-6
ISBN-10: 0-7582-2051-0

First Kensington Trade Paperback Printing: June 2010
10   9   8   7   6   5   4   3   2   1

Printed in the United States of America

To
Susan, Lauren, Paul, and Lisa

ACKNOWLEDGMENTS

Writing a book is a solitary endeavor. Getting one published, however, is not. It takes a team, and I am truly blessed with a great one. I owe a world of thanks to many people, dedicated and hardworking people, without whom this book would never have found its way into your hands.

And so I must say *mille grazie!* to all the wonderful people at Kensington Publishing who do so much to produce, promote, and sell my books. Special thanks to my editor, John Scognamiglio, for all his patience and guidance; to my publicist, Maureen Cuddy; to Kristine Mills-Noble, who designs my book jackets, and to George Angelini, whose beautiful illustrations grace them; to everyone at Jane Rotrosen Agency, particularly Meg Ruley and Christina Hogrebe, for their wise counsel and support, and Peggy Gordijn, who handles my books' foreign rights; to all my family, but especially my children, Andrew and Gabriella, and my wife, Corinne, who inspire and encourage me in so many ways.

And lastly, greatest of thanks, as always, to that greatest of publishers, He who makes all stories possible.

CHAPTER I

From somewhere, very far away it seemed, came the sound of a voice. Tender yet powerful, it was raised in song, the sweet melody caressing the air like a mother comforting her child.

The voice, and the piano that accompanied it, was the first thing the young man heard when he awoke, opened his eyes, and peered out into the blackness in which he was enveloped. At first he paid it no heed. How could he when, as so often happened to him, he was immediately beset by the dreadful feeling that the air was being squeezed out of his lungs? It was as if someone with a ponderously heavy boot was stepping on his chest, except this time it was heavier and more relentless than ever. Though curled into a ball, burrowed beneath the blankets as if in a cocoon, the young man was overcome by the sensation that he was laid out straight, suffocating, like someone who had been buried alive. In the inevitable moment of panic that ensued, he began to claw away the covers, struggling to escape until at last he emerged and lay there spent, gulping in the air while his heart pounded so hard that he thought it might burst.

The panic slowly subsided and his breathing became more regular, but the press of the boot against his chest remained. Lately, that particular sensation never went away completely; it dogged him every minute of the day and night, and he seemed always on the edge of succumbing to it. If he thought back, he could remember precisely the moment when it first began, but he had learned to avoid dwelling on the reminiscence of it, for it served only to torment him all the more and drain his precious energy.

At last, the young man sat up on the mattress—he no longer possessed the bed frame that once held it—and leaned his shoulders back against the wall. All was in shadows about him, the bedroom scarcely illumined by the faint sliver of daylight creeping over the top of the tightly drawn curtains. It was late morning, almost noon, but it still felt like the dead of the night. That's how things were for him. No matter now much he slept, he never felt rested, and his waking moments were passed in a perpetual state of exhaustion. Wearily, he closed his eyes once more and listened to the voice for a time.

It was a recording of Pavarotti, singing Schubert's "Ave Maria," that had awakened him. In a neighboring apartment—he had not been able to ascertain which one—some lover of opera had of late been playing his recordings at all hours. Though he himself was no great lover of opera, the young man had grown accustomed to hearing the music without truly listening to it. It was like a living sound track to him with ever-changing strains of sorrow and ecstacy, playfulness and passion, but one of which he had remained more or less oblivious. Now, however, for the first time, he found himself truly attending to the music, straining to hear each lyric, every note of the gentle tune.

". . . *Maria, grátia pléna* . . ."

On and on the tenor sang, his voice rising and falling with every heartfelt note.

The song was familiar to the young man, though he could not quite remember where or when he had heard it before. It kindled in his mind the flicker of some distant memory, but it was like something out of a sad dream that left in its wake only a sense of loss and sorrow, and the heaviness of regret, but no recollection of what had transpired in the subconscious.

"... óra pro nóbis peccatóribus ..."

He understood not a single word of it, and yet the simple beauty of the song moved the young man to the brink of tears, tears he choked back with great difficulty. The music evoked a hunger in him, one sharper and more insistent than the one gnawing at the pit of his stomach. Though he had not eaten in two days, deep within he realized that he was craving something other than food or drink, but precisely what he could not say. And so he listened all the more intently to the voice, hoping it would tell him.

"... nunc et in hóra mórtis. Amen ..."

The voice and the music finally died away, leaving the room in an unearthly silence that magnified all the more the young man's solitude. He sank back down onto the mattress for a moment, wanting with all his being to curl back into the protective shell in which he had slept, but he found that the covers no longer held any warmth. Not that it mattered, for he knew that the refuge of sleep would come no more to him that day. Against his inclination to remain there, he rolled his legs off the mattress and onto the floor, where he knelt for a time, wondering what he should do. At last he got to his feet, went slowly to the window, and drew back the curtains.

The January sky over Los Angeles was shrouded in dark, heavy clouds, and yet the gray daylight still hurt his eyes as he squinted and gazed out toward the marina. He had always loved the view from his apartment, the neat arrangement of the boats in their stately elegance, the sunlight reflecting off the water. It all made him feel special somehow, but the privilege of having it had come at a steep price. Once upon a time he had been happy to pay it, but those days had come to an end for him.

Now, as he looked blankly out the window, he scarcely noticed the view, for his thoughts had turned his attention inward. He was trying to recapture the sound of the voice, the one that had awakened him, to understand what it had been trying to tell him, but the recollection of it was just out of his reach. Hanging his head, he turned from the window and slouched off to the bathroom.

When he threw some water on his face and looked up into the mirror, it was a far older-looking, more careworn man than he expected to find staring back at him. The bloodshot eyes, the matted hair, the haggard unshaven face. The sight of himself was a shock, and he felt anew the too-familiar tightening in his chest and the quickening of his breath. He looked away and hurried back out to the corridor and into the living room. There the young man stopped for a moment to steady himself against the wall with one hand while he put the other to his head.

He looked about in dismay and bewilderment.

All was quiet and still as a tomb. Save for a solitary lamp in the corner, the room was empty, all the furnishings having been sold or repossessed, the faint indentations in the carpet the only evidence that anything had ever rested there. Where had everything—and everyone—gone? It seemed like only yesterday when that same room had been routinely filled with laughter and smiling faces. The smiles had come his way easily then. What had happened to drive them all away? He knew full well the answer, of course, but that knowledge comforted him little, so he closed his mind to it.

The young man continued on to the kitchen, where he stood for a time at the counter, the marble tiles cold against his bare feet, while he considered the unopened envelope addressed to him resting there. It had arrived yesterday via certified mail. He took the envelope and held it up before him.

"Jason Mirabella?" he wondered aloud, as if the addressee were a complete stranger to him. "Who's he?"

He said it only partly in jest, for his name no longer seemed to belong to him, but to someone else from some other place and time. It was as if he had been cast off from this world and set adrift, like a ghost trapped somewhere in the dark void between one life and another.

Jason dropped the envelope back onto the counter. There was no point in opening it, for he already knew it contained a letter telling him that he was being evicted from the apartment for nonpayment of rent. He had been expecting the missive for some time. The only surprise was that it had not come sooner.

The telephone rang, shattering the quiet and giving him a start. He was hesitant to answer it. Hardly anyone called these days, and even then, more often than not, it was someone looking for money. The electric company. The gas company. His landlord. The bars and restaurants who had once been happy to let him run up his tabs. Jason owed more than a few dollars to more than a few people. Having nothing left to give them, he decided to wait for the answering machine to pick up the call.

"Jay, it's Eddie," came the voice over the answering machine. "Come on, pick up, buddy. I know you're in there."

Jason took a breath and picked up the receiver. "I'm here."

"Hey, there you are," said Eddie easily. "I knew you were in there hiding someplace, screening your calls. So, what's the deal? Where's the party at tonight?"

Eddie was being kind. He was well aware of Jason's situation, and was just trying to keep things light. Jason appreciated it. Of all his friends, Eddie was the only one left who didn't run and hide every time Jason tried to get in touch. He was the only one still willing to help him in any way he could.

Jason glanced at the envelope on the counter.

"I don't know where the party is," he admitted with a sigh. "But I can tell you that it's definitely not here." He paused for a moment and closed his eyes, as if in prayer. "So, anything?" he asked.

There was an equivalent pause on the other end of the line.

"Nothing," Eddie finally said. "I floated your name to a couple of people here and at the studio, told them you were a marketing genius, that you'd be a perfect fit—but no takers yet. Beyond that, there's not much else to offer around here besides pushing a broom."

"I didn't think so," said Jason, his voice heavy with resignation. "Thanks, though. I appreciate your trying."

"Hey, don't get down," Eddie told him. "You've got to be patient. It's gonna take a while, so you'll just have to sit tight and wait for this whole mess you got yourself into to blow over. You know how it is out here. L.A.'s all about today. You just have to give people time enough to forget about yesterday. Understand?"

Jason replied that he did, but he said so with little conviction. Yes, he understood quite well what his friend was telling him, but he was not so sure that he agreed. Yesterdays, he had found to his great distress, had a way of darkening today no matter how hard one tried to bury them or hoped for them to drift away and vanish forever like clouds over the horizon.

Jason tried to listen as Eddie continued to give him words of encouragement, but he found his thoughts inevitably taking him back to the voice and the music, the sound of it echoing once more in the deepest chambers of his heart and mind. It haunted him with its calling, and evoked once more that same hunger, that same peculiar sense of longing that he could not quite name, but that would not leave him alone.

The more he dwelt on it, the more it began to dawn on Jason that perhaps this strange yearning welling up inside him was not so unfamiliar as he had at first led himself to believe. As he considered it more closely, he realized that it had been growing steadily stronger for many days, tugging at him with greater and greater insistence, but he had been like a child, his own stubbornness and pride blinding him to the truth. Now, as he half listened to Eddie, his mind awhirl as he tried to sort out what to do next, Jason found that he could no longer ignore its beckoning. He puzzled and puzzled over it, his thoughts adrift on a darkened sea, until all at once everything became clear to him, like the flash of a beacon on a distant shore, cutting through the night to show him where he had to go.

Home.

"Jay," said Eddie, "are you still there?"

"Yeah, I'm still here," said Jason.

"So, what do you think? What are you going to do?"

Jason turned the question over in his mind for a moment.

"I'm gonna clean myself up," he finally told him. "And then I'm going back."

"Where, back East?" said Eddie.

"That's right."

"Come on, you gotta be kidding," Eddie huffed. "How can you go back? You know you love it out here. Wasn't it you that always said that L.A. was your lady?"

"Maybe she was," said Jason. "But the lady dumped me, in case you hadn't noticed."

There was a long silence at the other end of the line.

"So, how long you think you'll stay away?"

Jason took the envelope once more and looked at his name.

"I don't know," he said. "I guess as long as it takes."

The next day found Jason Mirabella standing in the terminal of Los Angeles International Airport. Only after a diligent search of every pocket of his clothing had he been able to scrape together enough cash for the cab fare to get him there that morning. As he took his place in the line to the ticket counter, his bags in hand, it struck him that he was leaving Los Angeles with even less than he had brought there when he first arrived four years earlier. That day and all its promise seemed so long ago, almost as if it had been nothing but a dream. Jason shook his head to dispel the memory, leaving it for some other day's ruminations as the line moved ahead.

"How can I help you?" said the pleasant young woman when Jason finally made his way up to the ticket counter.

Once upon a time, Jason might have been ready with some playful rejoinder to the innocent question, but such confidence had long since abandoned him. Now it was all he could do to muster a smile.

"I'm looking for a flight to Providence," he told her.

Jason might have called ahead to make a reservation, he reflected ruefully, but his telephone service had been disconnected the previous day, not long after he had finished talking to Eddie.

"Hmm, let's see what we can do for you," replied the young woman, thoughtfully scanning her monitor as she tapped away at the keyboard.

While he waited, Jason looked around at the other passengers coming and going through the terminal. Black, white, Asian, Hispanic. It seemed like he was at the hub of the world, getting ready to fly off to the farthest end of one of its spokes.

"I can get you there," said the young woman after a few moments, "but nothing nonstop, I'm afraid."

"That's okay," Jason said. "I'm not in a big hurry. I'm just looking for the best available fare."

"I think we can manage that," she told him. "Are you looking for round-trip?"

Jason hesitated and looked about once more with despairing eyes.

"No," he sighed at last. "Let's make it one way."

Then he gave her his credit card and prayed that the charge would go through.

CHAPTER 2

"It can't be fixed."

Thus spoke Sal, the furnace guy.

The verdict was pronounced with an air of finality that, to anyone else, would have indicated that the issue at question had been officially closed. The tone of Sal's voice left no doubt as to where his thoughts stood on the matter, or the firmness of his conviction. He had examined all of the pertinent facts of the case, looked things up and down from every possible angle, considered them in every conceivable way, and finally rendered his judgment with the authority of a chief justice.

The furnace could not be fixed. Case closed.

Sal gave a grunt that conveyed an air of smug satisfaction, as if to announce that his long-held suspicions had finally been confirmed. Still down on one knee, he pulled back from the front of the furnace he had been inspecting and glanced over his shoulder at the gentleman standing behind him. The other man had observed the proceedings with keen interest, his eyes reflecting a modicum of concern, but not so much as to indicate that his state of mind had devolved into true worry.

The two were in the basement, a dark, confined, breathless place with a low ceiling and grimy stone walls. The space was just large enough to accommodate the enormous furnace, the oil tank, and a pair of sizable hot water heaters, but not much else. Apparently little thought had been given to the advantages of a large open basement by those who had constructed the house above over a century ago.

Sal turned back to eye the furnace and gave another satisfied grunt, further emphasizing his opinion that the mechanism had breathed its last.

Giulio Mirabella, however, the proprietor of the heating system in question as well as the house it heated, was not quite convinced, and was inclined to further consider the merits of Sal's case. With a furrowed brow, he looked over the shoulder of the repairman, who by now was gazing once more into the inner workings of the furnace, probing about with a flashlight in one hand and a screwdriver in the other.

"What do you mean it can't be fixed?" said Giulio, straining to see and understand exactly what the problem might be.

Sal gave an exaggerated sigh and turned his gaze upward, as if to say it was difficult for him to explain such things to mere mortals. He shone the light on the interior of the furnace and gestured for Giulio to take a closer look.

"See here?" he replied, wagging the screwdriver at the burner. "The whole thing is shot. Good for nothing."

Giulio eyed the apparatus with some skepticism. This was not the first time that the furnace had been declared dead upon Sal's arrival. In fact, the diagnosis was always the same whenever Giulio called upon him, as he had that morning, because the furnace had seen fit to engage in one of its periodic work stoppages. This time around it had chosen to go on strike just as a blast of arctic air had swept over southern New England, and winter had settled in over the region in earnest. It would not be long before the rooms upstairs grew chilly and guests began to complain. Nonetheless, despite the pressure to simply accept the repairman's gloomy assessment of the situation and proceed accordingly, Giulio was not ready to give in.

"There must be something you can do," he ventured.

Sal put down the screwdriver and flashlight, and pressed his hands together in a gesture of supplication. "Please, Giulio," he said. "Listen to what I say this time. It would take a miracle to fix this thing, and trust me, I'm no saint."

Giulio was moved by this last revelation, but he was still not convinced. He suspected that, despite the dire state of affairs with the burner, there was still a glimmer of hope that all with the furnace was not yet completely lost.

"Just figure out something to get us through one more winter, Sal," he implored him with equal fervor. "I know you can do it. One more winter, that's all I ask."

"Ayyy, you've been saying that same thing for years," groused Sal.

"Yes, and every year you've gotten us through," Giulio pointed out, sensing a change in the repairman's demeanor, a softening in his resolve that the furnace was beyond repair.

"Giulio, why won't you believe me?" lamented Sal. "You need a new furnace here. Even if I could get this one working again—and I'm not saying I can!—the thing is old and inefficient. You're throwing good money after bad. It's time to reinvest. Why can't you get that through your head?"

"I know, I know," sighed Giulio with a shrug. "You're probably right—"

"I *am* right!"

"Eh, maybe," Giulio went on. "But you see, I've grown accustomed to this old furnace. Yes, I know it gets a little moody sometimes, but it's like a part of the family to me. I can't just throw it out."

"Oh yes, you can," Sal noted, though by now it was clear to both men that he had lost the upper hand in the argument, if indeed he had ever held it. He turned back to the furnace and gestured at it with palms upward, then back to Giulio, his face twisted into an expression of acute consternation.

Giulio gave him a kind smile and patted him on the shoulder.

"I know you'll figure out something, Sal," he told him.

Sal let out a low growl before muttering something unmentionable regarding his customer's penurious bent. Pretending not to have heard, Giulio gave a nervous cough, turned, and started for the staircase.

"I'm making no promises this time!" Sal called after him. "No guarantees!"

"Of course," Giulio called back over his shoulder. "Just do the best you can for me."

With that he took hold of the handrail and briskly ascended the dusty wooden steps that led to the first floor.

When he stepped out into the back hall, Giulio was greeted by the sound of a vacuum cleaner running somewhere up on the second floor, and the clinking of the breakfast plates and silverware being collected in the dining room. In the living room, his son Raymond was whistling a tune while he changed a bulb in one of the light fixtures. In the study his daughter, Natalie, was on the telephone, booking a room for a prospective guest. It was late morning, nearly noon, and these were the goings-on of a typical day at the Bradley Mansion Inn.

Built in the late nineteenth century, Bradley Mansion was once home to a prosperous textile magnate and his family in a once elegant neighborhood on the edge of Providence. When the family's fortunes, and those of the rest of the neighborhood, eventually declined, the grand residence with its beautiful tall windows, high ceilings, and handcrafted woodwork throughout its many stately rooms gradually fell into disrepair. It changed hands several times and in the end was left abandoned. It was a story played out many times in the area, and what was once a stylish section of the old city had turned into a virtual ghost town.

As a young man, Giulio Mirabella had dabbled in a variety of trades, with only modest success at any of them, before he decided to try his hand as a property manager with a local real estate firm. It was during that time, nearly forty years ago now, that he had first come upon the mansion. By then it was a tired, faded image of its glorious past, and could be had for little more than a song. Eager to acquire some investment property of his own, he arranged for a tour of the house, intending to renovate it and convert it into commercial office space. Over the years, many of the other lovely homes in the neighborhood had likewise been converted into doctor or lawyer offices, funeral parlors, and other enterprises. That was how the money was to be made with these old properties, and the recently affianced Giulio had been keen to start making some of his own in the same way.

That at least had been the plan until Giulio invited his future wife, Vera, to accompany him on his first walk-through of the house. Together they had wandered about the empty old mansion like specters, moving through the spacious foyer into the dining room where the original chandelier still hung, and then out into the kitchen with its wide counters and ample cabinets, up the wide main staircase with its beautiful banister to the second floor, through all the bedrooms, many with their own fireplaces, and up the back staircase to the servants' quarters, then down again all the way to the back hall, past the study, and finally into the living room with its great fireplace and mantel, trying all the while to imagine how it all must have looked years ago in its original splendor.

As the two stood in the middle of the room, Vera had taken his arm while she gazed at the empty fireplace.

"Imagine what it must have been like to cuddle up here in front of a big fire," she had sighed, her eyes gleaming, "then to go upstairs and sleep in one of those bedrooms, then come down to have breakfast the next morning in that sunny little alcove off the kitchen or maybe in the dining room or even right here next to the front window. How wonderful it must have been."

The thought of it was indeed wonderful, and that was the moment when the idea for the Bradley Mansion Inn first sprang into Giulio Mirabella's imagination.

The rest was history.

Now, as Giulio made his way through the front hallway, he thought of his wife, as he often did when he made his daily tour of the premises. Vera had taken ill and passed away unexpectedly five years earlier, but to this day he still heard her voice, playfully chiding him for strutting about the inn like a sea captain inspecting his ship. The analogy was not so inapt, for Giulio had come to love the old place every bit as much as a sea captain loved his vessel. To him it was more than just a pleasing amalgam of wood and stone and plaster and glass; it was a living, breathing organism with its own unique personality and peculiar ways. There was the odd rattle and hum of the radiators (when the furnace was of a mind to work) and the way the wind sometimes whispered and moaned down the chimney. In the morning there was the lingering scent of burned wood from the previous night's fire in the fireplace, and the way it mingled with the warm aroma of coffee brewing at breakfast time. There were the ever-shifting patterns of sunlight streaming through the windows at different angles throughout the day, the way the mood of every room changed as the sun arced its way from east to west. Giulio particularly liked the way the soft light of the late afternoon sun beamed through the window over the staircase, illuminating the stairs and the landing while casting long shadows through the downstairs hallway, lending an air of mystery to the rest of the interior. Then of course there were the guests who came and let the house take them into its embrace and keep them safe and comfortable for a night or two. He took great pleasure in playing the host and seeing the house cast its spell on them.

Just the same, the operation of the inn was far from a pleasure cruise for its captain. Like a ship that had been too long at sea, the old house was in constant need of refitting. Today it happened to be the furnace that required repair, but on another day it might be the plumbing, or the window casings, or the electrical system, or the roof, or one of the doors, or any one of a thousand things. Then there was the condition of the paint and wallpaper to monitor, as well as that of the lovely old carpets and furniture. There was a fine line between old-style charm and dilapidation, and Giulio spent many of his days trying to navigate it. In doing so, hard decisions often had to be made to keep passengers and crew alike happy. It was a work constantly in progress.

Times were not always easy—it had taken years of struggle and sacrifice to make a go of the operation—and when he had lost Vera, Giulio had at first considered selling the inn and retiring, for he could not imagine managing it without her. Somehow, though, the house and the satisfaction of working with his adult children and keeping them close had kept him from falling to pieces. He felt an obligation to return the favor, and so he had stayed at the helm, but always while carrying with him the memory of his first and only mate.

A young Asian couple from Taiwan was descending the stairs arm in arm as Giulio made his way to the second floor. Bundled up for the cold, they appeared to be on their way out to do some sightseeing. The two spoke English well enough, but they were quite reserved in a nice way. From what he had been able to gather when they checked in the day before, Giulio believed they were on their honeymoon. He could not imagine why they had chosen to come to Providence in the middle of the winter when they might have visited other, far warmer climes in the United States, but he was glad to have them and broke out into a smile as they approached. The two smiled in return.

"Out to see the city?" said Giulio brightly.

"Yes," said the husband with a polite nod.

"This is our first time here," added his wife in a sweet voice.

"Ah, well then, enjoy yourselves," replied Giulio, always happy to be the first to welcome strangers to his little city. "And if you need a street map, or want to know where to find some good restaurants, or where to shop, or any other information, just stop at the study downstairs on your way out and my daughter will be glad to help you."

The couple nodded appreciatively and went on their way while Giulio continued up the stairs to the second floor. There, Mrs. Martinez, a middle-aged Guatemalan woman he had only just recently hired, was pushing the vacuum cleaner across the carpet that ran the length of the corridor. Mrs. Martinez was as capable and efficient a housekeeper as Giulio could hope for, but he found her a bit disconcerting, for she had a rather forbidding demeanor. She rarely spoke, and usually did so with caustic brevity. Indeed she tended to communicate more with her dark, expressive eyes than with words. Giulio could not be quite certain whether the cause of this reticence was an imperfect knowledge of the English language—her citizenship status was somewhat questionable—or an indication that she simply did not like him. He suspected the former, but could not rule out the latter. In any case, good housekeepers were hard to find, and so he saw fit to treat her with deference.

"Good morning, Mrs. Martinez," he said as he passed with caution, not wanting to appear to be checking on her work, even though that was precisely his job. "How are you today?"

The housekeeper turned off the vacuum cleaner just long enough to issue a curt "Good morning, Mr. Giulio" and a polite nod. Then in a matter-of-fact tone she added, "Chilly in here today."

This last remark she made while shooting Giulio a glance that one could only have described as accusatory. It had the effect of making him feel guilty for having kept the long depreciated furnace in operation against Sal's advice. As she resumed her vacuuming, Giulio mumbled something to the effect that he was working on that particular problem and hurried along to complete his rounds.

Later, after he finally made his way back downstairs, Giulio found his daughter in the study. Natalie, a sweater draped over her shoulders, was seated at the desk, wearing a worried frown as she entered the latest occupancy numbers into the computer. January was a notoriously slow month, and as usual the house was more than three-quarters empty. It could be nerve-wracking, waiting for the telephone to ring or for a guest to walk through the front door. The gnawing fear that the rooms would never be filled again hung heavy in the air, but Giulio had learned over the years how to weather the lean times.

"How are we doing today?" he said as he drew near to the desk. "I don't hear them banging down the door to get in."

"No, Dad, but it's still early," said Natalie with a smile that belied the anxious quaver in her voice. "Had a couple of calls about our room rates, but no reservations."

Giulio smiled warmly at his daughter, for he knew that she had a tendency to fret too much when the house was not full. Natalie handled most of the office duties for him. She was his middle child and the mother of two, both toddlers, and both the delight of their grandfather. Giulio was old-fashioned enough to sometimes wish that his daughter would stay at home with them and not bother working, but Natalie was a good reception-ist and an excellent bookkeeper. He would have been in trouble without her, so it was a comfort to him to know that at least the children were safe in the hands of her mother-in-law, who looked after them while Natalie and her husband worked.

"Don't worry," he assured her. "I'm sure by the weekend things will pick up." He leaned against the edge of the desk and looked out into the hallway. "Where is your brother?" he asked.

"He went to the hardware store," said Natalie. "He thought

the light in the living room just needed a new bulb, but I guess the whole fixture has to be replaced."

Giulio nodded thoughtfully. The need for such repairs arose constantly. Fortunately Natalie's older brother, Raymond, had developed into an excellent handyman and was quite adept at taking care of most of the daily maintenance and repair chores. Raymond helped him oversee the entire operation. Though not particularly imaginative, he had good business sense and was a hard worker, and he loved running the inn almost as much as his father. Giulio was grateful for that. He leaned over to get a peek at the computer monitor as Natalie went back to typing on the keyboard.

"Tell me," he said, "has anyone talked to Jason lately? I haven't heard from him since he called last month to say he wasn't coming home for Christmas."

"Not a word," said Natalie over her shoulder. "Don't worry, he'll call sooner or later. He always does."

"Maybe," said Giulio with a grunt.

Jason was the youngest of Giulio's three children. One could not rightly characterize him as his problem child; growing up, he had always been a good student—he was, in fact, the brightest of the three—and he had managed to stay out of trouble for the most part. Nonetheless, Jason had his own ideas about things and had always marched to the beat of his own drummer. Giulio had spent a pretty penny to put his son through college and business school, and had hoped for some return on his investment after graduation, but Jason had no interest at all in the family business. Instead he had gone off to California on his own to seek his fortune. Though it was a source of acute distress, Giulio had not tried to stop him, for he knew that there was nothing to be done for it. Giulio loved his children equally, but he had a soft spot in his heart for his younger son, and could not help but let him go his own way without complaint. Besides, by all accounts the move had paid off and Jason's career was beginning to soar. As much as it grieved him that he had moved so far away from home to work for strangers, Giulio could not begrudge his son's pursuing his own dreams and not those of his father.

Giulio felt a twinge of sadness at the thought of the great distance that separated him from his son, but he was suddenly heartened by the sound of pipes rattling in the walls. Then he heard the slamming of the basement door and footsteps in the hallway. A moment later, a scowling Sal appeared in the study doorway. Giulio looked at Natalie and gave her a nudge.

"Tell me," he said before Sal could say a word, "am I mistaken, or is that the heat I feel coming up?"

"Don't be surprised if they canonize me next week," grumbled the repairman, tossing the bill onto the desk.

Giulio gave a hearty laugh and patted Sal on the back, for once again he felt like Vera's sea captain. True, his ship had sprung a leak or two, but at least it would stay afloat and keep sailing for another day.

CHAPTER 3

Jason felt his shoulders sink back into the seat as the plane lifted off the runway and began to climb through the rain toward the slate-gray sky. Rising steadily, the plane banked gently to one side, giving him a brief glimpse of the city below. It pained him to watch it shrink from view, and for a moment he felt that familiar tightening in his chest, that awful grip of panic. He took a deep breath and slowly exhaled to calm himself. Then he put his hand to the window, as if doing so would help him hold on to the city a little longer, to take with him all the dreams he was leaving behind. There came a slight jostling of the cabin as the plane climbed ever steeper, a rush of water vapor across the wings, and then Los Angeles was lost behind the veil of clouds.

His ears popping from the change in air pressure, Jason stared out the window with forlorn eyes until the plane pierced the cloud cover and flew into the brilliant sunshine, the dome of crystal-blue sky stretching from horizon to horizon. The airliner was en route to Houston, the first stop on a zigzag journey across the country that would lead Jason home to Rhode Island. He would have preferred a more direct flight, but under the circumstances it was the best that he could manage. A tedious day awaited him, and there was little for him to do other than simply endure it.

Before long there came a chime from the public address system. The captain informed the passengers that the plane had reached its cruising altitude and that they were now free to move about the cabin. Jason unbuckled his seat belt and settled back, intent on closing his eyes and drifting away to wherever his thoughts would take him. Lately, though, his thoughts bore him ceaselessly into the past, the one place he was most anxious to avoid. And so, to pass the time, he found himself simply looking out the window at the endless expanse of sky, trying his best to think of nothing at all.

"Hey, buddy, you want something?" came a voice. It belonged to the man sitting beside him. A fortyish, burly sort, he had been perusing the morning newspaper ever since he took his seat just a few moments before departure. He gazed at Jason with friendly, inquisitive eyes, and nodded at the stewardess who had arrived a few moments before with the beverage cart. Lost in himself as he had been, Jason had not heard her ask if he would like a drink.

"Oh, sorry," he said, sitting up straight. He eyed the cart. At the moment, a good stiff drink might have suited him, but he had sworn off alcohol for the time being, and in any case he didn't have the cash to pay for one. "Ginger ale, please," he said.

"Dewar's and water for me, if you don't mind, darlin'," said the other man. He leaned toward Jason and gave him a wink and a nod. "I know it's a little early in the day for that, but even though I've flown this route a thousand times, I still need a little anesthetic now and then to get me through the flight—if you know what I mean."

Jason gave a faint smile in return, but inwardly cringed. He was not in the mood for conversation, no matter how pleasant, but he knew from experience that he had been seated next to a talker. The day before him was beginning to look even longer.

The beverages and peanuts dispensed, the stewardess pushed the cart to the next row of passengers. The man took a sip of his drink, then extended a beefy paw in Jason's direction.

"Name's Burt," said the man. "Glad to be ridin' with you." He made it sound as if the two had just met up on horseback and were getting ready to cross the prairie together.

"Jason," he answered reluctantly as the two shook hands.

"Ah, hell, that's another disappointment," said Burt with a sad shake of his head.

"I beg your pardon," said a puzzled Jason.

"Now, don't take it personal," Burt reassured him. "It's just that I keep hoping I'll sit next to an Ernie one of these days. Ya see, my little girl is only five and she just loves them two ragtop knuckleheads on *Sesame Street*. Damned if I wouldn't just love to come home, just once, and tell that sweet little thing that Burt and Ernie were flying together today. Course, the other Burt spells his name with an e, but that's no big."

Despite his disinclination to conversation, Jason could not help but give a little laugh. "I take it home is in Houston," he said.

"Yup," said Burt. "Just outside. I'm in insurance, property and casualty. Got a coupla big clients out in L.A., so I've got to drop in on them from time to time and make nice. How 'bout yourself? You goin' to Houston on business?"

"No, actually I'm on my way home, too," said Jason in a quiet voice. "I'm just connecting through Houston on my way back to Rhode Island."

"Sounds like you're taking the milkwagon route," opined Burt, pondering his beverage with a studied eye before downing another gulp. "What do you do for work back there in little ol' Rhode Island?"

"Nothing, right now," confessed Jason. "I've been in California for the past four years."

"Doing what?" said Burt with what seemed earnest curiosity.

Once again, Jason cringed. It was an innocent question, but one that made the back of his neck go hot with shame, inundating him with a wave of guilt. It made him feel like an exhausted swimmer who had suddenly found himself too far from shore.

"Well, I *was* in marketing," he admitted uneasily.

"Was?" said Burt.

"I'm moving back to Rhode Island—at least for now," said Jason with some hesitation.

"Who were you with out in L.A.?" asked Burt, persisting in this line of inquiry.

Jason did not reply right away. Had he wanted to, he could have simply evaded the question, or made up a fictitious name. Burt was a complete stranger to him, so what did he care? For some reason, though, Jason felt compelled to tell the truth. Still, he paused and took a quick look around at the other passengers nearby. Everyone seemed to be reading or listening to their music players or absorbed in conversations of their own. None, as far as he could see, had an ear inclined in his direction.

"Med-Device Technologies," he finally replied, keeping his voice low even though no one was paying him the slightest heed.

"Med-Device," repeated Burt thoughtfully. "That sounds familiar."

Jason remained silent.

"Say, I think I remember now," said Burt after a time. "I read about you guys in the paper when I was out in L.A. a while back. Weren't you the ones that were trying to sell that implant thing for people's hearts or blood or something like that?"

Jason only nodded, waiting with dread to see just how much of the story the other man recalled.

"Hmm," grunted Burt, eyeing him with a sober gaze. "You boys got yourself in some hot water, if I remember correctly. Really screwed the pooch. What was it now, something to do with the clinical trials, right? You didn't have anything to do with any of *that*, did you?"

Still Jason said nothing, knowing full well that the look on his face was answer enough. He waited for a rebuke, or the inevitable look of recrimination that he had grown accustomed to receiving. To his surprise, neither came. Instead, Burt simply downed the rest of his drink and considered the empty glass for a time before setting it down.

"Well, I suppose I wouldn't want to talk much about it either," he said. "And I can't say I blame ya for gettin' outta town. Probably would have done the same myself."

With that Burt pulled out his newspaper and opened it to the sports section. "Just tell me one thing," he added before he began to read, "that is, if you can. But what in blue blazes ever made you guys think that you could get away with it?"

Jason heaved a sigh.

"You had to be there," he finally said.

Then he turned to the window and lost himself once more in the empty sky.

CHAPTER 4

As he drove through the streets of Providence on his way back to the Bradley Mansion Inn, the bag of replacement parts for the living room light on the seat next to him, Raymond Mirabella cast a rueful look at the city's fledgling skyline. Providence was a far cry from Manhattan, he knew, but it had come a long way since he was a kid. Back then "downtown" consisted of a handful of buildings that one might consider tall, and aside from a few bright spots here and there, there wasn't much to brag about. Times had changed, though, and the city had undergone what one could only call a renaissance. Once the butt of jokes, Providence had suddenly blossomed into a vibrant, happening place. Old, blighted buildings had been torn down, the development of the riverfront areas had beautified the city, tourists were being drawn in, businesses were relocating there, and it seemed like a day rarely passed without plans being announced or ground broken for one sparkling new building or another.

This activity was, of course, all to the good for the little city and the surrounding regions. What grieved Raymond as he eyed the changing cityscape was that so much of the new construction sprouting from the revitalized Providence soil was for hotels. Big, beautiful, modern hotels with restaurants and shops and function rooms and nightclubs and all the modern amenities one might want. They were the future, which was not necessarily the type of competition you wanted when you derived your livelihood from a building that was essentially a relic.

The sight of them all brought a knot to his stomach.

Raymond loved helping his father run the inn; he had grown up in the business and he was good at it, but with the competition getting tougher every day, he could not help wondering how long it would be before a wrecking ball came swinging in their direction. If it was to survive, their little bed-and-breakfast operation needed to change, to adapt and grow somehow, but at this point he was at a loss as to precisely how to make that happen. And so he drove on, drumming his fingers against the steering wheel, hoping the needed solution would occur to him one day soon.

Natalie was still at the desk in the study, opening the morning's mail, when Raymond returned to the inn a short while later.

"Still cold out there?" she said as he tossed his coat and hat up onto the coat stand.

"Freezing," he grunted, shaking off the cold. "Thank God it feels like the heat's working in here again."

"Thank *Sal*," Natalie joked. "He left just a little while ago."

Raymond let out a groan.

"How much did it cost us this time?" he asked.

"Not too bad," said Natalie with a little sigh. "Cheaper than a new furnace, I guess."

"Yeah, I guess," muttered Raymond, "but I've got to learn how to take care of that thing myself. It keeps adding up." He sat on the edge of the desk and watched his sister sort the mail. "So, any calls while I was out?"

Natalie looked up at him with worried eyes and shook her head.

"It's been so quiet this month," she said. "What do you think it is?"

"I don't know," he told her. "But I'll tell you what, every time

I drive by one of those new places downtown I start to get *agita*."

"I know what you mean," said Natalie. "Do you think we're losing that much business to them?"

Raymond shrugged.

"It's hard to say," he replied. "Dad's always telling me that we shouldn't worry, that we have our own little niche here, and that the type of people who come to us don't want to stay in a big hotel, no matter how fancy it is. Who knows, maybe he's right. We started off pretty slow last winter too, and then we ended up having a pretty good year anyway. Still, I'd feel a whole lot better if we had a couple more rooms filled for tonight."

"So, what do we do?" said Natalie.

"I guess we just have to sit tight for now," replied Raymond, "and wait for the phone to ring."

"We?" Natalie chided him. "How about *you* sit by the phone for a while? I've been sitting here practically all day."

Raymond smiled and held up the bag of parts for the light.

"I would love to," he told her, "but I've got some other work to do."

"Yeah, right, go ahead, Mr. Fix It," said Natalie, waving him away.

Raymond gave a laugh, then went off to take care of the living room light.

CHAPTER 5

Jason stretched out his legs, folded his arms, and gave a yawn. He did so partly from boredom, but more so from nervous tension. He was sitting among the other passengers at a gate in O'Hare International Airport, waiting for the call to board the plane to Providence. The flight had been delayed for quite a long while and there was a palpable feeling of unrest in the air.

He glanced out the window at the planes lined up at the terminal. A light snow was falling from the darkening skies over Chicago, adding to the general angst, for everyone knew that if it started to come down heavily, the flight might be further delayed a very long time indeed. Jason had not seen snow since he moved to California, and the sight of the flakes drifting aimlessly to the ground caused him to consider for the first time the thin jacket he was wearing. It was cold where he was going, and he was obviously not prepared.

Jason tucked his chin against his chest and squeezed his arms more tightly about himself. He was shaking ever so slightly, and it felt like it was all he could do just to hold himself together, to not lose his resolve. It was not the cold or delay of the flight that was causing his anxiety, it was something else, a vague feeling of apprehension that had been growing stronger ever since he had departed from Houston, where he left Burt, the talkative insurance man, behind. Blessed with an empty seat beside him for the flight to Chicago, Jason had tried to stretch out and doze off to pass the time, but all the while he had been plagued by doubts. Doubts about what had become of his life, and what he was to do with it. Doubts about going home and facing his father. Doubts about what he should say to him, about how he would explain himself. What would his father think of him? Jason had wondered. What would they all think?

All these thoughts continued to gnaw at Jason's insides, filling him with dread, as he sat at the gate, waiting for the announcement. A part of him was hoping that it would never come, for the delay, if anything, was something of a relief to him, a sort of temporary reprieve from this sentence he had imposed on himself. There was still time to change his mind, the voices of doubt kept telling him, still time to come up with another plan, to go somewhere else if only he could decide quickly.

This was his last chance.

Jason lifted his head and looked at the other passengers sitting around him. Some were chatting—or in many cases, grumbling—quietly among themselves, while others paced about, talking nonstop into their cell phones. Across the way, in a row of seats directly facing him, he saw a young man and woman of his own age sitting together. Unlike the rest of the gathering, the two seemed quite unfazed by the delay. In fact, they looked perfectly serene. Her arm entwined about that of her boyfriend, the young woman rested her head lazily against his shoulder while she caressed his hand. In turn, the young man leaned closer now and then to kiss her gently on the head. The passage of time seemed not to bother the two lovers in the least. While everyone else felt trapped like caged animals, they were in a world of their own.

Jason envied that feeling of simple bliss the two were no doubt sharing. Once, not so very long ago as it seemed to him at that moment, he had known what it was like to feel that way with someone, to know with certainty that you were in exactly the right place at exactly the right moment in time with exactly the right person you were meant to be with. The more he watched the couple, the more keenly he felt the loss of what he once had, and so he turned his gaze from them. He stared out the window at the snow for a time, trying to lose himself in its swirling, twisting patterns, but instead found that his thoughts drifted inexorably back to those early days in California when it seemed for all the world like he could do nothing wrong.

"Stick with us, kid, and you're going to make it big."

That was what Phil Langway, senior vice president of marketing, had told him the day he offered Jason a job at Med-Device Technologies four years earlier. Med-Device was a young, up-and-coming company that designed and manufactured a variety of medical devices. Sales and market share were relatively small, but senior management had big hopes for a new product that was just being developed. They called it the ProCardia One, a high-tech surgical implant that was going to revolutionize the treatment of arteriosclerosis and other disorders. It was the first in a line of such products that Med-Device had on the drawing boards, and the one generating the most excitement. What ProCardia needed, and what Phil Langway was assembling, was a young, energetic team to help the company raise capital from outside investors, to guide the product through the clinical trials required to get FDA approval, and lastly to shepherd it into the marketplace, where it was a certain to be a winner.

Jason's salary, Langway had cautioned, would be modest in the beginning. Much of his compensation would come in the form of company stock. But then he had added, with a distinct gleam in his eye, that if things worked out for ProCardia as planned, and the company one day went public, they would all be able to retire very wealthy men.

Jason had not taken long to consider the offer. This was just the type of opportunity he had longed for ever since his first day of business school. Jason was one of those hardworking, driven people who only dream big, and the thought of returning to little Rhode Island, of working for no matter how short a time in the family's little bed-and-breakfast operation, had never been an option for him. From day one, he knew that he had to get out on his own, to go someplace where he could breathe and make his own way in the world. Having graduated near the top of his class, Jason had received offers from a number of older, more established companies, all of whom had offered far greater starting salaries, but none of the companies had excited him like this one. Here was the opportunity to get in on the ground floor of something big. And so he had jumped at the chance without a second thought, and made the move to Los Angeles.

From then on, the oyster that became Jason's life had seemed to hold nothing but a string of pearls. Jason loved his work, it was fast-paced and exciting, and he loved Los Angeles. He loved the weather and he loved the beaches. He loved the restaurants and the nightclubs. He loved everything about the city, but most of all he loved the women—and they loved him back.

How could they not? Charmed by his boyish good looks and his distinct Rhode Island accent, women had found him irresistible in those days. And if his looks and charm were not enough, there was the way he liked to throw his money around. Jason liked to play as hard as he worked. As his star rose at Med-Device, so did his salary, and he had no qualms whatsoever about spending as much of it as he could to impress whichever ravishing young lady he happened to find on his arm at any particular moment. He sent them flowers and expensive gifts. He rented a beautiful, ridiculously expensive apartment, zipped around town in a Lexus coupe convertible, wore the best clothes, and was on a first-name basis with practically every maitre d' in the city. He was the life of the party wherever he went, picking up dinner tabs or buying drinks for everyone. In those days, Jason Mirabella had been an easy guy to love.

Jason loved to play the field, rarely dating any one woman for more than a few weeks. His life was like a lavish buffet table laid out with one tempting delicacy after another; what was the point of lingering too long in one place when there might be something even better on offer further along the line? Besides, for all the women who had caught his eye, not one of them had ever come close to catching his heart. That would all change in a twinkling, however, late one Friday afternoon at Med-Device Technologies as he was getting ready to call it a day.

It was the end of what had been a particularly arduous week. Jason had been putting in a lot of long hours on the ProCardia project that week and he was feeling the need to go out on the town to blow off a little steam. It was just as he was getting ready to pull on his jacket and close up shop for the day when he saw what he thought must surely must be a vision walk by his office. She was blond and beautiful with long, lovely limbs and luminous brown eyes. Jason hurried to the door to get a second look, to make certain that he hadn't imagined her. He cautiously leaned out into the hall and watched her walk away, admiring all the while the swaying of her hips and the gentle bounce of her long hair falling about her shoulders until she disappeared around the corner. She was the most attractive woman he had ever laid eyes on, and he was instantly besotted.

"Whoa, did you get a load of that?" he had heard someone say. It was Sam, one of his coworkers. Entranced as he had been, Jason had not noticed that he too had been admiring the view from his own office across the hall. "What a babe. Did you check out those legs?"

"Who is she?" asked Jason breathlessly.

"Amanda Forsythe, you idiot," Sam laughed. "You've never seen her? She's Bill Forsythe's daughter."

Bill Forsythe was the company president. Jason worked primarily under Phil Langway, but now and then he sat in on meetings with Forsythe to keep him updated on the latest developments with ProCardia. The company president was a stern-faced, reserved sort who did not hand out compliments lightly. Just the same, though he had never said as much, he had always given Jason the impression that he was very pleased with the young man's work.

"I didn't know he had a daughter," Jason said just before Amanda suddenly appeared once more at the other end of the hall, walking back in their direction. The two young men instantly fell silent as she passed. Amanda flashed them a brief smile and said hello before continuing on her way. For all his experience with women, Jason had been utterly tongue-tied at the sight of her, and all he had managed to do was nod and smile in return. And then she was gone.

"Forget about it," Sam said at seeing the look on Jason's face. "You've got about as much of a chance with her as you do with the Queen of England."

"Don't bet on it," Jason had murmured, and in that moment he set his mind to finding a way to make their paths cross again.

As fate would have it, Jason did not have long to wait. To his surprise, when it came time to leave, he had found an annoyed Amanda Forsythe standing by her car in the company parking lot, a cell phone pressed to her ear. Jason could not help but overhear her explaining to someone that her car would not start, and that apparently it needed to be towed.

Wasting no time, Jason had been quick to introduce himself and offer his assistance, though he knew nothing about cars other than how to buy and drive them. There was, in truth, not much that he could do other than keep her company until the tow truck came. While they waited, though, the two had exchanged pleasantries, and Jason had become more and more enraptured with her by the moment. He loved everything about her, the way the sunlight played on her long blond hair, the sound of her voice, the soft brown hue of her beautifully tanned skin. Then there was the way she touched his arm when she laughed, making him melt inside, and giving him to wonder if perhaps the attraction he felt for her was mutual. This had emboldened him to offer her a ride home—she accepted—which en route led to an invitation to have dinner together—she accepted—and just like that, the romantic whirlwind had begun.

He fell insanely in love with Amanda, and she with him—or at least so he thought. In the passionate days and nights they would come to share, Jason would find in her embrace a sense of fulfillment and serenity he had never known. It was like he was part of some great harmonic convergence. Everything was coming together for him, success in his work, success in his love life. It was perhaps the happiest time of his life, and it seemed like it would never end.

But then had come the day at work, when Phil Langway had asked Jason to come into his office right away. Two other senior executives on the ProCardia project were already there, pacing nervously about, when Jason walked in. The two were clearly distracted and barely acknowledged him. For his part, Langway, looking drawn and anxious, had simply motioned to the chair in front of his desk.

"What's up, guys?" Jason had asked cautiously.

"Just close the door and have a seat," Langway replied. "We've got a big problem."

Jason sat down, never suspecting that, bit by bit, everything he had worked so hard to achieve was about to come unraveled.

The sound of the gate attendant, announcing that passengers could now begin boarding the flight to Providence, roused Jason from his brooding on the past and mercifully brought him back to the present. The present, however, was full of torments of its own, and once again he was consumed with doubts about what he was doing. He looked about at the other passengers who by now were hastily gathering their belongings together and hurrying to get on board the plane. There seemed no alternative for him, so reluctantly he stood and found his way to the back of the line.

A thin sheen of sweat was glistening on Jason's forehead when at last he settled into an aisle seat on board the plane and pulled the belt securely across his lap. He sat there for a time, trying to calm his breathing as he looked about at the other passengers and listened with growing apprehension to the soft whine of the idling engines. Across the aisle from him sat an elderly woman who seemed as equally unnerved as he felt at that moment. Her eyes squeezed shut, she was murmuring a prayer to herself while her trembling hands fidgeted with a string of rosary beads that lay across her lap. As luck would have it, the woman opened her eyes just in time to see Jason looking at her.

"Nervous about flying?" he said gently.

"Does it show?" she replied.

"Just a little," he said, mustering a smile, for the opportunity to comfort someone else made him feel a little better. "I wouldn't worry," he told her. "We'll be there before you know it."

"That's what everyone always tells me," huffed the woman, "but at my age, the thought of being six miles up in the air in a tin can doesn't exactly fill me with confidence."

Jason gave a little laugh and nodded to her rosary beads.

"Do those help?" he asked.

"They don't hurt," she said. "You want to give them a try. No offense, but you look as nervous I feel."

"I don't mind flying," Jason assured her. "I've just got other things on my mind."

The woman leaned in his direction and studied him for a moment with her sharp blue eyes. She had the face of someone who had seen more than a little bit of life, a kind, soft face that also evoked a certain hardness and, he suspected, resilience. She could have been just about anyone's grandmother.

"You don't look so good," she decided after a moment's consideration. "You look like you need to eat something."

"I haven't eaten all day," Jason acknowledged.

"Eh, I don't blame you," the woman said with a shrug. "The food on these things is garbage." With that she reached down into the bag at her feet and pulled out a small bundle wrapped in aluminum foil. "Why don't you have some of this pepper and egg sandwich?" she said, offering it to him. "My daughter made it for me this morning just before I left Oregon, but I probably won't be able to eat a thing until I get home."

"No, thank you," Jason told her. "I really don't think I can eat right now either."

"What's the matter, you feeling sick?" said the woman with genuine concern showing in her eyes.

"No," Jason said. He turned and looked away for a moment. "It's just that I haven't been home in a long time."

"Ayy," the woman exclaimed with a dismissive wave of her hand. "Don't you worry about a thing. Going home is the best thing in the world."

Before she could expound further, the plane pulled away from the terminal, gently jostling the cabin as it began to taxi toward the runway. A look of panic swept across her face.

"Just let me know if you get hungry and change your mind later on," she said, hurriedly tucking the sandwich back into the bag. Then she took up her rosary beads once more and closed her eyes.

As the engines began to roar and the plane accelerated down the runway, Jason smiled at the old woman and sighed. He wasn't sure if she was right, if going home would be the best thing in the world, but come what may, there was no turning back now.

CHAPTER 6

Giulio wrapped a scarf around his neck and tugged on his over-coat. The clock in the living room had just chimed four a few minutes earlier and he was preparing to go home for the day. He would have liked to stay a little longer, but having arrived very early that morning, he knew that he had reached his limit. Giulio could tolerate the cold of the often bleak New England winters as well as any man, but the shortened hours of daylight during those glacial months affected him more and more with each passing year. He was not one of those people who grew sad or depressed during the dark time of the year, but there was no question that his energy level took a precipitous drop every after-noon in tandem with the sun as it fell toward the horizon. Come sundown it would be a struggle to keep his eyes open, and he would want to crawl into a ball and go to sleep. This instinctive urge he well knew was simply nature's way. It was why creatures great and small went into hibernation during the gray, frigid months of winter. He had grown wise enough not to bother fighting it.

"Heading straight home, Dad?" said Natalie, coming out into the foyer to see her father off. His daughter was in noticeably brighter spirits than she had been earlier in the day. After lunchtime someone had called to book a room for that evening, and a short time later two others had reserved rooms for the coming weekend. After a shaky start, the day was ending on a hopeful note.

"I have a couple of stops to make," Giulio replied as he fished around for his gloves in his coat pockets. "I need one or two things at the market, and the dog needs food."

"Why don't you come to my house for dinner tonight?" she offered. "I hate it when I know you're eating all alone."

"Don't worry, I'm a big boy," he assured her.

"Then tomorrow tonight, okay?" she persisted.

"Okay," he agreed with smile.

"Good," said Natalie. "Now make sure you button up that coat, it's freezing out there."

The words had no sooner left her lips than the front door swung open and their two Asian guests came bustling in, chased by a ferocious blast of icy wind. The gust ripped through the foyer, tearing at their overcoats, the shopping bags they had clutched in their hands, and everything else in its path until the husband, with no small effort, pushed the door shut behind them. Laughing at their adventure, their cheeks flushed from the biting cold, they set down their bags for a moment while they shook off the cold. The two were smiling from ear to ear, particularly the wife, who bore that distinct look of satisfaction women often wear after a successful foray to the local shops and boutiques. Giulio chuckled inside, for she reminded him of a hunter who had just come back to camp flushed with victory after having bagged his first lion.

"A good day?" Giulio asked them.

"Very good," said the husband, his wife nodding in agreement. "Lot of fun."

"Wonderful," he told them. "Now come inside and get warm. We have a nice fire in the living room, and there's coffee and tea for all our guests." This he said while casting a questioning look at his daughter.

"Raymond's putting everything out right now," she told him with a reassuring nod.

"Excellent," said Giulio; then turning back to the couple, he added, "Please help yourself whenever you like."

With their shopping bags once more in hand, the ever-polite pair thanked Giulio, then Natalie, and then Giulio again before heading upstairs to their room to stow away their newfound treasures.

"You and your brother are in charge," said Giulio once they were out of sight. "I'll see you bright and early tomorrow."

"Drive careful," she told him.

Giulio smiled and blew his daughter a kiss before he opened the door and stepped out into the roaring wind.

Darkness had fallen by the time he arrived at home later on. All that was left of the sun was a faint orange smudge low in the western sky, but the streetlights were all lit and the windows of the neighboring houses aglow. A pair of grocery bags under his arms, he trudged across the crusty snow and ice that lay in patches on the hardened lawn. As expected, he saw in the living room window the silhouette of a dog. Despite the howling wind, it had heard the car pull into the driveway. Now, with paws on the sill and tail wagging, it eagerly awaited his master's return. It dashed for the door the moment Giulio began to mount the front steps and was there to greet him when the door swung open.

"*Mannaggia,* Sundance, give me a minute to get in the door!" Giulio chided the dog, putting down one of the bags so that he could give its ear a playful twist. "What have you been doing all day, boy, eh? Scratching up my windowsills with those paws of yours?"

Sundance, a high-spirited, mixed-breed Labrador retriever with white hair and orange-yellow ears, was bouncing up and down with excitement. He stuck his snout into the grocery bag on the floor, gave it a sniff, and then jumped up on his hind legs to get a look at the other under Giulio's arm.

"Down with you now!" laughed Giulio, shrugging him off. He picked up the other bag and went into the kitchen, where he set them on the counter.

By now Sundance, his tail wagging furiously, was waiting anxiously by the back door. When Giulio did not immediately look his way, he gave a whine and an impatient bark.

"What's the matter, you need to go outside?" Giulio inquired, though he knew of course the answer. "Trust me," he said, moving to the door, "you're not going to want to stay out there very long, but go ahead."

With that he turned on the outside light and opened the door a crack. In a flash, the dog bolted out into the backyard and ran off to find a suitable spot to conduct its business. Giulio closed the door and pushed aside the curtain on the window to get a look at the pale full moon rising behind the bony trees swaying wildly in the wind. A shiver raced up his spine. It was growing frightfully cold outdoors, and he was happy to be home. Letting the curtain fall closed, he turned and went back to the counter to unpack his groceries. It came as no surprise when, but a mere minute or two later, Giulio heard Sundance pawing at the back door, barking to be let back in. With a good-natured grumble, he opened the door for the shivering dog, gave him a pat on the head, and set to work preparing their suppers.

Giulio gave a yawn as he opened the bag of dog food he had brought home. The weariness was starting to set in on him, and he wondered for a moment if he should just go to bed and forget about supper. He knew of course that Sundance would feel otherwise, and the dog was right; they both needed to eat. So, with another yawn, he filled the dog's dish and placed it on the floor next to his water bowl.

"Aspetta!" he said, wagging a finger to make the eager dog

wait before he was allowed to eat. "What do you do for me first?"

Sundance dutifully sat.

"That's right," said his master with a tone of approval. He gestured at the dish. "Now you can eat."

While Sundance happily commenced gobbling down his food, Giulio went to the refrigerator to see what he might heat up for his own dinner. He did not keep a terribly great amount of food on hand, but there were one or two different things in the fridge that might suit his appetite that evening. After a few moments, his eye settled on a plastic container, which he pulled off the shelf and brought to the counter by the stove. He put the container down and took out a skillet, into which he poured a healthy coating of olive oil before placing it on the burner on low heat. While the pan warmed, he opened the plastic container. Inside were six big, beautiful red peppers roasted and filled with a zesty bread and meat stuffing, a perfect supper on such a cold winter's evening. Taking a big serving spoon in hand, he very carefully transferred two of the stuffed peppers to the skillet. Soon they were simmering in the oil, filling the kitchen with a warm, delicious aroma.

When the peppers were heated, Giulio put them on a dinner plate along with a piece of fresh bread. He set the plate on the table and poured himself a little glass of wine before settling into his chair. By this time a sated Sundance had wandered over from his empty dish. The dog crept under the table, gave a yawn of his own, and flopped down on the floor at Giulio's feet. Giulio peeked under the table and gave the dog a smile.

"You too, eh?" he chuckled. "I guess it's going to be an early night for both of us."

With that he straightened up and took a sip of wine before digging into his stuffed peppers. As he sat there enjoying his food, quietly contemplating the day's activities, Giulio listened to the relentless wind, the scratching of the bushes against the back windows, and the banging of the pipes as the radiators hissed to life even though he had set the thermostat quite low.

It was just then, at the height of a particularly violent gust of wind, that Giulio thought that he had heard over the tumult outside a bang reminiscent of the sound of a car door slamming shut. Sundance had obviously heard the same, for he immediately sprang up with a growl and ran to the front window to investigate. There the dog took to barking in the insane way he did whenever he observed someone or something passing by. Giulio tended to ignore the animal at such times, for most often it was only a neighbor or a squirrel or another dog Sundance had seen. This time, however, perhaps because of the immoderate weather, he was curious to see who or what might be prowling about the front of his house, so he pushed away from the table and got up to see what all the fuss was about.

By now, Sundance was jumping up and down, exuberantly spinning himself around in circles when Giulio finally came to the window. Giulio leaned close to the windowpane and peered outside, where he saw beneath the streetlight a yellow taxicab parked in front of the house. A lone figure, obscured in the shadows, stood at the back of the cab, struggling to pull some luggage from the trunk. One of the pieces of luggage tumbled to the ground and whoever it was stooped down to retrieve it. Curious as to who it might be, Giulio went to the door and flipped on the front lights. Back at the window, he nudged the dog aside to get a second look.

Giulio felt his heart well up inside him. The weariness that just a few moments before had been weighing on him so heavily vanished like a puff of steam, and at once he felt for all the world like jumping up and down himself.

"Jason!" he cried.

Then he grabbed his overcoat and hurried outside.

★　★　★

Out on the street, Jason knelt behind the cab, frantically trying to stuff everything back into his suitcase. He had under-
estimated the cost of the ride from the airport, and made the
mistake of opening one of his suitcases in the hope of finding
some extra cash with which to pay the driver. The bag had of
course fallen open and now it was all he could do just to grab
hold of everything before it was carried away by the wind. He
knew full well that he was making a spectacle of himself, and
that the driver was growing more impatient by the moment,
waiting for his money, but there was nothing to be done to
spare himself the humiliation.

It was, Jason could not help thinking with no small sense of
irony, a fitting conclusion to his journey. As if his stomach had
not already been a knot of nerves, the flight from Chicago was a
bumpy, nauseating affair from start to finish. At times it had been
so rough that he had thought for certain that the poor old
woman seated across from him would pass out from fright.
When the plane had finally landed and taxied safely to the terminal, she had mumbled a fearsome string of Italian invective of
which he understood not a single word, but nonetheless required no translation. He knew that she had accurately voiced
the sentiments of every passenger on board the plane.

Now, exhausted from the long journey and the ordeal that
had preceded it, his body shocked by the mind-numbing cold,
he fumbled in vain through his clothes for a few extra dollars
until, quite unexpectedly, he felt a heavy coat fall across his
shoulders. He looked up in time to see his father, wearing no
coat of his own, rush by his side to the driver's open window.
Jason's heart sank as he realized that his father was about to pay
the cab fare for him. Stripped of his last shred of pride, there was
nothing for him to do but watch until the driver had taken the
money and sped off down the street.

His eyes tearing from the wind, a lump coming to his throat,
Jason stood there shivering as his father turned to face him. He

had rehearsed this moment over and over again in his mind, but now that it had come, he found that he did not know what to say. He bowed his head and swallowed hard.

"Dad," he finally managed, his voice cracking. "Do you think I could come home and stay for a little while. It's just that I—"

Before Jason could utter another word, his father took him in his embrace and squeezed him for all he was worth.

"What kind of question is that?" said Giulio. Then he took hold of one of the bags and led his son in from the cold.

CHAPTER 7

Once, when Jason was just a little boy, he ran away from home.

It was a Friday afternoon, one warm day in late April, and Jason had been out in the yard, playing war games with his friends. Though he had been warned a thousand times not to do such things, Jason decided that it would be a wonderful idea to sit up on the top of his mother's car and pretend to be riding a tank. From that lofty perch, he would be better able to observe the enemy's position and fire at will. There were, however, certain tactical problems to consider, and his mind had quickly scrolled through the whereabouts of his family members. His mother, he knew, was busy in the basement, doing laundry. His father was at work, and his brother and sister out somewhere with their own friends. No one, he had concluded, would ever find out what he was planning to do.

And so, against direct orders from the parental high command, up he climbed and installed himself atop the roof of the car. There Jason remained, having a delightful time directing battle operations like George Patton, until he decided that it would be much more fun to relinquish command and get down from the car to take part in a hand-to-hand skirmish that had broken out on the front lawn. Eager to join the fray, he slid on his bottom down the windshield and onto the front hood of the car, where, in the process of swinging his legs over the side, he unthinkingly grabbed hold of the antenna. As his feet dropped toward the ground, it bent completely sideways. To his dismay, it failed to snap back upright, but instead stayed in that position, jutting away from the car like a spindly arm reaching out to drop a coin into a tollbooth basket.

Horrified at what he had done, Jason immediately attempted to straighten it back up, an effort that only succeeded in snapping it off at the base. Jason stood there aghast, his heart filled with dread, for he knew that he had committed a very grave transgression. He could only imagine the punishment he would endure for such a misdeed when his father got home. In the moment of panic that ensued, he took the only reasonable course of action he could think of.

He dropped the antenna and ran.

Fearful of the retribution to come, Jason scurried two streets over and hid himself behind the shed in a friend's backyard. He stayed there a very long time, until the sun began to set and the shadows closed in around him. Alone and scared, he curled up into a ball. He was fearful of the growing darkness, but equally fearful of going home.

By this time, of course, alarm bells had gone off at the Mirabella residence. With Raymond and Natalie in tow, Giulio set out to find his son while a frantic Vera remained behind on the front step lest, unbeknownst to them, her son came home to find no one there.

Jason grew ever more anxious as he crouched behind the shed and nighttime began to fall in earnest. His mind now playing tricks on him as he looked anxiously about, he imagined that all manner of apparitions and ghoulish creatures were gathering round. He was frightened out of his wits, and wished for all the world that he was back home, safe and snug in his own bed. He began to despair of ever finding himself there again, but then he heard his father's voice calling to him through the darkness.

Whatever punishment he might have to endure for breaking the antenna would surely be better than being devoured by the monsters of the night, and so Jason sprang up without another moment's hesitation and ran out to the edge of the street. On the other side, beneath the glow of the streetlight, his father was still calling out his name, looking about with worried eyes. Jason was struck by the look on his father's face. It was one of fear and not anger as he had expected. In the moment that passed before his father saw him standing there, he realized that what he had done in running away was worse than having broken the antenna, and he felt all the more the sting of guilt. It was worse than any punishment he had imagined. When his father rushed up to him and smothered him in his embrace, Jason wanted to explain himself, but without a single word, a relieved Giulio simply took him firmly by the hand and led him home.

The reception from his mother was not so muted, the fear/anger equation seemingly reversed the instant she realized that her youngest child was safe and sound. First she took him by the shoulders and screamed at him for scaring the daylights out of them all. Then she hugged him with all her might and cried, "Thank God! Thank God!" When at last she composed herself, she ordered him to wash his hands and take his place at the dinner table.

"What an idiot," his older brother, Raymond, had remarked when Jason slid meekly into his chair.

"Really," Natalie had chimed in. "You get the award for most stupid."

As he sat there, enduring their scorn, waiting for his father to sit down and for his mother to bring dinner to the table, Jason felt lower than ever he had in his young life. He knew that he had not heard the end of it, not by a long shot. All the same, despite the repercussions to come, he was happy to be home.

Later that night—he was sent to bed directly after dinner—Jason lay awake with the bedside light on. Upon hearing his father come up the stairs, he rolled over and squeezed his eyes shut, pretending to be asleep, for he did not wish to get into any further trouble. Giulio came into the room, kissed his son on the head, and turned off the light. He did not go back downstairs right away, but instead lingered outside the door in the hallway for a time. As he lay there beneath the covers, Jason could feel his father's eyes upon him and knew that it was no use pretending anymore. He rolled over, opened his eyes, and looked out at his father's silhouette filling the doorway.

"I'm sorry for what I did, Dad," said Jason through the darkness.

"I know," said his father gently in turn. "We'll talk about it tomorrow. Now go to sleep."

At that Jason closed his eyes and soon truly fell off to sleep, relieved beyond measure to know that he was home, safe once more in his own bed. His world had not come to an end after all.

Now, so many years later, the incident came afresh to his mind as Jason dropped his bags in the front hall and followed his father into the house. Like the little boy crouching in fear behind the shed, he had been filled with misgivings at the thought of coming home. Having finally crossed over the threshold, those misgivings started, if only slightly, to slowly abate.

"Sit down, I'll make you something to eat."

Though it was his clearly delighted father who had spoken as the two walked into the kitchen, somehow inside his head, Jason had heard his mother's voice. As he settled into a chair at the table and watched Giulio move about the stove, he could not help but be reminded of her. How often, he wondered, had he heard his mother speak those very same words to him? How often as a boy had he come home, cold and weary and stressed out from a hard day at school, only to find his spirits revived by the smell of something delicious cooking in the kitchen the instant he walked through the door? How often had it taken just a kind word or two from her—for she had a way, like all mothers, of knowing exactly what to tell him—to set his world right again?

It struck Jason then, guiltily so, that he had not thought about his mother in a great while. Precisely why not, he didn't know. In truth, he still missed her very much, but that was not something to which he would readily admit, not even to himself.

Jason reached down and scratched Sundance's head. The dog had not left his side since the moment he walked through the front door, and was now examining his master's son with unabashed zeal. It poked its snout up and down the length of Jason's trousers, sniffing in whatever curious scents he had discovered there with great gulping snorts. When it had concluded its quite thorough assessment of one trouser leg, Sundance gleefully changed sides and commenced examination of the other.

Giulio cast a glance over his shoulder.

"Ay, enough, you pest!" he called to the dog. "Go lie down somewhere and leave him alone now. He already knows you're happy to see him."

"That's okay," said Jason, giving Sundance's ear a tweak. "He's not bothering me."

Jason had told the truth, for if anything he found all the attention to be in some way reassuring. It was nice to feel welcome.

While Jason looked on, Giulio spooned two more of the stuffed peppers into the skillet on the stove and reignited the burner. In a little while, when the peppers were sufficiently warmed, he put them on a plate as he had done for himself, ripped off another chunk of bread, and brought the plate to the table.

"You want a little glass of wine with that?" he said, setting the plate and a knife and fork in front of Jason.

"Sure," Jason absentmindedly replied as he reached for the fork. Until he had smelled the peppers cooking, he had not realized how ravenous he was, and the sight of the food on his plate was too much to resist. He dug right in without another word while his father filled a wineglass for him.

"Maybe I should heat up the rest of these," remarked Giulio with a chuckle.

Jason took a bite of the bread and then another of the peppers before sitting back for a moment. It was simple fare, but somehow it was enough to rekindle the life in him. He gave a short, but audible sigh of relief before taking a sip of wine.

"These are good, Dad," he said. "Did you make them yourself?"

Giulio gave another little laugh.

"No," he replied with a shake of his head. "One of the lasagna ladies dropped them off for me yesterday."

Jason gave a little laugh of his own.

"They still coming around?" he said.

"Eh," grunted Giulio with a shrug, as if to say that there was nothing to be done about it, and that this was simply a burden he had to bear.

The "lasagna ladies," as Jason's father had come to call them, was the collection of widows and spinsters living in the neighborhood who took it upon themselves from time to time to bring him a home-cooked meal. Given the dearth of eligible senior bachelors in the area, and the fact that he had lived alone for many years, Giulio was considered a prime catch. And so it was that the lasagna ladies took turns following the timeworn strategy of treading the path through Giulio's stomach, hoping it might one day, at least for one of them, lead to his heart. On any given day, any one of them might show up at his front door, dressed to the nines of course, with a complimentary pan of lasagna, a tray of polenta and sausage, or on this latest occasion a container of delicious stuffed peppers. Competition for his affections had grown fierce over the years, but to date, despite their best culinary efforts, none of the eager throng had come close to winning them.

It was not that Giulio was ungrateful for their kind attentions, or that he was insensitive to their plight. He understood as well as any of them what it was to live alone day in and day out without someone there alongside with whom to share the ups and downs of life. And he was not averse to occasionally repaying their kindness by treating one of them to dinner at a local restaurant, or escorting another to some formal function. He was always a perfect gentleman, and though he often saw longing in their eyes, his relationship with all of them remained platonic. He was still very much devoted to the memory of Vera, his deceased wife, so he kept the others perpetually at arm's length.

Jason had always understood this about his father. Over the years, he and his siblings had more than once suggested that it might be time for Giulio to find someone to be with before it became too late, and he ended up living out his days all alone, but their advice had fallen on deaf ears. His father had his own ideas about how he wanted to live the rest of his life, and he would do things his own way regardless of the prodding of others. As he watched his father sit down across the table from him to finish his own meal, it occurred to Jason that that spirit of independence was a trait they shared in common. Strange, but perhaps for the first time he realized that it was not something he had just picked up off the grass.

For a time the two men ate in silence save for an occasional remark about the wind or the brutally cold temperatures that had fallen across the region. Now and then, Giulio would regard Jason with a thoughtful gaze, keeping him on tenterhooks as he waited for the inevitable flurry of questions about what had brought about this precipitous, unexpected visit. That he had not queried him outright on the subject led Jason to believe that his father already understood that there was something amiss and that he was content to let his son reveal it whenever he was ready to do so.

When the two had finished eating, Giulo pushed away from the table and began to collect their plates and utensils.

"Here, Dad, let me clean up," said Jason, getting to his feet.

"No," said his father, waving him away. "I'll take care of it. Go in the living room now and relax for a little while."

"Sure?" said Jason, wondering if perhaps he had been given a reprieve from having to explain himself that evening.

"Yeah," said Giulio. "Go on, and take the dog with you. I'm going to make us some coffee. Then you can tell me why it is that we've hardly heard from you for weeks and weeks, and what it is that suddenly brings you home today out of a clear blue sky."

With that he paused to consider his son for a moment with a sage eye before turning away to bring the plates to the sink. The ponderous weight of anxiety that had dogged him for so long pressed in on Jason once again. All the same, despite the tightening in his gut, he did as he was told, for in an odd way he felt relieved that the moment of truth had finally come.

Once in the living room, Jason turned on the television and flopped down on the couch with Sundance near at hand on the floor beside him. As he petted the dog's head and stared with disinterest at the television, exhaustion finally began to overcome him and he struggled to keep his eyes open.

By the time Giulio finally emerged from the kitchen with two steaming coffee mugs in hand, Jason had already slipped off into a deep sleep. At the sight of him, Giulio gave a grunt, as if to indicate that he was not surprised in the least. With a sigh, he took the coffee mugs back to the kitchen and poured them down the drain. After rinsing out the mugs, he went back into the living room, took a blanket from the closet, and gently tossed it over Jason so as not to wake him.

For a time, Giulio stood there, gazing down at his sleeping son with a look of joy tinged by worry. Then he kissed him on the head, turned off the television, and went upstairs for the night.

CHAPTER 8

The downstairs study at Bradley Mansion, which had been converted years ago into its present use as the main office, was the only place in the entire house where the Mirabellas could go to speak in private. The rest of the place, Giulio had constantly reminded his children over the years, belonged to their guests who were paying good money for a quiet, relaxed stay and had no desire to hear the family matters of others being discussed. Aside from this deference to his guests, Giulio was also one of those intensely private people who simply preferred that strangers not know too much about the goings-on within his family. And so, whenever there was a dispute to be settled, a grievance to be aired, or an important announcement made, all parties concerned were instructed to "take it to the study—and close the door."

Such being the case, Natalie and Raymond were instantly aware that there was something out of the ordinary to be discussed when the following morning, as the guests were having breakfast, their father called them into the study and closed the door behind them.

"What's going on?" Raymond asked straightaway.

"Is everything all right?" added his sister in a worried voice.

"Yes, everything is fine," Giulio assured them with a smile. "I just wanted to tell you both that your brother Jason has come home."

He waited to see their response. It was not quite what he had anticipated, for at first Raymond and Natalie simply exchanged glances.

"Really?" said Natalie at last. "When did he get back?"

"Just last night," replied Giulio.

"Did you know he was coming?" asked Raymond.

"No, he just showed up out of the blue," he said.

Giulio eyed his son and daughter. He could not be quite certain why, but the two did not seem particularly surprised by his announcement that Jason had returned. If anything, their somewhat muted reactions to the happy news led him to suspect that somehow they had been expecting it all along. How or why he could not say, but he did know that there was no point in asking directly. Giulio well understood that at times—and he sensed that this was one of them—he and his children stood on opposite sides of the generational fence. When circumstances caused the other side to close ranks, there was not much he could do but bide his time and wait for the inevitable loosening of lips.

"Where is he now?" asked Natalie.

"He's home, sleeping," said Giulio, rubbing his chin thoughtfully. "He was tired, especially with the jet lag and all, so I just let him rest."

"But what made him come home like that without letting anyone know?" said Raymond. "I mean, did he say anything?"

"No, not really," admitted Giulio. Then, with a shrug he added, "Actually, it was kind of late, so we really didn't get a chance to talk all that much."

Giulio would not say so, but despite his unquestioned elation at having Jason back home once more, he himself had been brimming with curiosity about the odd timing of his secretive return. It had taken only one look at his son to recognize that something was terribly wrong. The moment the night before, when the taxi had gone away and he first beheld him standing there, shivering in the cold, he had seen it in Jason's eyes and in the weary, drawn look on his face. It was almost as if the young man had been injured in some faraway battle and staggered all the way home, carrying within some dreadful wound that had all but put him at death's door. Something was clearly broken in his son's spirit, something that Giulio knew would need to be mended, but at that moment when he brought Jason into the house, he also recognized that first he would need to be coaxed back to life. That Jason had devoured his dinner so ravenously and then collapsed from exhaustion onto the couch, only confirmed this diagnosis. Perhaps when his son was feeling better, when his body and spirit were back in harmony, Giulio would learn the truth. Till then all he could do was protect him and be patient.

"Did he say how long he was going to stay?" asked Natalie. "We hardly got to see him the last time he came home."

"No, he didn't say," replied Giulio, "but I think it's going to be for a while." Giulio eyed his son and daughter again. "You know, Jason didn't tell me anything in particular, but I think maybe something went wrong for him out in California," he said. "I don't suppose either of you two knows anything that I don't?"

"How would we know anything, Dad?" answered Raymond. "You know how Jason is. He doesn't stay in touch with us any better than he does with you. Do you know how many times I've tried to call him and left a message, but never got a call back? He's like in his own world when he's out there."

It was a suitably evasive answer, thought Giulio, enough to convince him that his children might know more than they were letting on. Perhaps they had good reason for doing so, he told himself, but there was no way to know for certain, so he pressed them no further.

"Well, in any case, he's home," said Giulio. "Who know's how long he's going to stay? So I'd like for all of us to get together soon."

"Why not tonight?" suggested Natalie.

"Tonight?"

"Why not?" said his daughter. "I did invite you to come over for dinner yesterday, if you remember, and you did say that you were going to come."

"I did at that," said Giulio.

"So, bring Jason along," she said. "That is, unless he already has something else planned like he usually does."

"I don't think that will be the case," said Giulio.

Natalie turned to her brother.

"Can you and Donna make it?" she said.

"Sure, why not?" he said with a shrug. "I don't think we have any plans for tonight."

"Good, then it's settled," said Natalie, looking pleased with herself.

"I guess it is," replied Giulio. He smiled even though he felt that things were far from settled. Only time would tell, so he gave them a nod and went to the door. Then, with a slight, almost inaudible sigh, he folded his hands behind his back and strolled off to make his rounds for the morning.

CHAPTER 9

At the touch of something cold and wet against his face, Jason awoke with a start and opened his eyes. He had been having a rather strange dream in which he was lying face down in a painfully contorted position on the floor of some unknown place. At the same time, right by his ear, someone he could not quite make out was sweeping the floor at an absurdly brisk pace. It was the sound of the bristles scratching lightly against the floor as the broom swished back and forth that he most recalled. Upon opening his eyes, he immediately realized that the sound his semiconscious brain had interpreted as a broom, and the cold, wet sensation on his face that had so abruptly awakened him, shared a common source.

"Go away, Sundance," groaned Jason, squeezing his eyes shut once more at finding himself face-to-face with the dog.

Sundance, however, was obviously not of a mind to let him slip back into sleep. To the contrary, the dog seemed quite intent on disrupting his slumbers, no doubt with the aim of coaxing him to arise. And so, despite Jason's feeble efforts to shoo it away, it continued to sniff around his ears and nudge his nose against his face with increased fervor.

"All right, all right," grumbled Jason in annoyance when he realized that the animal had no intention of leaving him in peace.

With great difficulty, for he had been sleeping with one arm twisted beneath his body, Jason slowly shrugged off the blanket and sat up stiffly on the couch. He gave a yawn and wiped the cold drool from the side of his mouth with the back of his hand while at the same time trying to shake the pins and needles out of his other arm. Though he had slept like the dead, he did not feel particularly refreshed. If anything, he felt worse. It was almost as if the hours of deep repose had served only to awaken him to his true state of exhaustion. The urge to lie back down and go to sleep was great, but there was little point in trying so long as the dog continued to pester him. And so, with another yawn, he rubbed the sleep from his eyes, tossed the blanket aside, and got to his feet.

Sundance wagged his tail in approval.

Jason went to the bathroom and threw some water on his face. Reluctantly, he looked at himself in the mirror. His hair was a tousled mess, and the cushions on the couch had left a deep crease, like a scar from a saber duel, along the side of his face. He was a pitiable sight, but in some way he could not quite discern, he looked better to himself than he had just twenty-four hours earlier.

It was not until a few minutes later, when he came back into the living room, that Jason noticed the aroma of coffee in the air. With Sundance ever in tow, he followed the warm smell to the kitchen, where he found the pot of coffee Giulio had left for him on the counter. Next to it rested an empty mug along with the cream and sugar. In his near-comatose state, Jason had not even heard his father moving about the house earlier that morning, or at least he had no recollection of it. As he considered the coffeepot, Jason regretted having fallen asleep so soon the night before. There was so much more he needed to tell his father, and Jason had been ready to do so, but there had been no fighting the instinct to first close his eyes and rest his weary body and soul now that they had returned once again to the safe confines of home.

Jason poured himself a cup of coffee and gazed out the back window at the late morning sky. It was a beautiful sunny day outdoors with nary a cloud to be seen. He turned and looked over to the back door, where Sundance was spinning himself around in the way he did to indicate that he wanted to go outside. Jason took a sip of his coffee and smiled.

"Dad's right," he said to the dog. "You are a pest."

He walked over, intending to let it out to run around the backyard, but then he reconsidered. His body had a long way to go before it would be readapted to the New England cold; nonetheless he felt the urge to get outside for a little while and breathe some fresh air. A few minutes later, wearing an old winter coat and hat he dug out of the hallway closet, he put a leash on Sundance and the two headed out the front door to take a walk.

By this time, the winds that had roared like a wild beast all the previous night had calmed to little more than a whisper. Just the same, when Jason stepped outside, the sting of the icy air against his cheeks and hands—he had not thought to put on a suitable pair of gloves—was a distinct shock. His shoulders at once reflexively shrugged up against the cold, and he gave a shudder as his breath came out in short white puffs. His first instinct was to turn around and go right back inside, but after the initial jolt had worn off, and his eyes adjusted to the outdoor light, he became sensate of the brilliant sun beaming down on him. The faint warmth it brought to his face was enough to encourage him, so he buried his free hand in his coat pocket and, holding tight to the leash, tucked the other up under the sleeve. Then, with Sundance eagerly pulling him along, he set off on his trek.

Jason could not recall the last time he had walked around his old neighborhood; surely it was years ago before he went off to college. Still, as Sundance tugged him along, he instantly recognized the old houses and remembered the people young and old who had once lived in them. He remembered his childhood friends with whom he had played in the streets and in the yards, and the cranky old-timers who liked to scold them for running across their lawns. He remembered the snowball fights and the sledding in winter, and the endless games of hide-and-seek on the warm summer nights. He remembered it all as if it were yesterday. By now, he conjectured, every one of his friends had long since moved away, just as he had done. It struck Jason then to realize that he had lost touch with them all. Indeed, since going off to make his own way in the world, he had rarely given any of them a thought. Now, though, as he meandered aimlessly about the neighborhood, the names and faces flooded his mind, and he found himself wondering about where they all had gone and what had become of them.

Given his weary state, there was a limit to how far Jason could wander that morning, and it did not take overly long for him to reach it. When he felt the first hints of fatigue setting in, he immediately turned Sundance around and began to make his way back. They had just rounded the bottom of their street and started toward home when up ahead Jason saw a familiar couple walking out the front door of one of the houses. It was the McKinleys, an old couple who had lived in the neighborhood for as long as Jason could remember. Old Man McKinley, as the husband had come to be known, had always maintained his lawn and gardens with meticulous, almost fanatical care. Come springtime, not so much as the leaf of a shrub or a blade of grass was ever out of place. He was, of course, one of those cranky old-timers who took issue with the local street urchins frolicking on their front yards. That was how Jason had always remembered the old man, and so it came as a very great surprise to see him smile and wave a greeting as he and Sundance drew near.

"Well, if it isn't young Jason Mirabella," called Mr. McKinley amiably. "Out for a tour of the old neighborhood?"

"Yes, it seemed like a good day for it," replied Jason, amazed that the old man had even recognized him.

"Look at him," Mrs. McKinley said, giving her husband a nudge. "He's all grown up now. Can you believe it? It seems just like yesterday when you used to yell at him for running on your stupid grass."

"Ha!" the old man laughed. "He was an imp, just like the rest of them—but what I wouldn't give to see you all running across it again." This he said giving Jason a wink.

"My, how the time flies," his wife said wistfully.

Jason could not get over how much at odds his childhood memories of the two were with his impression of them now. Contrary to his boyhood recollections, they were actually a rather pleasant pair of characters.

"I saw your father going to work this morning when I went out to get my paper," Mr. McKinley went on. "He stopped and told me you had come back."

"I'm sure he's very happy," said Mrs. McKinley. "He's so proud of you. You know he talks about you all the time."

At these words, Jason felt a pang of shame, and his cheeks went hot.

"I'm happy to be here," he said, fidgeting with Sundance's leash. "It's been a while."

"How long do you plan to be in town?" asked Mr. McKinley.

"A few days at least," replied Jason with a shrug. "I have some catching up to do with a lot of people."

"Well, stop by and see us anytime," said Mrs. McKinley. "We'd love to hear all about what you're doing these days."

"Just make sure you don't step on the grass when you come," joked her husband.

"I'll be careful," Jason promised, mustering a smile even though he felt his insides twisting up once again into a nervous knot. Then he wished them a nice day, and continued on his way. He was suddenly anxious to get home, and he gladly let Sundance pull him along. The chance encounter with the old couple, pleasant as they were, had left him strangely drained. He simply was not yet prepared to face people, and he was eager to return to the refuge of the house.

When he finally made it home, it was with mixed emotions that he saw Giulio's car parked in the driveway. It was not so much that he wished to avoid talking with his father, but for the moment the energy to do so had left him. All the same, he put on a good face when he walked through the front door.

"Hey, there they are," said Giulio brightly. "I was wondering what happened to you two. Then I saw the leash missing, so I knew that you must have gone out for a little walk."

"Yeah, I just needed to get some air," said Jason, releasing the dog from the leash. "We didn't go far, just down the road a ways."

"That's good," said Giulio with an approving nod. "After being cooped up all day yesterday on the plane, you need a little exercise and fresh air to get your legs back under you."

His father paused and gave him a thoughtful look.

"Feeling better?" he asked. "You looked pretty worn out when you showed up last night. I was a little worried about you, to tell you the truth."

Jason gave a shrug.

"I'm fine," he answered. "But I'm sorry I nodded off on you like that. I know you wanted to talk."

"I still want to," said Giulio, "but that can wait till later. Meantime, I just came home to check on how you're doing, and to drop off a sandwich for you so you wouldn't have to go scrounging around trying to find something for lunch."

Jason was indeed feeling hungry again, so he was pleased to hear it.

"Thanks," he said. "What did you get me?"

"A grinder with salami and capicol' and a little lettuce and tomato," his father answered. "I left it on the kitchen table."

With that Giulio began to pull on his coat.

"I can't stay long," he explained. "I've got some things to do back at work, but I'll be home to get you later on, so get yourself cleaned up and take a little nap if you need one after you eat your lunch."

"What for?" asked Jason cautiously. "Are you planning to take me somewhere?"

"Your sister invited us over for dinner," said Giulio. "Raymond and Donna will be there too."

"Oh, sounds good," said Jason unconvincingly. The thought of seeing everyone just now was more than a little overwhelming. Still, he put on a brave face. "I'll be ready," he said.

"Good," said Giulio, heading for the door. "I took your bags upstairs to your old room, by the way, and I made the bed, so you can sack out there if you like."

Jason nodded his thanks and watched his father leave. The moment the door closed behind him, he started for the kitchen, but decided that his nervous stomach was not yet ready to let him eat again. All he wanted to do at that moment was lie down on his bed. He turned to the stairs, but found that just the thought of the short climb was too much for him, so instead he went back to the living room, flopped down once more on the couch, and quickly drifted off to sleep with Sundance curled up by his feet.

CHAPTER 10

"Jason!" cried Natalie when her younger brother walked through the front door with Giulio close behind. An apron tied around her waist, for she was still busy preparing dinner, she rushed over and gave Jason a hug, and a kiss on the cheek. Then she pulled away and gave him a playful swat on the arm.

"*Mannaggia,* it's about time you came home!" she chided him. "We were beginning to think that you had forgotten all about us while you were out in California living the high life."

"I tried to, but it turned out to be harder than I thought," said Jason with a smile. He had of course been kidding her, but deep inside he felt a pang at the thought that perhaps there was more than a bit of truth in what he said.

"Ayy, you can take the boy out of Rhode Island, but you can't take the Rhode Island out of the boy," laughed Giulio, a bottle of wine in one hand and a fresh loaf of bread in the other. He paused and gave the air a sniff. "Something smells good. What have you got cooking?"

"Nothing special," said Natalie, "just some chicken cutlets and macaroni. It'll be ready in a couple of minutes."

"And where are my grandchildren?" asked Giulio, looking about. "I haven't seen them in so long. They must be all grown up by now."

"It's only been three days," his daughter reminded him. "They're downstairs horsing around in the rumpus room with Michael and Raymond. Why don't you two go join them and I'll call you when everything is ready?"

"You go," said Giulio, giving Jason a nudge. "I'm going to open this bottle first so it has a little time to breathe before we have dinner."

While his father followed Natalie to the kitchen, Jason went to the door in the back hall and started down the stairs to the finished room in the basement. There Natalie's husband, Michael, was down on all fours, giving his son, Tommy, a pony ride when Jason poked his head around the corner at the bottom of the staircase. Raymond, meantime, was seated on the couch, reading *Horton Hears a Who* to Tommy's little sister, Jenna. The evening news was on the television, but no one was paying it any attention. Jason was stunned when he saw the two children. They were still both peanuts, but had grown so much since he had last seen them.

"Hey, look what the cat dragged in," said Raymond at seeing his brother. He hoisted Jenna off his lap and deposited her next to Tommy atop their father's back. "Hold on tight," he told her before jumping up from the couch.

The two brothers shook hands and briefly embraced in a way that expressed as much caution as affection. It was as enthusiastic a greeting as Jason could have expected, for things had always been that way between them.

"How you doin'?" said his older brother, giving him a nod and assessing him with a skeptical eye. "It's been a long time."

"I know," said Jason with a shrug. "Been busy, I guess." Hoping to deflect some of the attention away from himself, he asked, "Where's Donna tonight? I didn't see her upstairs when I came in."

"Working late," said Raymond of his wife. "She'll be by later on."

Michael, who had by now flattened himself on the floor to let his children safely off his back, picked himself up and came over to greet Jason. Tommy and Jenna, however, retreated to the corner at the far end of the couch.

"What are you two doing, hiding way over there like that?" said Michael to his children. "Come over here and say hi to your uncle Jason."

Reluctantly, the children came out from behind the end of the couch and stood at their father's feet, clutching the legs of his trousers as they gazed up at the newcomer. It was then, as he looked down at their sweet little faces, that Jason realized just how long he had been away. It was obvious that his niece and nephew no longer recognized him.

"Come on, say hello," their father prodded them.

"Hey, guys," said Jason brightly, patting them on their heads. "Nice to see you again."

The two murmured meek, perfunctory greetings, as small children often do when introduced to strangers; then they pulled away from Michael and scurried up the basement stairs to find their mother.

Jason had always considered himself rather thick-skinned, but even though their reaction to him had been perfectly understandable, he could not help feeling a little hurt. It must have shown in his eyes, for his brother-in-law was quick to give him a pat on the shoulder.

"Don't feel bad," Michael told him. "They just haven't seen you in a while, that's all."

"Hey, it's not their fault," said Jason. "These days sometimes I feel like a stranger even to myself."

"That sounds quite profound," snickered Raymond. "What did you do, think that up while you were doing Pilates one day?"

"Hey, you know how it is with us West Coast types," said

Jason, taking the dig with good humor. "I think that came to mind one day while I was meditating on the beach—or was it while I was doing my daily tai chi routine? I can't remember."

"You're no West Coast type," huffed Raymond, sitting down once more on the couch. "You're still a Rhode Island boy through and through whether you like it or not."

"Dad said something along those same lines just a minute ago," recalled Jason. "I don't know, maybe it's true."

"It's true. Trust me."

Jason settled onto the opposite end of the couch while Michael looked around the toy-cluttered floor for the television remote control. He found it hiding where one of the kids had accidentally kicked it under the couch.

"The pregame show should be coming on for the Friars any minute," he explained. "I think they're playing Georgetown tonight."

"Syracuse," Raymond corrected him. "Georgetown's next week."

"Whatever," said Michael. "So, what do you think? You guys feel like watching some hoops?"

"Hey, it's your basement and you've got the remote," noted Jason. "That makes you king."

"Go with the PC game," said Raymond. "Who wants to watch the news?"

Michael sat on the floor and leaned back against the couch. "Just trying to be polite for my guests," he chuckled.

While Michael scrolled through the channels to find the game, Raymond reached over and gave Jason a poke in the arm.

"So, what's the deal, little bro?" he asked. "It's nice to have you back, but what brings you home all of a sudden after all this time without telling anyone?"

It was the kind of question Jason had anticipated from his brother, and everyone else for that matter, but was still not prepared to answer.

"It's kind of a long story," he offered after a moment.

"I'm in no hurry," replied Raymond. "Take your time."

Jason was considering what to say next when, mercifully, Natalie came to the top of the stairs and called down to let them know that it was time to eat.

"I'll tell you all about it later," said Jason, getting to his feet.

"Can't wait to hear it," said his brother.

Then they went upstairs to dinner.

Giulio was in fine spirits when everybody was finally gathered around the table. While Natalie served the macaroni, he filled the wineglasses one by one and passed them along to the adults. Little Jenna and Tommy, of course, would have to make do with fruit juice when it came time for their grandfather to make a toast. When at last the wine was poured, Giulio broke out in a great smile and raised his glass to Jason.

"Here's to having everyone home together again," he said simply. *"Salute!"*

"Salute!" the others replied, clinking their glasses together—Tommy and Jenna of course with their sippy cups.

Jason returned their smiles, but inside, as he sipped his wine, he was a tangle of nerves and conflicted emotions. He knew that it truly was a good thing to once more be with his family, but the circumstances that had brought about the reunion, known only to him, were far from happy. The thought of these things weighed on him, and it was a weight of which he longed to rid himself, but he feared what the others might think of him were he to speak the truth just now. And so, for his sake as much as theirs, he put on a glad face, feeling all the while like an impostor in their midst as they all settled down to eat. To his dismay, the questions commenced almost the moment he lifted his fork.

"So, Jason," began Natalie, "it's great to have you home, but what's with not letting anyone know? You should have called to let us know you were coming."

"That's right," added Raymond from across the table. "I asked him the same question a few minutes ago. So, Jason, what was that long story you were about to tell me downstairs?"

Jason put down his fork.

"It really isn't a long story at all," he said with a shrug. "It was just kind of a spur-of-the-moment thing. I just needed to get out of L.A. for a while."

"How's things at your company?" asked Michael before he could elaborate any further. "What's the name again, Med-Tech, or something like that?"

"Med-Device Technologies," said Jason. Then, after a pause, he added, "They're doing fine."

"They?" said Raymond with a curious look.

"Hey," interjected Giulio, who had been keeping a watchful eye on the proceedings. "What is this, twenty questions? Let the kid eat his macaroni before it goes cold."

"Eat your food and all your vegetables!" exclaimed little Tommy, wagging a finger at his uncle Jason. It was a perfect imitation of a typical dinnertime performance by his parents, and everyone burst into laughter.

"So, what's happening at the inn?" asked Jason, seizing on the opportunity to steer the conversation away from himself once quiet had resumed. "Anybody see the lady in white lately?"

At that his father let out a groan.

"Oh, please," scoffed Giulio. "Don't start with that nonsense again."

The "lady in white" was a ghostly apparition that allegedly manifested itself from time to time in Bradley Mansion. Over the years, guests had reported seeing fleeting glimpses of a mysterious young woman dressed in a white gown, gliding down the hall or passing them unexpectedly on the staircase. Growing up, Jason and his siblings had all sworn to have themselves witnessed her floating about the premises, but in all his years Giulio had never once observed any unearthly visitors in his inn. He always pooh-poohed the whole thing as nothing more than the light and overactive imaginations playing tricks on one's eyes. His children were of course inclined to believe otherwise, and the lady in white had remained an ever-favorite topic of conversation, eliciting endless speculation as to who or what she might be.

As Jason had hoped, his inquiry about her prompted a lively discussion of the phenomenon, and at last he relaxed a little while he ate his dinner and listened to accounts of the most recent sightings. He did not know how long it would take for that particular topic to run its course. As long as it gave him time to decide just what he should say next, that would be enough.

CHAPTER 11

Jason and his father did not stay very late at Natalie's. Shortly before they had finished eating, Donna called to say that she would not be coming because her car would not start and she was stuck at work. After gobbling down a few last mouthfuls of food, Raymond bid everyone a quick good night and hurried off to pick her up. Not long afterward, when supper was finished, Natalie began to clear the table while Michael carried the kids upstairs to get them ready for bed. Giulio had taken that as their cue that it was time to go. Tomorrow would be another workday for everyone, so it was time for him and Jason to get on their way and let the young family settle down for the night.

Later, as his father drove them home across town, Jason reflected on the evening. All in all, things had gone as well as he could possibly have hoped. There had been one or two awkward moments, a few probing questions, but Giulio had managed to rescue him each time with a timely comment or an amusing anecdote before things ever went very far. It comforted Jason to sense that his father had been looking out for him, instinctively protecting him from his siblings' prying until he was ready to talk openly and honestly. All the same, he also understood that he could remain under his father's wing for only so long. He suspected that Raymond and Natalie already knew more than their seemingly innocent questions would indicate, but just how much he could not tell. In any case, he knew that he would not be able to hide from them or the truth forever.

Jason suspected that Giulio understood this as well. And thus it came as no surprise to him when, upon returning home and walking through the front door, his father straightaway directed him to take a seat in the living room. The tone of his voice told him that the time had come to clear the air. Jason had hoped to somehow put off this moment for a little longer, but apparently there would be no more waiting. Suddenly he felt that terrible, exhausting weight come crashing down on him once more. Like a condemned man, he dropped into a chair by the fireplace and waited in gloomy silence for what was to come. Sundance, perhaps sensing that there was serious business to be addressed, gave each man a halfhearted sniff, then slunk off to the kitchen, where he lay down beneath the table.

His father said nothing at first, but instead knelt by the hearth, opened the flue, and tossed some kindling and logs onto the grate. A strike of the match and the wood caught flame. Before long it went up in a crackling blaze.

"It's time for us to talk," said Giulio over his shoulder as he prodded the fire with the poker and the flames climbed higher.

"I know," sighed Jason.

Giulio leaned the poker against the hearth and put the screen back across the fire. Then he brushed his hands together and sat down in the chair opposite Jason. He fell silent once more and for a time the only sound in the room was the crackle and hiss of the burning wood. At last he turned his eyes from the fire and looked at Jason with the penetrating gaze of a father who knew when something was not right with his child, and was determined to get to the bottom of it.

Jason had seen that same look so many times before when he was a boy, but even now that he was a grown man, it still gave him pause. The little boy that still lived deep within him wanted with all his being to run away again like he had done that day so many years ago, but he knew it would be of no use, for there was no hiding from his father's eyes.

Giulio folded his arms, as if bracing himself, and leaned toward his son.

"It's time to tell me what happened to you," he said in a gentle voice. "I'm your father, you can tell me anything. Do you understand?"

At that Jason heaved a heavy sigh and bowed his head in shame and despair, for he found he could no longer look his father straight in the eye. He swallowed hard and struggled to hold back the tears welling in his eyes, but he no longer had the strength to fight them.

"Dad, I screwed up so bad," he said, his voice faltering. "I lied about something, something important—and I made such a mess of things."

With those words he buried his face in his hands unable to go on, until he felt his father's hand upon his shoulder.

"What did you lie about?" said Giulio.

Jason took a deep breath and looked away to the fire, ashamed all the more that he had broken down in that way.

"It had to do with a special project I was working on," he said, wiping his eyes dry with the back of his hand. "It was called ProCardia One."

"Yes, I remember you talking about it once," said Giulio. "Some kind of surgical implant or something, right?"

"That's right," answered Jason. "It was this incredible product we were developing that was suppose to revolutionize the treatment of cardiovascular disease—I mean, at least that's what we told everybody in all the marketing literature."

"But I take it there was a problem?" his father guessed.

"The problem was that it didn't work," said Jason ruefully. "At least not the way it was supposed to in some people."

"What happened?"

"At first, everything was looking great," Jason explained. "ProCardia was just sailing along through all the big clinical trials, just like everybody expected it to. Patients were doing well with it, and investors were lining up down the block. It was looking like a home run."

At that Jason paused and with a disconsolate countenance, rolled his eyes. "We were all going to be rich of course," he said.

"Was that important to you?"

Jason looked away.

"I don't know," he confessed with a shake of his head. "I guess so. But just when we thought we had it made, the results came back from two smaller studies the company had funded."

"What did the studies tell you?" asked Giulio, eyeing his son closely.

"Like I said, they were small studies," Jason replied, shrinking from his father's gaze, "but some of the patients in the studies developed severe complications after receiving the implant. Some of them almost died before the doctors could remove it. Statistically, when you considered them as part of the entire group of studies, the results weren't all that significant, but . . ."

"But people almost died," noted his father.

"Yeah," sighed Jason. "That's right."

"So what did you do?"

Jason shifted uncomfortably in his chair and heaved another sigh.

"I did what I was told," he said.

Somberly, Jason recounted for his father the day almost a year earlier when Phil Langway had called him into his office to tell him the bad news about the clinical studies. He described how he had sat there trying to make sense of what he had just been told while Langway and the others encircled him like a pack of angry wolves. Even now Jason could still hear their low, snarling voices.

"Do you have any idea what this means?" he recalled Langway telling him. "This could delay everything for years if we don't get FDA approval."

"Investors will pull out the second they hear of this," one of the others had said.

"The company stock won't be worth the paper it's printed on," lamented a third. "You, me, all of us, we'll lose everything."

"You have to do something," Langway had told him. "You can figure out a way. Just bury the numbers somehow. That's the kind of thing you get paid for, isn't it? That will give them time to fix whatever the problem is before we put ProCardia on the market."

Jason, his mind reeling, did not know where to turn or what to think. All he understood was that everything he had worked so hard for was about to fall to pieces, and he was gripped by a terrible fear. Fear of losing his job and all the perks. Fear of no longer being able to afford the lavish lifestyle he had come to enjoy. But worst of all, fear of losing Amanda, for would she still care for him if he lost it all and had to start out once again at the bottom?

"Just do what we say, and everything will be fine," he remembered Langway saying. "Trust us, no one will ever find out."

Jason paused at this point in his story and looked at his father.

"Let me guess what happened," said Giulio. "You did it—and somebody found out."

"It all came out six months ago," said Jason, shaking his head wearily. "Don't ask me who or how, but after that it was like I was caught in some kind of tornado of lawyers and lawsuits and investigations and reporters, and it just ripped apart everything in its path. I had been so afraid of losing what I had worked for, but in the end I lost it all anyway. My job. My friends. Just about everything I owned. It was like I'd lost everything that made me who I was."

Giulio arched an eyebrow.

"Everything that made you who you were?" he said. "Is that what they taught you in school?"

"I know, I know," sulked Jason. "It's just that it all came out in the news in L.A., with my name right in the middle of it, so suddenly I wasn't just broke, but I was like a leper. No one would come near me, never mind hire me."

Jason paused and shook his head again.

"I'm so sorry, Dad," he sighed. "I disgraced myself, and I disgraced my name. I wasted everything. All the years in school, all the work. All of it for nothing."

With that Jason turned away to the fireplace and stared forlornly at the dying flames while he waited for the inevitable rebuke.

For a time, his father made no reply. Instead he simply sat there, deep in quiet thought as he stroked his chin.

"So, what did you learn?" he said at last.

Jason looked at his father with uncertainty. "I don't know what you mean."

Giulio gave a sigh of his own and pressed the palms of his hands together in the way that he often did whenever he was about to say something of importance.

"Jason, nothing you ever do in life is a waste," he told him, "so long as you learn something from it. Now, what you did was truly disgraceful, and you have suffered justifiably because of it, but have you taken the time to stop and think about just how lucky you were?"

"*Lucky?*" snickered Jason. "How do you figure?"

Giulio settled back and smiled at his son.

"Jason, I believe that everything, even the most terrible and heart-wrenching things, happen for a reason," he said, "a *good* reason. Sometimes only God can know what that is, and he likes to keep his cards tight to the vest. But other times, if you take a step back and think things through, you can start to see the plan.

Now, let's look at you. Imagine that this scheme you and your bosses concocted had worked and that product had ended up being sold exactly as it was. How would you have felt if innocent people had died because the flaws in it had never been discovered and corrected? Imagine if it had happened to someone you know and care about. Would all the riches in the world have been worth it to you? Could you have lived with that?"

"No," Jason admitted. "You're right, I couldn't have. I guess I never thought of it that way."

Giulio gave a satisfied harrumph and got to his feet.

"Trust me, you lucked out, my friend," he said, patting Jason on the head. "But it's all over now, so stop worrying about it."

"But what do I do now?" said Jason, as much to himself as to his father.

"You need to find a way to make amends," said Giulio, "to put things right in your life again."

"Hmm, where do I start with that project?" muttered Jason.

His father gave a shrug and gestured at their surroundings.

"Why not stick around here for a while?" he said. "This is your home, you know, it's not a trap that you have to be afraid of getting caught in for the rest of your life. I know you have your own ideas about things, so stay as long as you want. Rest up, get strong again, and then make your plans. How's that for a deal?"

Jason did not take long to consider his father's offer. After all, where else was there for him to go?

"That sounds good," he said honestly. "Better than I'd hoped for." Then, barely above a whisper, "Thank you."

"Niente," said his father with a dismissive wave. Then he reached out and gave Jason a gentle swat across the top of the head, a playful gesture to let him know that everything was going to be all right. With that he bid his son a good night and headed upstairs to bed with Sundance close on his heels.

Jason remained by the fire for a while, drowsily watching it slowly burn down until all that was left was the orange glow of the smoldering embers. Though it had left him totally drained, he was relieved beyond words to have finally admitted to his father what he had done. Nonetheless his spirit was still deeply troubled. Yes, his father was right, he had indeed been lucky after all, but then again Jason had not told him the worst of it.

CHAPTER 12

One day after work, weeks after his ill-starred meeting with Phil Langway, but before things at the company had fallen apart for him, Jason accompanied Amanda on her daily jog along the beach. His girlfriend was a fitness buff—he was not—and like always whenever she coaxed him into running with her, it was a formidable challenge just to keep up. Her face perfectly serene, her slender arms and legs bronzed from the California sun, Amanda had loped effortlessly along, a picture of athletic beauty and grace.

Jason, on the other hand, was a different matter entirely. Five minutes into the run, his T-shirt already blotched with sweat, he was panting like a dog. His legs and lungs felt like he had swallowed fire. He was in agony, and it was only out of sheer pride that he managed to stay reasonably close until they came to the pier that marked the halfway point of their run. There Amanda stopped just long enough to turn around and quickly resume running in the opposite direction. Jason, however, had no choice but to wait for a few moments to gulp in a few breaths of air before jogging off after her at a considerably slower pace.

"Come on, slowpoke!" Amanda had playfully called over her shoulder.

Despite his abject suffering, Jason smiled and waved. That was how things had become for him. He was crazy about Amanda and willing to endure anything to be with her, be it a leg-shattering run on the beach or one of their many wallet-shattering nights on the town, for the payoff was always so much greater than the pain. He loved every second they spent together, and ached for her when they were apart.

Still, things had not been quite the same between them ever since Jason had agreed to take part in Langway's scheme. Amanda of course knew nothing of what he had done, but the nagging thought that it might come to light one day haunted the back of Jason's mind. For the first few days after he had manipulated the ProCardia data, every ring of the telephone or knock on his office door set his pulse racing, for he would be certain that the dreaded moment when he was to be exposed had arrived. He carried around inside him a constant dull ache of nervous tension that sapped his energy and eroded his peace of mind. Despite his best efforts to hide his disquiet, he often became moody and distant when he was with Amanda, brushing aside her inquiries as to what was bothering him.

As the days turned into weeks, though, and the ProCardia project went forward as planned, Jason began to relax a little, for it appeared that everything was going to turn out just as he had hoped. In time he learned to control his fears, and gradually they faded to the background of his consciousness. Now and then, they still arose to torment him, but he accepted that pain as the price he had to pay to keep Amanda—for he had convinced himself that what he had done he had done for her.

Amanda was already sitting back against a palm tree, sipping a bottle of water, by the time Jason finally straggled back to her. His shorts and shirt drenched with perspiration, he doubled over and rested his hands on his knees until he caught his breath. With a wince, he straightened up and limped over to her.

"Oooh, you poor thing," Amanda cooed at seeing his pained expression. "Are you going to be all right?"

"Actually, I think I'm dying," groaned Jason.

At that Amanda came close, took his face in her hands, and kissed him in a way that made his weary legs grow even weaker. Then she pulled away and gave him a furtive look that he could not possibly mistake.

"In that case, we had better get you home right away," she told him, "and get you out of those wet clothes."

Later, after they had made love, the two lay across Jason's bed, blissfully exhausted. By now the sun was setting, its fragile rays bathing them and the room in a soft, dreamlike glow. For a long while neither spoke, for they were content to simply rest there and enjoy the sweet languor of the moment. After a time, though, Amanda draped her thigh across Jason's legs and rested her head against his chest.

"Do you love me?" she said.

"Of course I do," said Jason, stroking her fine hair.

"Do you really?" said Amanda. "What would you do if—I don't know—let's say I told you my hair wasn't really naturally blond, but it was brown instead?"

"Well, I know for sure that it's not," said Jason with a knowing laugh, "but I would love you anyway, even if it weren't."

"Okay, but what would you do if someday I got fat and ugly?" she asked with a pout. "Would you still love me then?"

"I couldn't imagine you ever getting fat and ugly," he assured her, "but even if you did, I would still love you. I'll always love you."

At that Amanda grew quiet for a time. She sat up and looked down at him with a questioning gaze.

"What would you do if I told you that I was going to have a baby?" she said at last.

Jason sat up as well and looked into her eyes, wondering with a nervous twinge just where this line of questioning was taking him. He took her hand and brought it to his lips.

"In that case, I guess I would have to marry you," he answered truthfully.

"Well then," Amanda said softly, "I guess you're going to have to marry me."

She paused, waiting for his reaction.

At first Jason was dumbstruck as he took in the meaning of what she had just said. A wave of panic swept over him, but then it quickly passed only to be replaced by another completely different and unexpected emotion. To his utter astonishment, he found it was joy. Amanda, this breathtakingly beautiful woman, was carrying a child, *his* child! Their love had created an entirely new life. Suddenly Jason saw a whole new world opening up for them, a whole new way of living. The thought of it all was so wondrous that it left his face beaming as he reached out to take her in his arms.

"Amanda, do you really mean—"

Amanda laid a finger across his lips.

"No words," she said breathlessly. "Just show me that you love me."

Then, with a coy smile, she lay back and gently drew him to her once more.

When Jason awoke the next morning, he groggily reached out for Amanda, but found that he was alone in bed. On the nightstand, he found the note she had left for him explaining that she had needed to get up very early and had not wanted to wake him. Jason had overslept, so he hastily got himself out of bed, showered, and dressed. Before long he was hurrying out the door on his way to work.

As he sped down the highway, Jason felt like he was on top of the world. So many things were coming together for him. His career. His life. He thought about Amanda and how fortunate he was to have her as the mother of his child. It was all so perfect in so many ways. His love for her was honest and true, he told himself, and would have been no matter what her circumstances. That would have been enough on its own, but there were also practical advantages to their relationship that he could not deny. Though a huge investment, Med-Device Technologies was just one of her wealthy father's many enterprises. Who knew what other opportunities might lay ahead for Jason in the years to come? Could he be blamed for envisioning the comfortable life that marrying into her family would bring him?

When he arrived at Med-Device, those happy thoughts dancing in his mind, Jason strode across the parking lot, feeling lighter than air. He breezed into the building, bidding a cheerful good morning to everyone he passed in the hall. He was in a joyous mood and saw no reason not to share it.

It was then, just after he rounded the corner, that he saw that his office door was ajar. Inside stood a grim-faced Bill Forsythe, waiting with arms folded. For a moment, Jason imagined that Amanda had already spoken with her father and that he had come to Jason to demand an immediate explanation. This notion quickly evaporated when Jason nudged open the door and found three other men he had never before seen waiting there with the company president.

None looked happy.

Jason's heart went dead inside him, for he knew without being told exactly why they all had come.

"Good morning, Mr. Forsythe," he said, swallowing hard.

"Good morning, Jason," replied Forsythe with cool detachment. "Please come in and sit down. These men are federal agents. They have some questions they'd like to ask you about the clinical trials for ProCardia One."

Jason stepped inside and they closed the door behind him.

Later, after enduring hours of questioning culminated by the termination of his employment, Jason faced the further humiliation of being walked out of the building by two security guards. By this time, word of what he and the others had done had already spread like wildfire. There was not a man or woman who did not instantly understand just what it would mean to the company and to their own livelihoods. As he slouched toward the exit, carrying with him the few belongings he had been allowed to take, Jason bowed his head to avoid their icy, menacing stares. He knew full well what they were thinking. Jason Mirabella and the others had quite likely ruined them all, and he walked out of Med-Device Technologies a disgraced, discredited, and despised man.

For all that, when the guards unceremoniously abandoned him in the parking lot, sending him off into exile, Jason's first and only thoughts were of Amanda and the baby. He needed desperately to speak with her, to explain himself, to tell her what he had done and why. He rushed to his car in a panic, his cell phone pressed to his ear, but his call succeeded only in reaching her voice mail. Upon returning to his apartment, he ran inside, hoping to find a message from her on his answering machine, but there was none. He spent the rest of that day in self-imposed confinement, pacing about like a caged animal, his mind a feverish blur as he waited for her call to come.

When at last the phone rang, Jason sprang to answer it.

"Tell me it's not true," said Amanda the very instant he picked up the phone. Her voice was full of sorrow and bitterness, and the sound of it ripped Jason apart.

"Amanda," he pleaded. "Please let me explain."

"I don't want you to explain," she snapped. "I just want you to tell me that it's not true."

"Amanda, I—"

"Tell me!" she screamed.

There was a long, terrible pause. Jason wanted so desperately to say the words she wished to hear, to tell her that it had all been a misunderstanding, that it was all going to be all right, but he knew otherwise—and so he said nothing.

"Good-bye, Jason," she said.

"Amanda, please wait!" he cried.

By then, though, the line had already gone dead, leaving him alone in empty, agonizing silence.

The days that followed were a waking nightmare. Though Jason had agreed to fully cooperate with the investigation into the scandal at Med-Device, there was still talk of lawsuits and criminal charges that could lead to jail time. The legals fees to defend himself would be enormous. To pay for them, Jason drained what little he kept in his savings accounts, and one by one he began to sell all of his possessions. Too ashamed to let anyone at home know of his predicament, and too proud in any case to ask for help, he held out hope that somehow he would land on his feet and quickly start all over.

Throughout the ordeal, he tried to get in touch with Amanda, but she refused to return his calls. Frantic to see her again, he drove past her apartment building at all hours, hoping to find her at home, but for days her space in the parking lot was empty and the windows to her bedroom darkened.

Jason began to despair of ever seeing Amanda again until early one morning, as he drove past her building, he spied her car in the parking lot. Wasting no time, he turned into the lot and parked in the adjacent space. He was just getting out of the car when he saw Amanda emerge from the building with two small suitcases in hand. At the sight of him, she did not retreat indoors as he had expected, but instead boldly strutted past him on the way to the back of her car. There she opened the trunk and stowed the two pieces of luggage.

"You have nerve coming here," she seethed, slamming the trunk shut.

"Amanda, please listen," he begged her. "I know I made a bad mistake."

Amanda glared at him in incredulity.

"Mistake?" she spat. "Do you have any idea of what you did to my father? Of what you did to everyone, including me?"

"I know, Amanda," he sighed miserably. "What I did was wrong, but I can make up for it if you give me the chance."

"There's no making up for this," she said with deep venom.

With that Amanda pushed past him to open the car door.

"Wait," cried Jason, instinctively taking hold of her arm.

Amanda whirled around and slapped him hard across the face.

"Let go of me, you creep," she snarled.

Stunned, Jason released her and helplessly watched her get into the car.

"But where are you going?" he said.

"I'm going away," was all she would tell him.

"But what about us?" he cried. "What about the baby?"

Amanda rolled her eyes and gave him a look of utter disgust.

"Oh, please," she hissed. "As if."

Without another word she pulled the car door shut, revved the engine, and sped out of the parking lot.

Jason watched in anguish as she drove away. It was then that the true horror of what he had done set in on him. He squeezed his head between his hands, for suddenly he understood that not only had he lost her, but worse, their child would never be born. Stricken with grief and remorse, for there was no one to blame but himself, Jason stood there like a condemned man at the gallows. The breath strangled out of him, he fell to his knees, and his mind into darkness.

Now, six months later, as he lay awake in bed in his father's house, Jason dwelled on that final scene, pondering the terrible cascade of events his one foolish act had wrought. How, he despaired, could he ever make amends for something about which he could not even bring himself to speak? It was if he had been swept down a great rushing river and had tumbled over the falls. Until he found a way to catch himself, his life would be in perpetual free fall, plummeting endlessly toward the rocks.

CHAPTER 13

Something shattered the silence.

Startled from a deep, dreamless sleep, Jason sat up, rubbed his eyes, and strained to listen, hoping to discern what had awakened him. The sound, reminiscent of the roar of a jet airliner at takeoff, had by now already faded into the distance. Perhaps he had only imagined it, Jason thought at first, but a few moments later he suddenly heard the roar again growing louder and closer by the moment. Reaching out to the window, he parted the curtains and immediately understood. It had snowed overnight, the world outside now blanketed in white. The snowplows were out clearing the streets.

Jason gave a yawn and flopped back down on the pillow as one of the plows rumbled by the front of the house. He had been home three days. As with each of the previous mornings, he had slept well past the ungodly hour his father typically arose to go to the inn. The thought that Giulio had gone off to work while he had lounged in bed like a schoolboy on a snow day gave Jason a twinge of guilt, but there was nothing for him to do about it. Though he had done little else but sleep these past days, there remained deep inside him a seemingly bottomless well of fatigue. Sometimes simply thinking required more effort than he cared to muster, and Jason had spent much of the time on the couch, dozing when he wasn't watching the inane offerings on the television. It seemed he had no choice but to heed his father's admonitions to just rest for the time being and do nothing else.

Jason had not needed to be convinced of the wisdom in his father's advice. Whatever his outward appearance, he knew that inside he was a collection of damaged goods. This morning, however, he realized that he had not awoken filled with complete dread at the thought of what the day might bring. The boot against his chest seemed to have eased ever so slightly, and for the first time he suspected that he was beginning to heal, that perhaps the deep well of fatigue was finally starting to empty. To be sure, he remained a far cry from his old self, but as he rolled out of bed and set his feet on the floor, he realized that it was already becoming just a little easier to face the day and to keep the inner demons that preyed on him at bay.

When Jason came downstairs, he found Sundance curled up on the couch. The dog lifted its head as he passed, gave a rather dramatic yawn, and promptly curled back up to sleep.

"And good morning to you too," chuckled Jason on his way to the kitchen.

As always, Giulio had left a freshly brewed pot of coffee plugged in on the counter. Jason poured himself a cup and stared out the back window.

From what he could see, six inches or more of the white stuff had fallen, the snow lying like a white quilt across the yard and clinging to the tree branches above like great clumps of cotton. Though he now liked to consider himself a Californian, Jason had not been away from New England winters long enough to be able to admire the simple beauty of the snow without reminding himself of what a nuisance it could be. Once again he thought of his father, and once again felt a stab of guilt. The sun most likely had not yet even risen when Giulio trudged out alone through the snow to clean off his car that morning. Inwardly, Jason scolded himself. Had he been awake, he at least might have gone out and done that little service for him. He knew that at this point his father expected nothing from him. Just the same, Jason loathed the feeling that he was turning into a freeloader.

When he had downed the last of his coffee, Jason stood there for a minute, drumming his fingers on the counter. There was, unfortunately, no undoing the past, but there was always the present in which to make amends. And so, against his father's advice to just rest, he went upstairs, pulled on some warm clothes, and headed outside to shovel the drive and the walks.

Later, when he came back inside, his cheeks flush from the brisk air and hard work, Jason stood in the hallway, stamping the snow off his boots. He had forgotten how strenuous shoveling snow could be, and he was remarkably tired and hungry. Nonetheless, despite the heavy weariness in his limbs, he felt very much invigorated. The fresh air and exercise had done him a world of good and put him in a better frame of mind. His stomach rumbling for lunch, he started for the kitchen to see what he might prepare for himself, but en route another idea presented itself. It would require the use of his father's car—Giulio had driven his pickup truck to work, and left the sedan in the garage as he often did in bad weather—but Jason was certain that he would not object. The matter decided, he took the car keys from the hook on the kitchen wall, pulled his coat and hat back on, and promptly headed out the door once more into the cold.

Jason knew that if you arrived at Graziella's Bakery after eleven thirty in the morning, you took the very real chance of finding nothing left to buy. The bakery, owned and operated by Jason's aunt Gracie and uncle Ernie, made what many considered the best Italian bread in the city. The golden brown crust of Graziella's bread was just the proper crispness, the warm delicious center of the loaf just the right texture. Wise bread connoisseurs from the surrounding neighborhoods invariably lined up at the bakery door every day before it even opened for business. There they would wait with mouths watering as they breathed in the heavenly aroma of the baking bread wafting from the ovens inside. It was a rare morning when every scrap of bread (Uncle Ernie's specialty) and all the cakes and cookies (Aunt Gracie's) were not sold out well before noon. When the last loaf of bread went, no more was baked, and the doors closed for the day.

And so it was that Jason was not surprised to find the doors already locked when he arrived a little while later at the bakery. He pressed his face against the window and peered inside. Apparently the inclement weather had not prevented the local faithful from buying their daily bread, for inside he could see Aunt Gracie and Uncle Ernie cleaning up for the day, his aunt cackling away at her husband like she always did.

Jason smiled. One of his favorite childhood memories was of Sunday mornings after Mass when Giulio would drive the family across town to get their bread for dinner and a treat (*if* they behaved!) for dessert. No matter how busy the morning might have been at the bakery, there was always a loaf or two of bread and a little tray of Italian cookies set aside just for them. Aunt Gracie was his mother's sister. She and Uncle Ernie had no children of their own, and whenever the family came through the door, the two made a great fuss over Jason and his siblings. There would be hugs and kisses and cheeks pinched so hard his eyes would tear up. And then, while the adults chatted, Uncle Ernie would let the kids "help" by putting them to work sweeping the floor or wiping the counters. Of the three, Natalie would make a proper show of it more often than not, but it would not take long before sweeping the floor turned into something more resembling a hockey match whenever Raymond and Jason got their hands on the brooms. Sometimes the family stayed for just a few minutes (who could put up with their commotion!) before heading home. Other days they all went upstairs, where his aunt and uncle lived, for coffee and pastry. No matter what they did, Jason could remember nothing but pleasant times in that place.

Happy as those memories might have been, Jason could not now help feeling a little sad. Running a bakery, even a little one like Graziella's, was hard work, and the years were slowly beginning to catch up with his aunt and uncle. They wouldn't be able to run the business forever by themselves. With no son or daughter to one day take over the operation for them, what would become of the place?

Jason gave the window a knock.

"We're closed!" Uncle Ernie called over his shoulder as he pushed the broom along the floor.

Jason knocked again, this time a little harder.

Aunt Gracie, who had been occupied wiping down the glass on the front of the display case beneath the cash register, straightened up and looked in mild consternation toward the window.

"We're closed!" she called just as her husband had done. Then she paused and took a step toward the window to get a better look at the smiling stranger standing outside. Her face lit up. "Oh my God," she cried. "Ernie, look who it is!"

In a flash the door swung open and Aunt Gracie pulled Jason inside. There were hugs and kisses and, incredibly, she still pinched his cheek. Uncle Ernie, who was a bit more reserved than his wife, simply smiled and shook his hand before giving him a warm pat on the shoulder.

"It's good to see you, Jason," he said.

"Your father told us you were back home," said Aunt Gracie, giving his cheek another pinch. "We were wondering how long you were going to wait before you came to see us. What took you so long?"

"Ayy, it's only been a few days," noted Jason with a shrug.

"Well, who knew how long you were going to stay?" replied his aunt. "We were worried you'd be on your way back to California before we got a chance to see you."

"No, I'm going to be hanging around for a while," said Jason. "Besides, I wouldn't have gone without stopping by."

"So, what brings you home?" asked Uncle Ernie. "Just back for a little vacation?"

"Actually, I'm between jobs right now," said Jason tactfully. "So before I looked for something new, I figured it would be a good time to come home and visit for a while." He paused and gave the air a sniff. Though there was no bread left in sight, the sweet smell still lingered everywhere. He feigned a sigh and looked about with sad eyes. "And I was hoping to maybe get a nice fresh loaf of bread somewhere," he added, "but it looks like you're all out."

"Ayyy, what a zoo we had in here this morning!" exclaimed Aunt Gracie. "They came in like a swarm of locusts the minute we opened the door. We were practically sold out by nine o'clock!"

"Happens every time it snows," said Uncle Ernie with a shrug.

"Why didn't you make a few extra loaves?" inquired Jason, though he already understood that that was simply not how they operated. "I bet you would have sold a bunch more today."

"Eh, I was going to," said Uncle Ernie with a dismissive wave, "but we really don't need the extra dough."

Uncle Ernie was one of those people who loved to play with words—that is, whenever his wife gave him a chance to talk—and Jason laughed at the pun. Aunt Gracie meantime just rolled her eyes.

"See what I have to put up with?" she lamented. "He tells stupid jokes like that all day long." At that she shook her head before leaning closer to scrutinize Jason's face. "Hey," she said with concern, "you look a little peaked. Have you eaten today?"

"Not much," Jason admitted. "I figured maybe I'd grab a sandwich or something while I was out."

"A sandwich?" scoffed Aunt Gracie. "Your uncle and I are going out to lunch as soon as we're done here. We're going to the Post. Why don't you come with us and tell us all about what you've been doing out in California?"

Jason was not all that anxious to talk about California, but he was famished and the invitation to lunch was too good to pass up. After pitching in to help them finish cleaning up, he gladly accompanied them to the restaurant.

The Post was not the type of establishment Jason had grown accustomed to frequenting during his heyday out West. Run out of the function hall of a local V.F.W. post, its only decor was the few commemorative plaques on the walls and the red-and-white-checked cloths on the tables. There was no maitre d' to greet them, no one to check their coats, just a sign asking patrons to please wait until a waitress seated them at an empty table. Despite its lack of ambiance, the place was packed with lunchtime diners. One whiff of the delicious smells drifting out of the kitchen reminded Jason why. The food was superb. This was not a place to see and be seen; it was simply a place to eat, and eat well.

Jason had not dined there in years. Just the same, as he followed his aunt and uncle to their table and looked about the crowded room alive with talk and laughter, he saw among the patrons more than one familiar face. He could not quite remember any of their names—and he suspected that they probably did not remember his—nonetheless they exchanged nods of greeting with him. Though small gestures, they had the effect of making Jason feel welcome. It was a good feeling.

"So, what looks good?" asked Jason after he settled into a chair and opened his menu.

"Everything's good here," his aunt assured him.

"They've got the stuffed calamari today," Uncle Ernie pointed out.

"Do they still have the polenta?" asked Jason, scanning the menu.

"Ooh, that's really good here too," said his uncle. "Tell you what, I'll get the calamari, you get the polenta, and we'll get some extra plates to share a little bit. Deal?"

"Fine with me," said Jason.

His uncle smiled and leaned closer.

"In Roman times," he explained, "that's what they used to call a little *squid* pro quo, if you know what I mean."

Aunt Gracie looked with disdain at her husband and gave a groan.

"And to think they shot Lincoln," she muttered.

Jason could only smile.

CHAPTER 14

For all the slipping and sliding on the roads, and the aggravation of having to shovel the steps and walkways, there was a certain undeniable magic about waking up to find the world outside suddenly covered in a thick shroud of snow. Giulio often thought that snowstorms were nature's way of masking the drab, barren landscape during the winter months until God was ready to warm the earth and beautify everything once again come spring. New-fallen snow, Giulio found, had a way of putting people in a different frame of mind. It made them slow down a little, if only for a moment or two, to take in the altered scenery and breathe in the fresh air scrubbed clean by the falling snowflakes. It had a way of renewing a person's spirits, almost as if it made you become a child again, at least on the inside.

On such days, Giulio understood that there was no better treat than to arise from bed and come downstairs to enjoy a nice cup of coffee and a leisurely breakfast by the warmth of a crackling fire. And so the first order of business that morning at the inn was to get the dining room and living room fireplaces blazing well before the guests began to roll out of bed. Giulio loved the smell of the burning wood and he kept the fires stoked until well after breakfast. Come the afternoon, he would rekindle them once more before everyone returned for tea time.

The second order of business for the day concerned Jason.

Giulio was exceedingly pleased to have his son home, but anxious nonetheless to see him get back on his feet and engaged in some new productive activity as quickly as possible. The days of recuperative rest at home were all well and good for the time being, for life had obviously thrown him down quite hard. For now he required gentle handling, but the time would come very soon when Jason would have to climb back into the saddle and start moving forward again on his own. Otherwise, Giulio fretted, he might slip into stagnation and throw away months, if not years, before he righted himself.

The more he mulled the matter over, the more Giulio became convinced that the best thing for Jason would be to get himself back into a regular routine, however light it might be at first. At the same time, he understood that his son did not need the pressure of rushing out on a job search, especially considering his most recent employment experience. What he needed was an easy entry back into the world, someplace to start over, to get his hands a little dirty again from honest work, and gradually regain his confidence.

The obvious choice, by Giulio's reckoning, was his own family business.

Giulio knew his son too well to believe that Jason would take to the idea of coming to work at the inn with much enthusiasm, if any at all. With a little gentle prodding, however, he might be convinced to at least give it a try for a little while. After that, who could say where things might lead him?

His mind made up, Giulio intended to discuss his plans with Raymond and Natalie straightaway after breakfast, but before he could call the two into the study, an officer from the state fire marshal's office showed up unannounced to make his annual inspection of the building. Giulio had no choice but to escort him around the premises while Raymond hurried off to tend to a leaky pipe in the kitchen. Natalie meantime found herself on the telephone for much of the morning, trying to resolve a discrepancy on an invoice from one of the inn's vendors when she wasn't fielding a sudden burst of calls from prospective guests.

That's the way things went for much of the day. It seemed like every time Giulio finished dealing with one matter and had a free moment to talk with his children, another that required his immediate attention, or that of Raymond or Natalie, would immediately present itself. The parade began with Victor, the milkman. Victor loved to talk about politics or the economy or whatever else happened to be on his mind whenever he found a willing ear. He lingered for near fifteen minutes, kibitzing about the cold weather before discreetly dropping the hint that he would need a check soon to bring their account up-to-date. Not long after Victor had gone on his way, the requisite check in pocket, Carl, the mailman, showed up with a certified letter requiring a signature. Over the years—none of the Mirabellas could quite recall how or when—it had become a daily tradition to offer him a "quick" cup of coffee when he dropped off the mail. It was a rare day when Carl did not accept the offer before heading off to complete his appointed rounds. This day proved no different, and a few more elusive minutes slipped away. No sooner had he gone than Mrs. Martinez reported her discovery of a loose piece of carpeting in the second-floor corridor that she advised, in her own inimitable fashion, be secured before someone "trip and fall and hurt themselves very, very badly."

Lunchtime offered no respite. Before Giulio could close the study door for a few moments of privacy with his children, the Fremonts, a very pleasant middle-aged couple in town to visit their daughter at Providence College, presented themselves. The two were enjoying their stay well enough, but the wife was in a bit of a tizzy over having misplaced a favorite earring somewhere in the house. The Fremonts avowed that they had thoroughly searched their room for the earring, and had made a cursory inspection of the downstairs, but to no avail. Giulio guided them to the living room, where the wayward bauble was eventually recovered from its hiding place between the sofa cushions.

On and on it went all day in the same fashion with scarcely a minute to catch one's breath. Before Giulio knew it, the clock in the living room was already chiming three, and he was at a loss to explain where the hours of the fast-waning day had flown. By this time, he and the others had started to feel more than a little ragged, and the effort to go about business wearing a smile for the benefit of the guests proved considerable. Though the timing was perhaps not the best, Giulio decided to seize advantage of a brief lull in the hustle and bustle and called Natalie and Raymond into the study.

When the three were gathered together and the door closed, Giulio wasted no time, but got straight to the point.

"When I think he's ready," he told them, "and if he wants to of course, I'm planning to put your brother on the payroll and have him come to work with us for a while."

The announcement was greeted with a deafening silence interrupted only by the clattering of the pipes as the heat came up.

"To do what?" Raymond finally said.

"Whatever he can to help us," said Giulio tersely, for he was a little miffed at the indignance he perceived in his older son's voice.

Natalie, who was no stranger to playing the family diplomat when she sensed tensions on the rise, intervened at once.

"But what about his job out in Los Angeles?" she asked.

"Jason's not going back to Los Angeles," replied her father. "At least not right away. And unless I'm very mistaken, the two of you know more about the reason why than you've been letting on these past few days."

"Jason hasn't told us anything," said Raymond truthfully. "Not that he ever does."

"Then he can tell you when he's ready," answered Giulio, irked by the coolness of their reception to his plan. He folded his arms and tapped his foot. "Say, what's the problem with you two, anyway?" he asked in growing agitation.

"What did you expect?" complained Raymond, his voice full of frustration. "Me and Natalie got left here holding the bag all those years while you paid God knows how much to put Jason through school. And then what does he do? He flies off to California without so much as even offering to give even just a little bit back, to work here just a few months, a year maybe. Was that too much to ask?

"But let's face it, the kid never wanted anything to do with this business. And that's fine. But now something's gone wrong with his big grandiose plans, and we're supposed to turn cartwheels with joy because he wants to just waltz into the operation after we've been here busting our humps to make it work all this time?"

"What's the problem?" griped Giulio. "First you complain that he hasn't given anything back. Now you're going to complain when he *does?* I thought you'd be happy to have him back."

Raymond gave a dismissive wave and rolled his eyes, as if to say it was impossible to make his father understand.

"It's not that there's a problem—not really," interjected Natalie. "It's just that this is so out of the blue, that's all. And of course we're happy he's back."

Her words did little to soothe her father's mounting annoyance.

"Jason is my son and your brother," he told them in no uncertain terms. "He's a part of the family, and there will always be a place for him in this family business. The same goes for any of you. Got it?"

Raymond bowed his head for a moment and gave a sigh of resignation.

"Look, Dad," he said, looking up. "We get it. It's not that we have anything against Jason, or that we don't want him back. It's just that the pie here is only so big. If you cut it up into too many pieces, we're all gonna go hungry. Do you know what I mean?"

"Then we'll all have to go on a diet for a little while," snipped Giulio.

With that he turned and marched out of the study.

Later, after he had rebuilt the fire in the living room and was satisfied that the afternoon tea was properly arranged, a still-peeved Giulio pulled on his coat and hat, bid his son and daughter a curt good night, and headed out the door for home. The sky had darkened, in keeping with his mood, and he surveyed his surroundings with a sour gaze, for the snow had started to come down again.

"Rotten snow," he grumbled.

Then he trudged down the walk to brush off the truck.

CHAPTER 15

"**T**o do what?" said Jason to his father.

The two were sitting at the kitchen table where Giulio had just proposed the idea of his son coming to work at the inn. The irony that the suggestion had elicited the exact same response as that of his older brother did not escape him. The only difference was in the tone with which each had uttered it. In contrast to Raymond's indignance, Giulio detected a hint of alarm in his younger son's voice.

For his part, Jason was indeed feeling the sudden grip of panic at the thought of his father's offer. Up to that point, the day had gone so well for him. After saying good-bye to his aunt and uncle, he had taken a ride around the city for no other reason than to simply reacquaint himself with his hometown. He cruised through Federal Hill and downtown past the financial center and the hotels overlooking Kennedy Plaza, then up College Hill onto the East Side, a fashionable section of the city. There he wove his way through the old-moneyed neighborhoods with their stately brick homes until he found himself on Thayer Street. Lined with shops and restaurants, the street had once been a favorite haunt of Jason's, and he had cast a wistful eye at the university students walking up and down the snow-covered sidewalks. Seeing them had brought back to him pleasant memories of more carefree times. Later, he had looped

around through the north end of the city and made his way
back across town past the statehouse before finally heading
home in time to catch a quick nap before his father returned
from work.

Thinking back, the ride around the city had been the best
part of Jason's day, even better in some ways than his lunch with
Aunt Gracie and Uncle Ernie. Perhaps it was the sensation of
being in control of the car that had made it so, or maybe it was
the freedom to steer himself in whichever direction he chose.
Whatever it was, something about being behind the wheel of a
car again relaxed him and for a little while stole his thoughts
away from Amanda and all the troubles he had left behind in
California.

Now, though, things felt as though they were spinning once
more out of his control and the dark clouds of anxiety suddenly
swirled back in around him like a gathering storm. His disqui-
etude obviously showed in his face, for his father immediately
reached out and patted him on the shoulder.

"Relax, Jason," Giulio reassured him. "I'm not asking you to
take over the place, and I'm not suggesting that you start right
away. I just think that it's going to be time very soon for you get
back out there and start doing something constructive again. I
know you've gone through a tough time, but when you get
thrown from the horse, you have to climb right back on because
if you wait too long, you might never ride again. Do you understand what I'm saying?"

"Sure, I understand," said Jason unconvincingly. "It's just
that . . ."

"What?" asked his father.

Jason shifted uneasily in his chair, for he could not dispute
the truth of what Giulio had said. Just the same, the thought of
going to work at the inn filled him with an odd, but distinct
sense of dread, one he could not readily explain to himself, let
alone to his father. It was not that he had anything in particular

against his family's business, but something inside of him had always rebelled at the idea of being trapped there under the thumbs of his father and older siblings. He had always needed to get away, to find a different way through life and perhaps one day build something that he could call his own. As things were, it had been hard enough for Jason to swallow his pride and come home from California in defeat. This would be a far more bitter pill.

"I know that you're right, Dad," he finally said, nervously rubbing the back of his neck. "I do need to get out and start doing something new soon. It's just that I don't think I would fit in very well. I mean, you and the other guys have your own way of doing things. I'd probably just get in the way and gum up the works."

Giulio smiled, for he saw right through his son.

"Jason, I know that what we have is just a boring little business that's not going to make anybody rich. It's nothing compared to where you've been and what you've seen. But you know, small as it is, with all its boring little problems, it has its virtues too. There's something to be said for a business where you get to meet people from all over the world, to take them in and show them a little hospitality, to make them feel welcome. It's a good feeling that you can't put a price tag on."

Giulio paused and eyed Jason for a moment.

"And if that isn't enough," he went on, "you might consider that we really could use a little help right now."

"What do you mean?" Jason asked.

Giulio gave a shrug.

"Times are changing," he said. "There's a lot of competition out there, a lot more than there used to be. We run a good place, but you and I both know that that's not always enough in any business. When everyone always has their noses to the grindstone, nobody's looking around to see how you might do things better and keep the big guys from eating you alive. The truth is that we could use an extra set of eyes and maybe some fresh ideas right about now. Of course, an extra pair of hands wouldn't hurt either."

With that Giulio threw up his hands and nodded at Jason as if to ask what he thought of the whole thing.

For a long time Jason did not respond, but simply sat there, turning things over in his mind. His initial inclination to run and hide had subsided, but he was still filled with apprehension. He gave a sigh and shook his head.

"I don't know what to say, Dad," he said at last. "Of course I want to help, but right now, where my head's at, I just don't know how much of a commitment I could give you. I don't want to waste anybody's time."

Giulo leaned closer and looked at him with kind eyes.

"I'm not looking for a commitment," he said earnestly. "And I'm not looking to put you on the spot. But you know, if you did this, even for just a little while, who knows, it might help us both."

Jason let out a little groan of consternation, for despite his many misgivings, he was finding it difficult to say no to his father.

"*If* I said yes," he asked reluctantly, "when would you want me to start?"

"Whenever you're ready," Giulio told him. "Tomorrow's Friday, and then there's the weekend. Why don't we wait and see where your head is at on Monday?"

"And what about Raymond and Natalie?" he asked. "How are they going to feel about this?"

Giulio gave a little cough to clear his throat.

"Oh, don't worry about them," he said with a reassuring smile. "Trust me, they're going to be very excited to have you around."

CHAPTER 16

Late Saturday morning, the doorbell rang.

Jason was alone in the basement when he heard it. He had been down there in the laundry room for some time, trying to work out precisely how to operate the washing machine. It was, to his best recollection, the first time in his life that he had ever attempted to do any such thing, and he was feeling just a little hesitant. From what he could see, it did not seem to be a particularly complicated affair. Load the clothes, throw in some detergent, close the door, and press the button. How hard could it be?

Nonetheless, for all his years of higher education, he found the task a bit intimidating. As a youngster, of course, Jason's idea of doing the laundry encompassed little more than dropping his dirty clothes—when he remembered to pick them up—into the seemingly magic basket his mother always left on the floor by the foot of his bed. The rumpled, dirty clothes would inevitably vanish from it, only to miraculously reappear sometime later cleaned and folded in his bureau drawers. He had never given much thought to precisely how that marvelous process worked, but had found it quite convenient.

In this regard, Jason had not come much further as an adult. The very notion of stooping so low as to do his own laundry would have been laughable to him when he was living the high life out in Los Angeles. Back then he left such mundane domestic chores to Mrs. Aranchez, the Mexican woman who also cleaned his apartment. In those days, he did not even bother to put his dirty clothes into a basket, magic or otherwise, but instead simply left them for her in piles wherever he happened to drop them on his bedroom floor. Just the same, the clothes would without fail reappear in their proper place, clean and folded as always, without his ever giving the matter of how the slightest thought. He had enjoyed very much the convenience of that arrangement as well.

Jason had been thinking about Mrs. Aranchez when the doorbell first rang. Indeed, he had thought of her the moment he opened his eyes that morning and looked about at the burgeoning mess on his bedroom floor. He had been living out of his suitcases since he came home, and it was beginning to show.

Dismayed at the sight, he had flopped back on the pillow and stared at the ceiling for a time, pondering his life and wondering what he should do next. Part of him longed to be back in Los Angeles, back to his old life—and he fully intended to get it all back one day—but another part of him recoiled at the memory of what had driven him away, of facing it all again. He simply wasn't ready. It seemed clear that he would be staying put in Rhode Island for a while, and despite his reluctance, throwing his lot in with the family business for the time being. That meant it was time to get his little corner of the world in order, and ready himself to make a good impression come Monday morning.

Sadly, in Jason's mind, there was no one he could turn to other than himself to set things in motion. He certainly could not have asked his father to do his laundry, and he had no money with which to pay someone else to do it for him. And so, after rising from bed and getting himself dressed, he had knelt on the floor and gathered his dirty clothes together. With a bundle almost too big for his arms to encompass, he teetered toward the top of the stairs, losing one or two items along the way, and made his way down. Thus had Jason embarked on his first foray into the mysterious realm of the basement laundry room.

Now, as he heard the doorbell ring a second time, Jason looked apprehensively at the washing machine's control panel. He had not been quite able to ascertain just how many clothes constituted too large a load, so he had stuffed in as many articles as he could manage, poured in double the recommended amount of detergent, and set the knob to large before closing the lid. Taking a deep breath, he hesitated for just a moment before finally pressing the Start button.

The sudden lurch of the machine as it came to life and the sound of the water rushing into it gave Jason a start. He fretted for a moment that he had done something wrong, but this fear quickly passed when he correctly surmised that this was simply what a washing machine sounded like when one turned it on. Satisfied that he had met with success in this new venture, he bounded up the stairs to answer the door before the bell rang a third time.

Jason opened the front door to find two rather prim older ladies standing on the doorstep. At first he did not recognize the pair, bundled up in their scarves and winter coats as they were, but then he saw the foil-covered pans each was carrying and he knew them at once. They were the Signorelli sisters, Alba and Louise. Spinsters both, they had lived in the neighborhood since long before Jason was born, and were charter members of the league of lasagna ladies who occasionally provided for his father's nutritional needs.

"Good morning, Ms. Signorelli—and Ms. Signorelli," said Jason awkwardly. He could never recall which of the sisters was Alba and which was Louise, and so had never been quite certain as to how to address the pair when he encountered them together. To call them by their first names would have felt impolite, in any case, so he had always stuck with the more formal address.

"Well, good morning, Jason," replied one of them. "What a surprise to see you. We didn't know you were home."

"Alba, how would we know?" huffed one of the sisters, Louise evidently. "It's not like he's supposed to send us his vacation schedule."

"Oh, so you're home on vacation, is that it?" said Alba.

"Not exactly," said Jason with a little cough. Then, opening the door wider, "Would you like to come in? I mean, it looks like you have your hands full."

"We can only stay a minute," said Louise as the two sisters stepped into the front hall.

"Yes, this is just a quick visit," seconded Alba. "We knew we were going to be passing by this way today, so we made a little something for your father." She held up her pan. "These are some manicott' that I made."

"And *I* made the meatballs to go with them," her sister was quick to add. "Not to mention the sauce."

Alba rolled her eyes.

"My sister thinks nobody in the world can make a sauce like her," she said with a dismissive shake of her head.

"I would have made more of both if I'd known you were home," said Louise.

Jason took one look at the sizable pans each was holding and gave a smile.

"Don't worry," he told them. "It looks like you both brought plenty for my father and me."

Louise leaned closer and looked with hopeful eyes past Jason's shoulder to the living room.

"He's not home, is he?" she asked. "Your father, that is."

"Actually, he's out running some errands," explained Jason. "I think he was planning to take the dog to the vet for a checkup and then maybe stop by the inn for a little while before coming home."

This news was greeted with obvious disappointment. Alba pursed her lips in consternation while her sister sighed, "Oh, well."

Jason gestured to the pans.

"Would you like me to take those for you?" he offered.

Alba managed a smile and started past him toward the kitchen.

"Oh, that's all right," said Louise, following close behind. "We know where the kitchen is. We'll just tuck these into the fridge and be on our way."

There was nothing for Jason to do but get out of the way and watch the two ladies march straight off to the kitchen. Along the way, as they passed through the living room, the two looked about with keen eyes, scrutinizing every inch of the place. Once in the kitchen, they stood in front of the opened refrigerator, whispering to themselves as they assessed its contents and re-arranged things to their liking to make space for the manicotti and meatballs. Jason kept his distance, leaving the two old ladies to have their fun.

"Well, that's done," said a satisfied Alba, brushing the palms of her hands together when they reemerged from the kitchen

"Things look a little better in there," added Louise.

"I'm sure my father will be very grateful," Jason told them. "That was really nice of you both to go to all that bother for him."

"Eh, what bother?" said Alba with a wave of her hand. "What else is there for old biddies like us to do?"

The three of them began to walk toward the front door. The sisters, however, did not leave right away, but instead lingered in the hall for a few minutes, chitchatting about the cold weather and the exorbitant cost of heating oil. They were dragging their feet, Jason rightly guessed, in the hope that his father would at last make an appearance.

"So, what are you planning to do while you're home on vacation?" said Louise, extending their stay just a little longer. "Something fun, I hope."

Jason gave a little chuckle and nodded toward the basement door.

"Well, at the moment I'm doing my laundry," he said.

"Doing your own laundry, how nice," said Louise with little conviction. "It's good that men do these things for themselves these days—I guess."

"What you need is a good woman, a wife to look after you," opined Alba, wagging a finger at him. She looked at her sister, then back to Jason. "Maybe one a little younger than us two—but we *are* available."

"I'll keep that in mind," laughed Jason.

"Good boy," she said, patting his hand. "Now just make sure that you sort your laundry properly."

"Sort?" said Jason.

"Of course, silly," said Louise. "You know you have to separate your whites from your colored clothes. You don't want to end up with pink underwear, do you?"

The possibility of such a result had never occurred to Jason when he was stuffing the clothes willy-nilly into the washer. He gave a nervous cough to clear his throat and cast another glance at the basement door.

"No, of course not," he said.

"That's good," said Alba. "Well, we should get on our way and let you get back to your own business. Tell your father we said hello."

"And don't forget to tell him about the manicott' and meatballs," added Louise.

"I won't," he assured her, smiling despite his mounting alarm at the thought that his undergarments were changing hue even as they spoke.

With that the two ladies said their good-byes and were soon on their way.

Jason stood at the door, watching them make their way back down the steps, praying that neither would slip and fall. Then, as soon as the two had successfully navigated the icy front walk and were safely installed in their car, he slammed the door shut and fled to the laundry room on winged feet.

CHAPTER 17

"**Y**ou know, that wouldn't have happened if you had sorted those *before* you put them in the washer," noted Giulio a little while later that afternoon.

They were sitting in the living room where Jason was forlornly sifting through the basket of laundry, disentangling the discolored underwear from the rest of his clothes while his father read the newspaper. Sundance, meantime, had his nose stuck in the basket and was sniffing its contents with great interest.

"Now he tells me," Jason muttered, tossing a pair of rose-tinted underpants onto the pile he was making. He pulled out another and held it up for examination. "What am I supposed to do with these?" he wondered aloud.

"You could try bleaching them, that might work," offered his father. "Or you could just wear them. After all, who's going to see them but you?"

"You never know," sighed Jason.

"Oh, well, in that case, I guess you could always go to Walmart and buy some new ones if you had to."

Walmart, thought Jason, trying not to sulk, but failing miserably. Wasn't it just yesterday that he was buying the best tailor-made suits in Los Angeles without giving a thought to the price? It was perfectly indicative of his present situation that he could no longer afford to shop at even a discount store for new underwear. His humiliation, if not complete, was rapidly descending to that status.

"But save the old ones," Giulio added. "They're good for washing the car. Just don't use them on the windows."

"Why not?"

"They leave streaks."

Neither the advice nor the humor was of much consolation to his son.

While Jason finished putting his clothes in order, Giulio tossed the newspaper aside and went to the closet from which he produced what looked like a thin black suitcase. He brought the case back to the couch, where he opened it and, to Jason's surprise, carefully lifted out an old violin and bow.

"What's that?" said Jason with great curiosity.

"It's a violin. What did you think it was?"

"I know it's a violin," said Jason. "What I meant is, what are you doing with that one? You don't play the violin."

"Not yet," said Giulio, taking the bow and drawing it across one of the strings. The instrument responded with a frightful scratch and screeching noise that brought to mind the sound of music only in the most rudimentary sense.

"Sounds wonderful," said Jason, wincing.

"I'm just getting started," admitted his father. "I've just been toying around with it really. I haven't even taken any lessons yet, so you can't expect too much."

"Lessons?"

"Of course," said Giulio. "How else am I going to learn?"

"Just seems like a lot of bother to go through, that's all," said Jason with a shrug. "No offense, but aren't you a little old to be taking music lessons?"

His father gave him a withering look and pointed the bow in his direction like a foil.

"Your academic record notwithstanding, you have a lot left to learn, my friend," he said coolly.

With that Giulio pulled the bow across the strings once more, this time producing a slightly more tolerable sound. Encouraged, he paused and looked the violin up and down before fiddling with one of the tuning pegs. He gave it a twist and drew the bow across the strings once more to test the result. The quality of the tone was better still, but far from symphony quality. Nonetheless, Giulio looked over the violin with evident satisfaction.

"It's a fascinating instrument," he said, more to himself it seemed than to Jason. "I've always loved the sound of it. Have you ever watched someone play, I mean someone really accomplished? It's like magic, the way a good violinist can take this little wooden thing and make it sound like a living creature crying or laughing. Just the way their fingers move across the strings is incredible to watch." He paused for a moment. "Anyway, it's winter, so it seemed like a good time to learn something new."

"What's so important about that?" said Jason.

Giulio chuckled and laid the violin and bow back down in the case.

"Learning new things," he told his son, "is what makes it worth getting out of bed in the morning. When you get to be my age, and you start to feel a little past your prime, it's the one thing, more than anything else, that can make you feel like a child again. Doesn't matter what it is, just so long as it stretches your brain in a new direction."

"Lately, my brain feels just about as stretched as I'd want it," said Jason with a rueful smile.

"Give it time," said Giulio.

With that he snapped the violin case shut and returned it to the closet. While there, he took out his coat from the hanger and began to pull it on.

"Heading out again?" said Jason.

"Just taking the dog out for a little walk," said Giulio.

At the sound of the word *walk,* Sundance's ears pricked up and he dashed over to his master's side, his tail wagging furiously. By the time Giulio grabbed the leash hanging from the door knob, the dog was bouncing around and whimpering with excitement. It was all Giulio could manage just to snap the leash to its collar.

"I'll be back in just a little while," he told Jason. "I'm planning to go to the four o'clock Mass at Blessed Sacrament later on. Why don't you come with me?"

"Don't you usually go to the eight on Sunday morning with all your cronies?"

"Eh, usually," grunted Giulio. "But this time of year, everybody's down in Florida, staying warm. So, what do you say?"

Jason put the clothes aside and flopped on the couch. There he reached for the remote control, switched on the television, and began cycling through the channels to see what might be worth watching.

"No, thanks, Dad," he said. "Maybe another time."

Giulio did not press him on the subject, but instead gave another grunt and went on his way with Sundance tugging him along.

"So, are you coming to Mass with me or not?" he asked again when the two returned from their excursion a short time later.

By now, Jason was resting quite comfortably on the couch.

"Come on, Dad," he groaned. "I really don't feel like it. Besides, I haven't gone to Mass in years."

"Maybe now would be a good time to start going again," his father pointed out.

"Are you kidding?" scoffed Jason. "The floor would probably start shaking if I set foot in the place."

"Please," Giulio urged him. "Just do this once for me as a favor."

"Why, what's the big deal, Dad?"

Giulio gave a sigh.

"If I show up at Mass by myself," he explained, "the lasagna ladies are bound to see me sitting alone. Before you know it, I'll end up sitting with one of them and then we'll have to chat after Mass, and there'll be the whole go-round about getting together for dinner, and then it turns into this whole big production, if you know what I mean. I'm just not in the mood for that tonight. As it is I'll have to give the Signorelli sisters a call later on to thank them for that food they dropped off."

"Must be hard to be so much in demand by the female persuasion," Jason needled him.

"Someday it might happen to you," said his father. "So, come on, what do you say? Don't make your old man have to beg."

Jason gave a sigh of his own.

"All right," he finally relented. "But you're gonna owe me for this."

Giulio looked very pleased.

"How about I treat for dinner after?" he offered. "I'm thinking manicott' and meatballs."

"Who'd have guessed?" said Jason, dragging himself off the couch. Then he went to get his coat.

Jason had only been half joking when he said he feared that the floors would start to shake were he to set foot in the church. As he blessed himself with the holy water, he hesitated in the vestibule and hazarded a look inside with apprehensive eyes as his father walked in ahead of him. Up on the altar, he could see the altar boys moving about, making preparations for the Mass, while the organist played a soft, contemplative melody.

They had arrived early, the pews only just beginning to fill. Giulio might have found a seat just about anywhere as close to the altar as he liked. Instead he genuflected in the aisle and slid in on the end of the very last pew. There he looked back over his shoulder and nodded for Jason to join him.

Jason stepped inside.

There was no discernible movement of the floor beneath his feet. Just the same he felt suddenly anxious and a little sad for some reason he could not quite put his finger on. Then, as he walked toward the pew, he listened more closely to the song the organist was playing. It was the "Ave Maria," the very same song that had come to him from out of nowhere that morning back in his apartment when he had finally decided that it was time to come home. At once he understood why it had sounded so familiar then, for he now recalled that the vocalist had sung it at his mother's funeral Mass in that very same church. That had been the last time that Jason had come to Mass.

Jason slid into the pew next to his father, who had knelt down to say a prayer. He did not immediately join him, but instead simply sat there quietly, thinking about his mother while he absentmindedly looked about at the people filing into the church. It was then that his gaze fell upon a young woman sitting by the side wall at the far end of the pew just in front of them. It was the motion of her head that had caught his attention. One moment she was staring up quite intently at one of the church's stained-glass windows with its vibrant colors set aglow by the late day sun. The next she was looking down at something on her lap, her face lost to him behind a cascade of fine dark hair. When Jason leaned forward to get a better look, he saw that it was a sketch pad of some sort that the young woman held. She was drawing the window.

Intrigued, Jason watched intently as she looked up once more and pushed the hair away from her face. She was quite lovely, he saw that right away, but it was something else about her that captivated him. Absorbed as she appeared to be in her task, she exuded a distinct aura of serenity that he felt drawn to in a gentle, but powerful way. In a different place at a different time, he might have thought to approach her. Then again, he would have felt guilty at disturbing someone who appeared to be so much at peace.

The young woman kept at her work, and Jason kept watch on her, until the cantor invited the congregation to rise to greet their celebrant. Jason felt his father give him a nudge, prompting him to stand as the priest walked in and the opening hymn commenced.

Later, when Mass was over, Jason walked slowly by his father's side, hoping to catch the young woman's eye as they filed out with the rest of the parishioners. To his disappointment, she did not walk their way, but instead ducked out one of the side doors. Jason emerged from the church just in time to see her walking away down the sidewalk.

"Well," said his father, giving him another nudge as he buttoned up his coat. "That wasn't so bad, was it?"

"No," replied Jason. "I guess it really wasn't."

"Good," said his father. "I'm glad you think so. Now maybe you'll decide to do it a little more often."

Jason looked out once more down the sidewalk, but by now the young woman had disappeared into the shadows of the gathering night.

"Who knows?" he told his father. "Maybe I will."

CHAPTER 18

Giulio did not give Jason a formal job description for his first day of work at the Bradley Mansion Inn. Come Monday morning, his only instructions to his son were to simply observe as much of the operation as he could for the first few days, lend a hand when he was able, and over time try to identify any areas where they might improve. There were already plenty of able hands on board to manage the day-to-day tasks, Giulio explained. What was needed was someone with a different perspective, someone who might pick up on the little things that everyone else was overlooking. How could they operate more efficiently? In what ways might they improve their service? Were they making the best use of their staff? Most important of all, how could they entice more people to come and stay at their bed-and-breakfast? In short, Jason's mission was to put his education to work for the family, but first he would need to learn the ropes.

Rule number one, Jason very quickly learned that morning, was that calm and quiet were to be maintained at all times come what may. This edict, long ago issued by Giulio, was to be most devoutly obeyed in the early hours at the dawn of the day when the guests were still abed. Nothing could ruin an otherwise pleasant night's stay more quickly than to have one's peaceful slumbers disturbed by loud talk in the hallways or the clattering of pans and utensils in the kitchen while breakfast was being prepared. Guests who came downstairs tired and grumpy were not likely to return for a second visit no matter how generous a breakfast they found awaiting them, and so Giulio made certain that those in his employ went about their business with the quiet deliberation of monastic monks.

Not wishing to disrupt anyone's routine, Jason did his best to just stay out of the way and watch while Raymond got to work first thing, setting out coffee and muffins for the early risers. Meantime in the kitchen, Lana, the weekday chef, prepared the main breakfast of eggs and sausages, bacon and home-fried potatoes, and other standard fare, all of which would be set out very nicely in buffet style a little later in the dining room. Lana was a forty-something woman who worked just the few hours it took each day to get breakfast out on the table and clean the kitchen. She was, Jason would discover, just one of several locals who worked at the inn during the course of any given day. Roger, another, was at that same moment in the study with Jason's father, giving him his morning report. Roger was a re-tiree who often worked what the Mirabellas referred to as "the watch." The watch comprised the overnight hours between dusk and dawn when very little happened at the inn, but when it was nonetheless essential to have someone reliable on hand in the unlikely event that something went awry during the night.

A yawning Roger was just getting ready to leave when Jason walked into the study.

"All present or accounted for, Giulio," said Roger, barely above a whisper, as he pulled his coat on. "Just another quiet night."

"Those are the kinds I like," answered Giulio. He gestured to Jason. "Roger, I don't think you've met my son Jason yet."

Roger extended his hand and gave Jason a smile.

"Nice to meet you, Jason," he said softly as the two shook

hands. "Coming to work for the family business like your brother and sister?"

"For a little while at least," said Jason with a shrug.

"Well, you'll like working here," said Roger, giving Giulio a wink. "The hours can be kind of long, but at least the boss lets you sleep on the job sometimes."

Giulio chuckled and gave Roger a pat on the back.

"Have a good day, Roger," he told him.

"Thanks, you too," said Roger through another yawn. "Nice to meet you, Jason."

Giulio closed the door behind Roger and turned back to Jason with a hopeful countenance.

"So, how are things going so far?" he asked brightly.

"I haven't done anything yet," admitted Jason. "Not that there's a lot for me to do. Ray seems to have everything under control. Honestly, right now I just feel like I'm in the way."

Raymond did indeed seem to have everything under control, and he had been going about his routine with quiet efficiency, as if wanting to emphasize the point. Though he had greeted Jason cordially enough when he arrived that morning, something in his demeanor told Jason that his older brother would have preferred that he had not been there at all. It was to be expected, so Jason made no mention of this to his father.

"Why don't you help me get the fires going?" Giulio suggested. "Then later on we can all get together and talk when Natalie comes in."

Mondays, Jason discovered, were generally a slow time at the inn. On this particular morning there were only a handful of guests in the house. The weekend had been reasonably busy with most of the rooms booked by Friday, but the vast majority of those visitors had checked out on Sunday. There would therefore be only a few people coming down for breakfast. Just the same, there was no telling precisely when everyone would decide to roll out of bed. Despite the small numbers, the fires would have to remain stoked and the breakfast laid out for the duration of its normal hours just as if there had been a full house.

After helping to get the fires going, there seemed little else to do but wait, so Jason went to the living room and sat on the couch. Laid out on the coffee table were several daily newspapers. To pass the time, he picked up the *Wall Street Journal* and began to scan the headlines. It was not long after, though, when his brother poked his head around the corner.

"Pssst," he whispered, shooting Jason a sharp look and a nod, before glancing back over his shoulder.

Jason took the hint that the room and the newspapers were off-limits. He folded the paper, tucked it back neatly with the others, and walked out of the room just as the first guests of the day were coming in with their morning coffee.

Later, when breakfast was over and Natalie had arrived, Giulio brought them all together into the study. Leaning back against the edge of the desk, he motioned for everyone to take a seat. He did not speak right away, but instead took a moment to rub his chin thoughtfully. It seemed to Jason that his father was a little on edge and perhaps anxious to choose his words carefully. For Jason it was a terribly awkward moment, but one he knew could not be avoided.

"Well then," Giulio finally began, pressing his palms together, "I just wanted to have a little team meeting now that we're all here." He looked at Raymond and Natalie. "Jason, as you two already know, is going to be working for us for a while."

At that announcement Natalie leaned over and gave Jason a little applause.

"Welcome aboard," she said.

"Thanks," said Jason.

Raymond gave him a half smile.

"I hope this means that I don't have to shovel the snow out front anymore," he quipped.

"Well, it certainly means that you won't have to do it all by yourself anymore," replied Giulio.

Jason threw his hands up.

"Hey, Dad, you didn't say anything about me shoveling snow," he pretended to complain. "I didn't know that was part of the deal."

The jest had the intended effect.

"Well, in that case you better make sure to read the fine print, my friend," chuckled his brother.

"Ah, now you see," Giulio continued, looking pleased that the ice seemed to have been broken more easily than expected. "That's just the sort of thing I wanted to talk about. While he's with us, I want your brother to learn everything about what each of us does here. We all have our own way of doing things, and that's fine, but who knows, maybe he can use all that education of his to help us figure out how to do things a little better. Let's think of him as a consultant."

"A bed-and-breakfast consultant," mused Natalie. "That has a nice sound to it. Maybe you're starting a whole new profession, Jason."

"Who knows, you could be right," said Jason. "Maybe someday when I'm an authority I'll write a book about it."

"Well, before you can write the book, you'll have to do some hands-on research," harrumphed Giulio. He turned to Raymond. "Why don't you help your brother get started by giving him a little tour of the house so he can get to the know the place again? I'd do it myself, but I have a couple of appointments downtown."

Raymond gave a shrug.

"Sure, why not?" he said, getting to his feet. "Come on, Mr. West Coast, I'll show you around the empire."

Jason got to his feet as well, and the two left the study.

It came as no surprise to Jason that his brother seemed to know every square inch of the enormous house like the back of his hand. After all, he had worked there for their father all those years even before Jason went off to college. What struck Jason the most, however, was something else he noticed about Raymond as the two wandered up the stairs and along past the bedrooms on the second floor. There was a distinct pride in his older brother's voice that one could not miss as he described all the work the family had done to renovate and maintain the rooms, especially work that he himself had performed. Raymond seemed to take pleasure even in pointing out ongoing work that still had yet to be completed, for there was always something that needed to be repaired or replaced.

"That room we finally finished last year," he said, gesturing to one bedroom door. "I put the tile in the bathroom myself."

"The window casings in that room need to be resealed," he said of another.

"We spent a bundle redecorating this one," he said of a third.

As he listened, it became clear to Jason that his older brother was far more invested in the place than he had ever been. Raymond's heart and soul were truly in it. Jason's heart, on the other hand, had always led him in another direction. The house and the business had never held any great attraction for him. Just the same, he could not help feeling strangely sad, as if he had missed out on something important of which he might have been a part.

"So here we are again," said Raymond when they finally made it back downstairs to the living room.

"Is everything in order down here, Mr. Fix It?" Jason kidded him.

"Oh yeah," said Raymond with a shrug. "The fireplace works fine. The furniture is still in good shape. The rugs are getting a little frayed around the edges maybe, but not too bad. The only thing that bothers me is the light fixtures in this room."

"What's the problem?" said Jason

"I don't know," said Raymond. "I've had to replace some of them lately, but they still don't work right. I think maybe there's a problem with the wiring in these walls. God only knows how old it is."

He paused and studied the walls with a questioning look before turning back to Jason.

"Anyway," he continued, "that ends the tour for today. I hope you enjoyed it."

"Thanks, Ray," said Jason. "I did."

"No big," said his brother. Then he fell silent and scratched the back of his neck for a moment. It seemed to Jason that he wanted to say more, but then thought better of it. With a nod, Raymond turned and started for the kitchen.

Jason was prepared to let him go on his way, but there was something he needed to do first. He took a deep breath.

"Wait, don't go yet, Ray," he said. "I need to talk to you about something. It's about why I came back."

Raymond looked at him with the hint of a smirk. "Is this that long story you were supposed to tell me the other night at Natalie's?"

"Yeah," said Jason, his cheeks flushing.

"Save it," said Raymond. "We already know all about it."

"How?" said Jason, taken aback. "Did Dad tell you?"

"No," said his brother coolly. "I found out for myself back in December when you didn't come home for Christmas. I never said anything to Dad, but I figured something was wrong, so I went online and Googled your name. Sure enough, it showed up in an article about your company. When I read about what had happened, I tried to get in touch, to see if I could help. Natalie tried too—but like I said you weren't returning anybody's calls."

There was a hint of bitterness in Raymond's voice, one for which Jason could not blame his brother.

"It was a bad time for me," said Jason with a sigh. "I had to figure out some things for myself."

"Yeah, well, there's still a few things to figure out if you're gonna be staying here," replied Raymond. "But I guess we can talk about that some other time. Right now, we've got work to do."

With that his brother went on his way.

"How did it go?" said Natalie brightly when Jason returned to the study.

"Okay, I guess," said Jason. "But I get the feeling Ray might be happier if I were back in L.A."

"Oh, don't worry about him," huffed Natalie. "You know how Big Brother is, always needing to be in control. Besides, I think he's got something on his mind that he's not telling anybody."

"I know how that is," said Jason gloomily. "I've had some things on my own mind that I've been wanting to tell people— but I think you already know that."

Natalie leaned close and kissed him on the cheek.

"I do know," she told him gently. "But you're home now, so forget about it."

She took him by the arm and led him over to the desk.

"Maybe this will cheer you up," she said, pointing to the computer. "See, I've already got you up on the payroll."

"Wow, this is an exciting moment," said Jason deadpan at the sight of his less than impressive take-home pay.

"It is!" laughed Natalie. "Now you're officially part of the family business."

"Great. When do I get my first check?"

"Why, what are you going to do, go to Disney World?" she joked.

"Nope," replied Jason. "I'm gonna go to Walmart."

CHAPTER 19

Jason took a bite of his meatball grinder and gazed out the window. He was sitting in his father's pickup truck on a street by a little park on the east side of the city. The park was situated atop a steep ledge from which one could look directly out over downtown Providence. At its edge a statue of Roger Williams stood watch with his hand outstretched, conveying his blessing onto the city he had founded.

The park was one of Jason's favorite places in the city, though he had not been there in years. He could remember coming there sometimes as a little boy when his father would take the family out for a Sunday afternoon drive. Jason loved running around the park with his brother and sister, but best of all was standing at the foot of the giant statue, looking down with it at the city. It made him feel like he was on top of the world. The memory made Jason smile, for now the park did not seem nearly so lofty a spot as it once did to him as a little boy, but he still enjoyed the view all the same.

Jason had decided to spend his lunch break there that afternoon simply as an excuse to get out of the inn for a little while. Despite the size of the house—and it was indeed a rambling place—it seemed that he and the rest of the family were always working in very close quarters. The study proved to be the only place in the house where he could go to make a phone call or simply sit and think. The only problem was that the room was shared by three other people, particularly Natalie who had no qualms about making it known that she considered it her own domain. This arrangement did not seem to bother Giulio or Raymond in the least, but it was something of an inconvenience for someone like Jason, who had long been accustomed to having a private office all to himself. To remedy the situation, he had prowled about the house whenever he could, in search of any place at all that he might be able to make his own. A little used, but ample-sized closet on the third floor had caught his eye, but taking over even that small piece of territory would require some delicate negotiations. Until then, the occasional drive to the park at lunch was the only way to fulfill his need for a few moments of solitude.

The lack of privacy aside, Jason could not complain. Against all his expectations, he had not found working for his family as dreadful as he always imagined it would be. As the days had passed—they were well into February by now—he had settled fairly easily into the daily routine of helping the others run the operation. Theirs was not a terribly complicated enterprise, but he came to appreciate very quickly the eye for detail that it required. As with any business, success relied on a compilation of many small things. The smile that greeted a guest at check-in. The way the bed was turned down just so at night. The selection of books and board games in the parlor. The spotless linens on the breakfast table. The air of calm and relaxation that required so much hard work to achieve. Jason did not feel a great calling to this particular line of work, but for the moment it fulfilled a need and made him feel useful again.

Working again served another important purpose. It distracted Jason's mind from the troubles he had left behind in Los Angeles, and most pointedly his brooding over Amanda and their child. The morning when he first awoke was always the worst for him. For some reason, just then in those early hours, the guilt of what he had done would inevitably settle in on him all over again. It was like a weighted vest that he was forced to don each morning and wear throughout the day. As time went by, so long as he stayed busy, he found it easier to bear the load, but the strain of it was always there, sapping his strength. He longed to be rid of it, but how to do so eluded him.

Jason turned his face upward and closed his eyes. Though it was quite chilly outside, the sun shone bright, warming his skin. For a moment he was back in California, lazing on the beach on one of those carefree days before everything had gone wrong. The memory made it all the more dismaying when he opened his eyes once more and looked about at the snow and ice covering the landscape.

"What am I doing here?" he wondered aloud.

The invisible, ever-present weight beginning to press down on him again, Jason quickly finished his sandwich and headed back to the sanctuary of work.

When Jason returned he found Natalie at her desk, busily scribbling something onto a sheet of paper. At seeing him walk in, she put the pen down and hastily shifted the sheet aside to the top of a thick stack of papers. These she gathered together, bound them with an elastic band, and tucked them into a file folder, which she in turned dropped into the satchel at her feet.

"Whatcha got going?" said Jason, nodding at the satchel.

"Oh, that's nothing," she said vaguely.

"Sure looked like something."

"It's not, trust me."

"Then it can't hurt to let me have a peek," said Jason impishly, his curiosity now thoroughly piqued by her evasiveness.

"You can't have a peek," she insisted.

"Why not?"

"Because you would laugh."

"I could use a good laugh right about now," said Jason. "But I promise I won't. So, come on, show me what you've been doing."

Natalie squirreled up the side of her mouth in an expression of mild irritation. Reluctantly she reached down into the satchel and pulled out the stack of papers. She held them tightly against her chest for a moment, almost as if she was hugging a child, before finally turning them face-out for him to see.

Jason leaned closer to get a better look. On the top page he saw rows of neatly aligned text running in a column down its center. Before he could read it, Natalie quickly flipped to the next page and then one by one through the others; all of them contained similar writing. It took Jason a moment before he suddenly realized what he was looking at.

"Poetry?"

"You don't have to look so surprised," she snipped. "I know I didn't go to college like you, but that doesn't mean I can't compose a sentence."

Jason smiled.

"I'm not surprised," he told her. "Actually, I think it's pretty cool. How long have you been writing?"

"For a while now." Natalie shrugged. "Not that I'm any good at it yet. It's just something I do when I get two minutes to myself—which as you know isn't very often around here."

"Still, it looks like you've written a lot," said Jason. "Have you ever tried to get any of them published?"

"Oh God, no," laughed Natalie. "I wouldn't even think to try. I've never even let anyone else read them."

"Why not?"

Natalie looked down at the stack of papers and ran her finger across the top page.

"I don't know," she said thoughtfully. "I guess it's because they're so personal. It would be too embarrassing."

"But just think, Nat. Maybe someday you could become a rich and famous poet," he kidded her.

"There might be some famous poets, but I don't know how many rich ones there are," she pointed out. "Besides, I don't care about any of that. These are just for me right now."

The notion that someone could invest the time to produce such a body of work without seeking the reward of money, or at least some recognition for the trouble, puzzled Jason. He had been schooled in the ways of the business world, trained to analyze the risk and potential rewards of an enterprise, and to choose the avenue that showed the greatest promise of producing a profit. What was the point without it?

"It seems a shame to not at least give it a try," he said.

"Try writing a few lines yourself someday," she suggested, dropping the papers back into the satchel. "Then see how you feel about it."

Natalie turned her attention to the top of the desk.

"Anyway," she continued, "I haven't been just wasting the day writing. I did book some rooms for this weekend."

"Excellent," said Jason with a nod of approval.

"And I took a message for you from somebody at *Rhode Island Life*," she said, passing him a slip of paper.

"Really?" said Jason with interest. "What did they want?"

"They said they're doing a piece on bed-and-breakfasts for one of their upcoming issues and they wanted to know if they could send someone out to take a few pictures of the place. I guess whatever little marketing plan you've got started is already working."

"It isn't much of a plan at this point," said Jason, looking over the number. "All I did was send out some information about us to the local rags. I was hoping for something like this—I mean it's free publicity—but I didn't think it would happen right away. Must have got lucky."

"Hey, don't fight it," said Natalie. "What is it that they say, sometimes it's better to be lucky than good, right?"

"Maybe," said Jason. "But it never hurts to be good, too."

CHAPTER 20

"Looks like someone's getting ready for a hot date tonight."

It was early Friday evening and Jason was leaning against the frame of the open bathroom door, watching his father finish up shaving.

"Nope," said Giulio with an air of nonchalance. "This one's just lukewarm."

His head tilted back at a slight angle, Giulio eyed himself in the mirror as he carefully dragged the razor across the last remaining patch of shaving cream on the skin just underneath his jawline. That accomplished, he swished the razor in the sink and put it aside. Gazing back into the mirror, he turned his head from side to side to assess the thoroughness of his work. Satisfied that it was up to standard, he threw some clean water onto his face and grabbed the hand towel hanging next to the sink.

Jason laughed to himself, for the scene brought him back to his childhood. How many times as a small boy had he stood in that same doorway, watching his father go through his morning ablutions? As with most little boys, the sight of his father shaving was a source of endless fascination. Standing off to the side, gazing up in wide-eyed curiosity, little Jason would study him with rapt attention, intrigued by every step of the ritual. The washing of the face with steaming hot water. The lathering of the shaving cream onto the skin. The precise tilt of the head in front of the mirror so as to be able to watch the first swipe of the razor as it cut a path through the cream like a plow clearing away a layer of freshly fallen snow. The razor itself, of course, was an object of particular fascination, and despite ample warnings not to play with it, Jason had more than once nicked his face trying to imitate his father.

"So, who is she?" Jason asked. "Anybody I know?"

"No," answered his father, running the towel over his face. "Just a friend who I've owed a dinner to for a while."

"Ah, a lasagna lady, I take it," Jason snickered.

Giulio gave a grunt in reply before he tossed the towel aside and opened a bottle of aftershave. He shook a small amount into his hands and rubbed his palms together.

"As a matter of fact," he mused as he briskly patted his face, "now that I think of it, it seems to me that she might have a daughter your age. I'll set something up for you if you're interested."

Jason put up his hands in a defensive gesture. "No, thanks, Dad. That really won't be necessary."

"Just trying to help," said his father. "It wouldn't hurt to meet someone, you know, maybe think about settling down someday."

Jason would have liked to tell his father that once, not so long ago, he had given very serious consideration to settling down, but that was something about which he was still trying to avoid thinking, never mind discussing.

"Someday—maybe," he said. "Just not tonight."

"Why not tonight?" said Giulio on his way out of the bathroom.

Jason stepped aside.

"Well, for starters I'm going over to Ray's house later on to watch a ballgame," he said as his father walked by.

Giulio stopped and looked at him, his chin jutted out in an expression that conveyed mild surprise but also approval.

"Hmm, to Raymond's house, that's good," he said thought-fully, "especially since there's not much here to give you for dinner."

"Ayy, I can fend for myself," huffed Jason.

"So you say," replied his father. Then he continued on to his bedroom to get dressed.

A short while later, a dapper-looking Giulio descended the stairs and went to the closet for his coat. Sensing the possibility of a nighttime walk, an expectant Sundance followed close behind, his tail wagging a mile a minute.

"No, sorry but you're staying home, my friend," Giulio told the dog as he tugged his coat on. "Now get away from me before I walk out of the house with dog hair all over my pants."

Jason walked over and took Sundance by the collar to allow Giulio safe passage to the front door.

"And what time are you planning to come home, young man?" he asked his father before he could leave.

"Heh, don't worry," replied Giulio. " I'm sure I'll be back well before you."

"Make sure," Jason kidded him. "Otherwise I'll get worried, and then I'll have to send the police out looking for you."

"Right, Dad," said Giulio with a tip of his cap. He went to go, but paused for a moment. "Hey," he said, suddenly very serious. "I'm glad you and brother are getting together tonight."

"Me too," said Jason.

At that Giulio gave him a nod and headed out the door while Jason hurried back upstairs to finish getting himself ready to go out.

"Come on in," said Raymond a little while later, when Jason came to the door. "The Celts are just about to get started."

Raymond's wife, Donna, was in the kitchen, cutting up a homemade pizza when Jason walked in. Jason had caught the pleasant aroma of it even before he stepped into the house. He loved that scrumptious smell, the way it hung in the air and surrounded you like a comfortable blanket. It reminded him of his mother, who loved to make homemade pizza of her own.

Donna put down the knife she was using and came over to greet him.

"Hey, there he is," she said warmly, brushing her cheek against his.

Donna and Raymond had been married just two years. Despite being the oldest child, Raymond had put off taking the plunge until well after Natalie. All the same, it seemed to Jason like they had been together forever, for they were obviously very happy. As yet there were no children in the picture, but they often spoke of wanting them someday.

Donna gave his arm a squeeze and beamed a smile.

"It's been so long since we've seen you," she said. "How are you?"

"Actually, I'm starving," he told her with a smile. "The smell of that pizza is killing me!"

"Well, you two go sit in the den and watch the basketball game," she replied, shooing them away. "I'll bring it in for you in a minute when it's all cut up."

Jason went into the den and settled onto the little couch while Raymond brought in a handful of beer bottles from the refrigerator. He carefully put them down, cracked one open, and handed it to Jason before sitting down on the opposite end of the couch. There he stretched out his legs and opened one for himself.

"Cheers," he said, raising his bottle to Jason.

Jason replied in kind and the two clinked their bottles together. Shortly after, Donna brought in the pizza on a serving plate and set it down on the coffee table.

"There's more in the pan on the stove," she explained. "And I'm making a salad too, so you guys can help yourselves whenever you want."

At that she grabbed a small piece of pizza for herself and went back out, leaving the two brothers to themselves.

They wasted no time, but dug right in, for the aroma of the tomatoes and sausage and peppers was far too much to resist. Soon they were contentedly munching away while they chatted about the ballgame. Raymond did most of the talking at first, for he was an avid Celtics fan. Jason had of course by now evolved into a Lakers fan, which provided fuel for some lively repartee. Jason was happy that there had been a game on for them to watch. In truth, he had never really socialized all that much with his older brother. They were just far apart enough in age that they had always seemed to occupy separate worlds, a feeling that had become more pronounced as the two grew into manhood and had taken very different paths through life—at least to this point. And so there had often been a brief period of awkwardness whenever they found themselves together in such situations. Talking sports had always proved a good ice breaker.

They would not spend the entire evening talking about just basketball of course. It was inevitable, especially for two brothers working together, that sooner or later the conversation would take a turn toward business. Jason had hoped against reason that it would not. He was still not certain as to how he fit into the family's little operation, and even less so when it came to wondering how his brother felt about the same subject.

"So, how's it going?" Raymond eventually asked when the game went into halftime. "How do you like working with the rest of us?"

"It's okay," said Jason with a shrug. "I mean, I'm still learning about things."

Raymond put down his beer and cracked open another.

"Eh, what's to learn?" he said, taking a sip. "A smart guy like you with all that education should be able to run a place like ours with your eyes closed."

Jason could not decide if it was a hint of sarcasm he detected in his brother's voice, or something else entirely, for Raymond had spoken with what seemed to him an air of resignation. It was as if some unpleasant thing his brother had suspected had been found to be true. Whatever it was, it seemed to darken his brow.

"Hey, there's way more to this business than meets the eye," Jason answered cautiously. "You know that better than I do."

Jason paused and leaned forward to take another piece of pizza. By now, though, the platter was empty, so he sat back and contented himself for the moment with a sip of beer.

"Anyway," he continued, "it's just like any other business. I can see that it's got its own problems, its own challenges. Bottom line, though, is that if you want to be good at it, and be successful, it takes a lot of hard work and people who know what they're doing."

This remark seemed to please Raymond, for his countenance brightened once more. He settled back for a time and laced his fingers behind his head.

"You know," he said, "even if it wasn't under the best of circumstances for you, you made Dad really happy by coming home—and especially since you've been working for us. You can see it in his eyes."

Jason gave him a dismissive wave.

"Bah, he just likes having someone around to take care of the dog for him," he said. "He cares more about that thing than me."

At that the two shared a laugh.

"Seriously, though," said Raymond. "He really is happy about it. But what do you think, is this just a flyby, or are you planning to stick with us for a while?"

Jason did not respond right away, but instead took a deep breath and exhaled.

"Honestly, Ray, I'm not sure about anything right now," he said truthfully.

Raymond gave a little laugh.

"Welcome to the club," he said. Then, getting to his feet, he gave Jason a swat in the arm and beckoned for him to follow. "Come on, I want to show you something."

Jason followed Raymond downstairs into the basement. There he was surprised to see the little workshop his brother had created for himself. Occupying the entire corner of the room, it contained a table saw, lathe, sander, and all manner of woodworking tools about which Jason knew absolutely nothing. Roundabout were an unfinished bench, a small table, a corner shelf unit, and other pieces of furniture in various states of partial completion. Beneath the workbench on the floor lay a small patch of fresh sawdust, evidence of recent work on one or another of them.

Jason gaped at the collection.

"Did you make all these yourself?" he asked, quite amazed.

"Oh yeah," answered Raymond, as if it had been the simplest thing in the world. "It's just a little hobby of mine."

"I never knew you did anything like this," said Jason, still very much in awe. "It must be so much work. How do you find the time?"

"Eh, you do a little bit here, a little bit there," answered Raymond. "And it's not work. Tell you the truth, it's more like therapy for me. Whenever I've got something on my mind, doesn't matter what it is, I just come down and get to work for a little while and before you know it the time just seems to fly by, and my head's clearer. It's kind of like when you daydream sometimes while you're driving. All of a sudden you get where you were planning to go, but you can't remember anything at all about how you got there. Know what I mean?"

Raymond gestured to a sizable piece standing covered in a sheet off to the side of the others.

"This is the one I've been working on the most lately," he said, pulling away the sheet to reveal a chest of drawers.

Jason came closer to get a better a look. The top and sides were already completed, and the legs attached below, but only two of the five drawers were finished. Just the same, though he knew virtually nothing about furniture, Jason could tell that it was going to be a beautiful piece. He ran his hand across the top, admiring the craftsmanship of it, the finely sanded wood smooth to his touch.

"So, what do you think?" said Raymond.

Jason marveled at his brother.

"I'm impressed," he gushed. "Honest to God, I really am."

Raymond smiled.

"Thanks," he said modestly. "Like I said, it's just a little hobby."

"Hobby?" laughed Jason. "You should think about selling some of these."

"Sell? Nah," replied Raymond. "I'll just give them away as gifts."

"Why? Look at all the work you've done. I bet you could make some good money for these."

Raymond just shook his head.

"I don't do this for money," he said. "It's just good for the soul, know what I mean?"

Jason nodded his head to indicate that he understood, but in truth he wasn't completely sure that he did.

Raymond smiled at him and nodded to the stairs.

"Come on, West Coast," he said, tugging the string to turn off the light over the workbench. "Let's go up and see if there's any more pizza left to eat before the second half starts."

Jason gave a last look over his shoulder at his brother's work, all of it once more hidden in the shadows, then followed after him up the stairs.

When Jason came home later that night, Giulio was sitting in his chair, watching the late news. At seeing him come through the door, he nodded his son a greeting and turned his attention back to the television.

"Told you I'd be back before you," he said smugly. "Good time over at Raymond's?"

"Yeah, it was good," said Jason, flopping down onto the couch. "How was dinner?"

"Fine."

Sundance, who had been stretched out by the fireplace, wandered over and rested his chin on Jason's knee. Jason gave him a scratch behind the ears, and the dog looked up at him with affection. For a time Jason just sat there in silence, thinking about Raymond and his furniture, Natalie and her poetry, and even Giulio with his violin.

"Something on your mind?" said his father, shaking him from his ruminations.

"No, not really," replied Jason. "It's just that I was thinking that I don't really know some people as well as I thought I did. I keep finding out that there's way more to them than I realized. What does that say about me?"

Giulio chuckled and turned his attention back to the television.

"It says that you're learning," he said.

CHAPTER 21

Though it had taken a great deal for Jason to swallow his pride and come home from California, he would have been hard-pressed to deny that there were without a doubt certain benefits to living once more under his father's roof. Not least of these was the cost of the rent, which in his case was zero. Once he had begun to earn some money from the inn, Jason had offered to start contributing to the household expenses, but Giulio would hear none of it.

Jason's take-home pay from the family business was not terribly large, but there was nothing like free room and board to help one acquire a modest pile of cash in a comparatively short amount of time. Further contributing in this regard was Jason's nascent frugality, a side effect no doubt of living with his father. Since coming home and starting work, Jason had lived very much as a hermit, rarely venturing out of the house at night unless it was to visit one of his siblings or perhaps his aunt and uncle. Save for the investment in a proper winter coat, a wool sweater, and a pair of shoes better suited to the ice and snow, he spent precious little on himself.

Given the combined effect of these factors, it did not take very long before Jason accumulated a fair amount of surplus cash that he hoarded diligently. Once upon a time, in what seemed another life entirely, those same funds would have quickly burned a very large hole in his pocket, particularly if he had spent it on Amanda. This time around he chose a more practical use for his hard-earned money by sojourning to an office supply store, where he purchased a modestly priced laptop computer.

The purchase of the computer served a number of purposes. Foremost was that it gave him a virtual office that he could take anywhere he liked. At work, for instance, it allowed him, without imposition, to help Natalie find ways to better utilize her accounting software and to develop some reports to better track and predict the inn's occupancy numbers. That he could now do so without competing with her for time on the inn's lone personal computer gave his productivity a tremendous boost, and him a feeling of satisfaction at being able to earn his keep in some small, but tangible way.

At home, it served a much different purpose. With its Wi-Fi capability, Jason discovered that he was able to obtain Internet access through someone else's system close by in the neighborhood. Often late at night, he would find himself sitting up in bed, perusing the online editions of the *Los Angeles Times* and other publications just to keep tabs on what was happening back on the West Coast. It was a bittersweet exercise that tended to bring back memories, pleasant and ugly alike. The longer he remained at home, the more he craved to relive the former, but still feared facing the latter. Now and then, as he watched the days go by on the calendar, his heart would grow heavy at the thought that, by now, he might already have been a father, and he would struggle to push those melancholy thoughts to the back of his mind. At such times he would feel very much as though he were standing on the middle of a bridge somewhere between his past and present lives, longing to move toward one side, but feeling hesitant just yet to distance himself too far from the other.

Very early on, Jason established an e-mail account. Though

he looked upon it as a way to reach back and reconnect, he had gone so far as to use it just once to send a message to his friend, Eddie. It had read simply:

Still breathing—just barely.
J.

No response had ever come.

Jason had taken that as a dismaying sign that perhaps he was meant to remain trapped in this state of limbo, like a sailing ship adrift on a breathless sea, moving neither forward nor back, for the rest of his days. The winds of life, however, never stay becalmed forever, as Jason would discover one afternoon when they unexpectedly freshened and nudged him in a new direction.

On that particular day, Jason was not in his bedroom or in the inn's study with Natalie. He was instead ensconced in his little hideaway in the closet on the third floor of the Bradley Mansion. In it he had surreptitiously cleared some space and installed a small table and chair. It was not much of an office by any stretch of the imagination, but it was better than nothing.

At the moment, Jason was working on his laptop computer with some inexpensive Web site development software he had purchased. The inn was listed on a variety of referral sites on the Web, but lacked a proper site of its own. It was another one of those projects that everybody knew needed to get done, but for which no one had the time or energy. Jason saw it as a way for him to make another very useful contribution to the cause, and he was eager to get something up and running as soon as possible.

He had just gotten down to work when he was suddenly startled by a soft knock on the door. This was something of a puzzlement to the young man as he had been certain that no one at all had taken notice of his clandestine appropriation of the little-used closet. He sat very still for a moment and strained to listen, suspecting that perhaps he had only imagined it.

There came a second, more insistent knock.

Reluctantly, Jason reached out and opened the door. There in the corridor stood Mrs. Martinez. How in the world she had known that he was there escaped him, but then again he suspected that she already knew every inch of the house as well as any of them. The housekeeper did not speak right away, but instead stood there for a time, surveying his cramped quarters with a rather disapproving air before shaking her head and giving him a baleful look with her dark, piercing eyes. There were moments, and this was one of them, when Jason found her every bit as intimidating as he knew his father did.

Jason gave a nervous cough.

"Um, can I help you, Mrs. Martinez?" he said, trying his best to maintain some semblance of dignity despite his humbling surroundings.

Mrs. Martinez pursed her lips in a sour expression.

"Your sister look for you downstair, Mr. Jason," she informed him in her thick accent. "Somebody here to see you."

"Oh, very good. I'll be right down," said Jason. He hastily closed down the laptop before adding, *"Gracias, Señora,"* hoping the little flourish of Spanish would send her away with a more favorable impression of him.

Mrs. Martinez turned away and rolled her eyes.

"De nada," she muttered before returning to her duties.

Natalie was taking a call on the telephone when Jason poked his head into the study and nodded to her with questioning eyes. She put the speaker to her chest.

"Where have you been?" she whispered. Then, waving him back out the door, "In the living room. The photographer from *Rhode Island Life* has been waiting for you."

Jason had known that the editor of the publication was sending someone out to take some pictures of the inn, but he was certain that it had been arranged for the next day instead of that very afternoon. He scratched his head for a moment in puzzlement before hurrying off to the living room to introduce himself.

For some reason, Jason had been expecting to find a man when he walked through the archway into the room. Instead it turned out to be a young woman he discovered waiting for him there. Turned to one side so that he saw her in profile, a camera bag slung over one shoulder and her coat under her arm, she was looking with interest at one of the paintings hanging near the baby grand piano in the far corner.

Jason stopped dead in his tracks.

Even before she turned to face him, he recognized her. The dark hair, the slender figure, the delicate lines of her chin and lips, but most of all the tranquil air about her as she studied the painting. It was the very same young woman he had seen that day he went to Mass with his father. Astonished to find himself suddenly in her presence, he stood there like a dunce, momentarily speechless.

"Hello," he finally managed to say. "I'm Jason Mirabella. Sorry to keep you waiting."

The young woman turned away at once from the painting and approached him with her hand outstretched. Jason offered his own in return and the two shook hands. Her grip was soft and warm, and yet surprisingly strong in a gentle way that intrigued him. As he looked into the tranquil blue of her eyes, it was only with great reluctance that he was able to release it.

"Claudia Loren," she said pleasantly. "And please, I'm the one who should be sorry. I know that our appointment was for tomorrow, but I had to come by this way today, so I thought I'd just take a chance and stop by. I hope you don't mind. If it's not a good time, I can always come back tomorrow."

Jason was trying very hard not to stare at her, and not succeeding very well.

"No, it's quite all right, believe me," he assured her. "You came at a good time. Things are pretty quiet right now—not that they ever really aren't around here."

"You're sure?"

"Completely," he said.

At that he paused and gestured to her camera bag.

"Please," he told her. "Whenever you're ready, I'd love to show you around."

"My God, this old place is so beautiful," mused Claudia, her eyes roaming about with obvious pleasure. "It must be so nice to be able to come to work here every day."

It was a short time later. The young woman had already taken photographs of the parlor and dining room, and she and Jason were now ascending the main staircase to the second floor to view some of the guest rooms.

"It has its moments," Jason replied with a modest shrug even though he was very pleased by her reaction. It was odd, but for the first time in memory he was feeling a bit of pride and plea-sure of his own in his family's establishment. In truth, he was thoroughly enjoying showing her around, though he wished he knew as much about the house as his brother Raymond, for Claudia seemed fascinated by its every detail.

"Did you grow up in the business?" she asked with what seemed sincere curiosity.

The question surprised Jason in a pleasant way, for till that point all her interest had been directed solely toward the house and her purpose there.

"You might say that," he told her, "though honestly I only came back to work here a few weeks ago."

They paused at the top of the landing before turning to as-cend the second flight of stairs.

"Where were you before?" she said.

"I spent a few years working out in California," Jason answered.

It occurred to him then that he would rather not go into any detail about his experiences there, so he quickly turned the focus away from himself.

"How about you?" he asked. "How long have you been working for *Rhode Island Life*?"

"Actually, I don't really work for them," she told him. "I just do this as a freelancer whenever I have the time."

"What do you normally do?"

"I'm a graduate student at RISD."

RISD—she said it so it sounded like riz-dee—was the Rhode Island School of Design.

"Ah, that explains it," he said just as they came to the top of the stairs.

Claudia stopped and looked at him.

"What do you mean?" she asked.

"I think I've seen you before—at church," Jason explained, hesitantly. "It was at Blessed Sacrament, just before Mass one afternoon, and you were sitting there making a sketch of one of the windows. Do you belong to the parish?"

Claudia gave a little laugh and looked away for a moment before shaking her head.

"No," she confessed. "To tell you the truth, I'm not even Catholic. I don't belong to any church. I just happened to go there one day because someone had told me how beautiful it was inside, and I just wanted to see it for myself and maybe draw some of it. I ended up sitting there for a long time, just looking all around because it was so amazing. But then people started coming in and before I knew it the music was playing and the Mass started. I felt funny about just getting up and leaving—so I decided to stay."

"That must have been the day I saw you," said Jason with a smile.

"Maybe," she said with a vague expression.

"Why, have there been others?" he asked with sincere curiosity of his own.

"I've been going every week," she said to his surprise. Then, leaning closer, she added inquisitively, "Do you?"

"Go every week? Um—well, not exactly," Jason admitted with a shrug.

Claudia looked past him for a moment with a faraway gaze. It was as if she had suddenly drifted to some distant place that he could not see.

"I kind of like going," she said softly, as if to herself. "I'm not sure why."

As quickly as she had drifted away, she suddenly came back to herself.

"That's not against the rules, is it?" she said, cringing. "I mean, going to Mass if you're not a member. I have been putting some money in the basket every week."

"Don't worry," Jason kidded her. "So long as you cover your expenses, you're good."

At that the two shared a laugh and then continued on their tour.

For Jason it would all end too soon. Before he knew it they were coming back downstairs. As luck would have it, Giulio happened to walk through the foyer just then on his way back in from some errand. At the sight of his son and the pretty young woman with him, he gave an approving nod and stopped to greet them.

"Well, who have we here?" he said amiably, doffing his cap.

"Claudia, this is my father," said Jason.

"It's nice to meet you, Mr. Mirabella," she said, shaking his hand.

"Giulio," he told her with a warm smile. "And the pleasure's all mine." He nodded to her camera. "Official business?"

"She came to take some pictures of us for that magazine I told you about," said Jason.

"Well, I hope you make us look good," said Giulio.

"It would be hard not to," replied Claudia. "This place is wonderful."

"Thanks, we try," said Giulio, clearly charmed.

Jason give a little cough.

"Well, I guess I should leave you two to your business," said his father, taking the hint.

"Wait," said Claudia before he could go. "How about a picture of the two of you? It's good to have at least one people shot."

Before either man could object, she had the two of them dutifully standing side by side in front of the big grandfather clock against the wall in the front hall. When at last Claudia had finished taking the picture, Giulio said his good-byes and discreetly slipped away to allow Jason to walk her to the door.

"Thank you for showing me around," Claudia told him as the two slowly ambled out onto the front step together. "I think I got some nice shots."

"I'm looking forward to seeing them," Jason told her. With that he looked down and kicked pensively at a piece of ice on the step, trying without luck to think of something clever to send her away with.

"Well, I'm really glad you came today," he told her at last.

"Me too," she said. "It was fun."

With that, she said good-bye, and Jason watched her begin to make her way down the steps.

"Hey," he called after her when she reached the walk.

Claudia stopped and turned around. "What?"

Jason swallowed hard.

"I was just thinking," he said, "that it might be nice someday to maybe see those pictures you've been drawing at the church. I mean, I bet they're beautiful."

Claudia did not answer right away, but looked at him thoughtfully for a time, as if she were turning something over in her mind, before giving him a shrug.

"Maybe we'll see each other at Mass sometime," she told him with the hint of a smile before she turned once more and went on her way.

Jason smiled in return and watched until she had reached her car. He stayed there until she started the engine and pulled away from the front of the inn.

"Maybe we will," he said to himself when she was finally out of sight.

Then he went back inside, wondering how he should spend the rest of the day—and the rest of the week.

CHAPTER 22

"Looks to me like someone's getting ready for a hot date to-night," said Giulio.

It was Saturday afternoon and he was leaning against the frame of the open bathroom door, watching Jason shave himself in front of the mirror. Sundance had wandered in as well and was now seated on the floor beside his master's son, looking up with marked curiosity at his lathered face. The dog gave a high-pitched whimper of displeasure. The mask of shaving cream was apparently making it uneasy, and it was anxious to see Jason's face restored to its former state.

"Nope, not me," replied Jason.

He gave the dog a wink and drew the razor down the side of his cheek. Eyeing himself in the mirror, he gave the razor a swish in the sink to rinse off the cream and proceeded to shave the patch of skin immediately adjacent to the first.

"I'm not sure," he added, "but I was just thinking about maybe going to Mass later on, that's all."

His father gave a grunt of incredulity.

"Mass?" Giulio harrumphed.

"Yeah, Mass," said Jason. "There something wrong with that?"

"Not at all," replied Giulio with a shake of his head. "It's just that the last time I asked you to come with me—which I suspect was the first time you had gone to church in quite a while—I practically had to drag you out of the house."

"Well, I was tired that day," said Jason, unconvincingly.

"And you're feeling better rested today, I take it."

"You might say that."

"And what makes you suddenly want to go to Mass?" asked his father, casting a skeptical eye at him. "Something in particular on your mind?"

Jason shrugged.

"No reason," he said. "I just felt like I might want to go."

Jason paused for a moment and ran his fingertips over the two swaths of shaven skin to determine if they were sufficiently smooth. Satisfied, he moved on.

"You, um, planning to go yourself today?" he asked, trying to sound offhanded.

"Nah," replied Giulio. "Some of the guys are back in town, so I'm going to the eight o'clock tomorrow morning and then to breakfast."

"That's nice," said Jason, relieved by this news. "It's good that you have friends you can do things like that with."

"You're welcome to join us tomorrow if you don't feel like going by yourself this afternoon," his father offered.

"Oh no, that's okay," said Jason quickly. "I mean, who knows, I may not even go to Mass at all. Like I said, I was just thinking about it."

"What's to think about?"

"Nothing," said Jason with another shrug. "It's just that I might decide to do something different."

"Like what?"

"I don't know, Dad," he said, growing a little irritated. "What is this, twenty questions? I might go to Mass, I might not. I just thought maybe I'd get out of the house for a little while. That a problem?"

"No problem at all," Giulio answered him. "Just making conversation."

"Fine," breathed Jason, trying to refocus on the task at hand.

"But you do seem a little on edge," his father observed.

Just then Jason nicked himself with the razor.

"Ow!" he said with a wince.

At that a startled Sundance sprang up and put his paws on the edge of the sink, trying to get a better look at what had happened. In the process he knocked the can of shaving cream and the bar of soap to the floor, causing an instant commotion as only a high-spirited dog is able to do.

"Dad, I'm not on edge, I'm trying to shave," said Jason testily, elbowing the dog aside. He put his face closer to the mirror to evaluate the damage. It was only a small cut, a single droplet of blood burgeoning from the breach in the skin, but it was just big enough to be an annoyance.

"You're right," said Giulio, taking Sundance by the collar. "I'll get the two of us out of your way. We're making you nervous."

Jason gave an exasperated sigh.

"You're not making me nervous," he said. "And I'm not on edge. I just haven't made up my mind yet about what I want to do tonight. Okay?"

Giulio nodded his head, as if something suddenly made sense to him.

"Ah, that'll do it to you," he said.

"What?"

"Indecision," replied Giulio. "Trust me, insanity and indecision live next door to one another."

Jason gave a little laugh, for right at that moment his father was driving *him* insane.

"In that case, I think I've been living in that neighborhood for a while now," he said.

That much, Jason reflected, had been particularly true for the past three days since Claudia Loren had come to Bradley Mansion. Since the moment they parted company that afternoon, he had not been able to make up his mind about anything at all to do with her. For starters, his once prodigious confidence in dealing with the opposite sex had abandoned him completely, and now he was beset by nothing but doubts. Jason had sensed a mutual attraction between them, but he knew that it might well have been only wishful thinking on his part, for his decided attraction to her could easily have clouded his judgment. And what of her parting comment about meeting after Mass someday? If not an invitation, had it at least been an indication of interest, or had she simply been trying to be polite so as not to make him feel foolish? He replayed the scene over and over in his mind, wondering which was true. More pointedly, he brooded over the question of whether he should even consider trying to approach her again regardless of the answer. After all, what would she think of him if ever she came to know the truth about his past? Would it be worth the trouble? For all his deliberations, he simply could not decide.

"Come on, Sundance," said Giulio, his voice bringing Jason back from his ruminations. "Let's get out of the way and let the man think."

Afterward, when Jason had showered and dressed, he came downstairs and into the living room, where his father was watching a golf tournament on the television. Beside him on the couch the violin case lay open.

"Getting ready for your next symphony?" Jason asked.

"Carnegie Hall," Giulio quipped, taking the violin and bow in hand. "What about you? Make up your mind yet about what you're doing?"

There was something about the way he posed the question that gave Jason to believe that his father was asking about more than just his plans for the night, but more than that he was not prepared to discuss. He glanced at the clock on the mantel and saw that it was nearing four o'clock.

"I guess I'll be heading out," was all Jason said.

"Where to?" asked Giulio.

"I don't know," he replied with an ironic laugh. "I think maybe I'll just drive around for a while and see if I can't find a way out of that crazy neighborhood I've been living in lately."

"Just don't come home too late," Giulio told him, "otherwise I'll get worried and have to send the police out looking for you."

"Right, Mom," Jason said with a smile.

Then he grabbed his coat and headed out the door.

CHAPTER 23

"**H**ey, I heard it's really beautiful in there," Jason called out.

He was standing out on the sidewalk near the side entrance to the Church of the Blessed Sacrament. It was just after Mass, and he had hustled down the steep steps out front and around the corner of the church to station himself precisely at that spot. Having worried and waited all week for this moment, he had been quite intent on getting there in time.

At the sound of his voice, Claudia Loren, who had just stepped outside the church amid the other members of the congregation, stopped and looked across to him with an expression of what seemed to Jason only mild surprise. Her arms wrapped around the sketch pad she had brought to Mass, she beamed him a smile and descended the steps.

"It really is beautiful," she called back. "You should try coming in more often to appreciate it."

Jason could not help but return her smile and, as the two approached each other, the indecision and doubts that had plagued him the past few days began to recede.

"You sound a lot like my father," he told her when at last they were face-to-face.

"I bet he's a very wise man," she said.

"He has his moments."

Claudia stepped closer and looked up at him with her soft blue eyes.

"So, what brings you here tonight?" she asked, giving him a sideways glance.

"I came to Mass, of course," he answered with a grin. "I was sitting just a few rows in back of you the whole time."

This time Claudia looked truly surprised.

"You were? Why didn't you let me know you were there?"

"You were drawing when I came in," Jason explained with a shrug. "I didn't want to interrupt."

It was true. Jason had preferred to watch her from a distance, marveling all the while, as he had the first time he saw her, at that same aura of serenity she seemed to evoke when absorbed in her work. It stayed with her, even after she put the pad aside when the opening hymn of the Mass began to play. There was something profoundly attractive about it and her, something he longed to draw closer to. At the same time he could not help feeling that somehow it would be wrong for him to disturb her, so he had stayed away until now.

"I wouldn't have minded, you know," said Claudia softly. "It would have been nice to have someone to sit with."

"I'll remember for next time," he told her.

The two stood for a moment without speaking. It had been a miserable day, the skies dropping a mixture of snow and rain, and the ground and streets were covered in a messy layer of slush. By now the precipitation had let up, but the damp cold hung heavy in the air, and their breaths came out in little puffs of white.

Jason dug his hands down deep into his coat pockets and nodded to her sketch pad.

"So, did you get much done tonight?" he asked.

"A little," she said. "Would you like to see?"

"Why else would I have come?" he said with a grin.

"I don't know, maybe to say your prayers?" she replied playfully. Then with a sly gaze, "Then again, maybe you came to ask me out for a cup of coffee, which would be kind of nice right now because I'm freezing out here."

Jason feigned surprise.

"Hmm," he said thoughtfully, pretending to mull it over. "Honestly, nothing of the sort ever entered my mind, but now that you mention it, that might be kind of nice." He paused. "Actually, I'm kind of hungry. What would you say to having a little dinner together, and save the coffee for later?"

Claudia smiled and nodded. "I thought you'd never ask."

Not long afterward, the two were sitting in the cozy warmth of a booth at a little Mexican restaurant in the north end of the city. It was a lively place, and the room was full of talk and laughter and piped-in mariachi music. Sipping bottled beer while they waited for their dinners to arrive, the two leaned close over the table to talk. By this time, with some prodding from Jason, Claudia had opened her sketch pad to let him see her work. One by one, she had been flipping the pages over, each with a drawing of a window, or statue, or perhaps an intricately crafted section of the ceiling that one's eye might tend to overlook. Her eye seemed to capture everything, from the dove of peace over the pulpit to the little owl carved into the top of one of the columns flanking the doors at the back of the church.

"That's the sacrament of matrimony," said Jason, marveling at the sketch she had drawn of the stained-glass window high above the pews inside the church. The window was one of seven to be found on the walls of the church, depicting each of the holy sacraments. From what Jason could see, she had captured every detail. "This is really beautiful."

"Thank you," said Claudia with a modest shrug.

Jason could only shake his head in wonder as he looked them over.

"My God, these are all fantastic," he gushed. "You're so talented. Do you ever sell any of your work?"

At that Claudia gave a little laugh.

"No," she said, pushing a strand of her dark hair away from her face. "I could never do that."

"But why not?" said Jason. "If these are any indication, I bet you could make a name for yourself in no time."

"I really don't care about making a name for myself that way," Claudia told him. "And my work is not nearly as good as you think. But I love art, and when I'm done with my master's, I just want to teach. Who knows, maybe I'll be able to help other people make names for themselves. That would be enough for me, really." She closed up the pad and tucked it aside. "Anyway," she said, "these are just for me right now."

At that Jason smiled.

"What is it?" said Claudia.

"Someone I know, who writes poetry, told me that very same thing not too long ago," he said. "Maybe poets and artists have that in common."

"Art is art," she said with a shrug. "If you write with a pen, or draw with it, it's all about expressing a part of yourself that you might not want others to see—at least not until you're ready."

"And when is that usually?"

"Well, sometimes never," Claudia laughed. "We artists can be quite shy, you know."

Now it was Jason's turn to laugh.

"You shouldn't be, not about anything," he assured her. Then, hesitantly, "But, um, is that why you go to Mass by yourself?"

Claudia arched an eyebrow and gave him a skeptical look.

"Are you trying to ask me if I have a boyfriend?" she said.

"Well, kind of, I guess," said Jason with a chuckle.

Claudia paused for dramatic effect.

"Not at the moment," she finally answered.

"Why not?"

"I'm picky," she said with a shrug, the corners of her mouth curling into a captivating smile that Jason found more and more irresistible the longer he was with her.

"You can afford to be," he told her, unable to resist gazing into her eyes. "But why do you keep going back to church all alone?" he wondered aloud. "Just to draw?"

"Well, I guess it was at first," Claudia admitted. "But there's something else, too."

"What?" said Jason.

"I don't know what it is about it," Claudia replied. "I mean, I don't even understand all the rituals and prayers, but there's something comforting about it, you know? Besides, I never feel like I'm alone there. It's kind of a nice feeling, actually."

Leaning closer, Claudia put her elbows on the table and propped her chin up on her hands. For a time she studied him with a steady gaze, as if she were about to make him the subject of one of her drawings.

"So, what about you?" she said thoughtfully. "Do you go to church every week like a good Catholic boy?"

"I don't, not really," confessed Jason. "At least, I haven't until recently."

"Why not?"

"I don't know," he told her. "I think maybe I just got caught up in worshiping some false gods for a while."

Claudia gazed at him all the more intently.

"I remember you saying the other day that you had worked out in L.A. for a few years," she said. "Is that where you found them?"

"Honestly, I don't know if I found them out there or they just followed me from here," laughed Jason.

"What made you go out West in the first place?" she asked.

Jason sat back and took a sip of his beer.

"I just never really wanted to work for my family," he told her, "at least not back when I was going to college. So when a company in L.A. made me a good offer right after I got out of business school, I decided to take it and ended up staying. I liked it out there. I'd like to go back someday."

"What made you come home?"

Jason felt his heart beat a little quicker, the heaviness of indecision pressing in around him, for he did not know how much of the truth he dared tell her. It was the first time in months that he had allowed himself once more to feel even the faintest spark of attraction to or from a woman, and he was anxious not to say anything that would extinguish it so soon. Still, there was something about Claudia that made him want to tell her everything, and trust the chips to fall where they may. His courage, though, failed him.

"It's really just a long, boring story," he finally told her with a rueful grin. Then he fell silent.

Claudia sat back and smiled at him in a kind way.

"And let me guess," she said gently, "you don't want to talk about it, right?"

"Not really," Jason said. "Not just yet."

She gave a little laugh.

"Too much sharing on the first date?" she said, giving him that same sideways glance as she had when he met her after Mass.

Jason gave her a sideways glance of his own.

"Well, maybe it might be a good idea to leave a little something left over for the second date," he replied with a note of hope in his voice.

"Hmm, I'll have to think about that," she teased him. " I mean, right now I only know that you're into business, and I'm into art, and they say the two are very hard to mix, you know."

"Has that ever stopped anyone from trying?" Jason asked.

"Why should it?" said Claudia.

A grinning Jason was about to reply that he could think of absolutely no reason at all, but before he could speak the waitress arrived with their orders.

CHAPTER 24

The telephone rang.

It was late the next morning, and Jason was still lying in bed. He had been awake for quite a while, thinking about Claudia and going over and over in his mind everything about the evening just past.

The night had ended, he had thought at the time, far too early. After leaving the restaurant, he had given Claudia a ride back to her car at the church. Along the way, he had suggested stopping at a club or some other nightspot to have a drink and maybe listen to some music. To his keen disappointment, though, Claudia had declined his offer, telling him that she had work to do and that she really did not want to get home too late.

It had seemed a classic brush-off, and Jason had taken her refusal as a signal that perhaps the night had not gone nearly as well as he had perceived. A bit crestfallen, he had hesitated to even suggest that perhaps they might get together again some other time. But then to his surprise, Claudia herself had proposed the idea. Telephone numbers were exchanged, and early as it was, the night had ended for him on a hopeful note.

Now, though, as he lay in bed, Jason was once again beset by many of those same doubts that had plagued him before. Had she been serious? Did she really want him to call? Should he even go through with it and risk inevitable rejection when sooner or later she learned the truth about him? These questions and others swirled around inside his head, and he felt anew the boot against his chest, for he simply could not make up his mind about any of them.

The telephone rang again.

Jason gave a sigh. It was chilly in the room, and he was reluctant to pull himself from beneath the warm covers. Just the same, he had heard Giulio taking the dog out for a walk earlier, so he knew that only he was home. With a grumble he threw aside the covers, got to his feet, and went to his father's bedroom to answer the phone.

It was Claudia.

"Hey, how long were you going to make me wait before you called?" she playfully chided him. "I've been sitting by the phone all morning!"

"My bad," said a pleasantly astonished Jason.

Claudia was waiting on the doorstep to her apartment when Jason drove up to the house in his father's pickup truck. It was a bright, clear day, and she was wearing a pair of stylish sunglasses, her face turned up to receive the warmth of the sun. At seeing him pull into the driveway, she broke into a smile and waved before walking down the steps to the front walk.

Jason could not help but smile in return as he watched her approach. When they had spoken earlier, he had not bothered to ask her where she wanted to go or what she wanted to do. In truth, he did not care. It was enough just to know that she wanted to see him again, and so he had showered and dressed in a mad rush, scribbled a note to his father that he would be back later in the day, and grabbed the keys to the truck.

Now, as he watched Claudia draw nearer, Jason realized that he was forgetting his manners. He jumped out and hurried around the truck to open the passenger's-side door for her.

"Hey there," she said breezily, as she stepped past him and climbed in.

"Hey there back," answered Jason, smiling ear to ear as he breathed in the delicate scent of her perfume.

"Sorry to call you like that," said Claudia when she had settled in. "I hope I'm not ruining your Sunday."

"Completely," Jason joked. "But I'll get over it."

With that he closed her door, came around to his side of the truck, and climbed in behind the wheel. He started the engine and gave her a nod.

"So, what did you have in mind for the day?" he asked. "Anything special?"

"Well," she began, "I was thinking about last night, and how you seemed to enjoy looking at my sketches."

"I did," said Jason truthfully. "Very much."

"In that case, what do you say to taking a look at some real artwork?"

"As good as yours?" he said with a skeptical air.

"At least," laughed Claudia.

"Okay, then," he said, putting the truck in gear. "Show me the way."

A short while later, after a brief ride across town, the two walked in through the main doors to the Rhode Island School of Design Museum. As a graduate student, Claudia did not need to pay for admission, so she waited by the entrance to the galleries while Jason purchased a pass for himself. There she peeled off her coat and draped it across her arm.

When he finished paying and turned to look for her, Jason saw for the first time the snug-fitting jeans and knit blouse she was wearing. It was a simple but very appealing ensemble that clung rather nicely to her slender figure. As Jason tucked away his wallet, he was hard-pressed not to stare.

"Coming along?" beckoned Claudia.

"Absolutely," he said.

Claudia smiled and gave a contented sigh when at last he came to her side.

"I love this place," she told him.

Then she touched his arm and led him inside.

The two wandered everywhere that afternoon, from gallery to gallery, the museum much larger than it had appeared to Jason when they first arrived. There was, in truth, too much for him to appreciate in such a short amount of time, and he felt a bit overwhelmed. Claudia, though, seemed to be in her element. No matter what work of art they happened to find themselves regarding, be it a piece of Roman sculpture or a painting by Monet or Cézanne, she seemed to know something about it. It was like having a private tour guide to whom Jason very much enjoyed listening, even if he was largely unacquainted with what she was talking about.

Eventually they stopped for a rest and sat on the bench in the middle of an enormous gallery housing an equally enormous collection of paintings from the twentieth century. Jason stretched out his legs, and looked about, not knowing which to consider, for many of them struck him as simply odd. In truth, it was of small concern, for his attention in any case was more focused on Claudia, who was sitting now quite close to him.

"So, what do you think?" she asked, her shoulder brushing against his as she looked about. "Aren't all of these just amazing work?"

"They are," said Jason, inclined to agree, for he would not have known just how to describe them otherwise. "But I couldn't help wondering how much people get paid for doing paintings like these."

Claudia laughed to herself.

"What's the matter?" Jason asked.

"You really do have a businessman's mind, don't you?" she teased him.

"What's wrong with that?"

"Well, money is nice," she told him. "And of course everyone dreams of getting paid for their work, but it's not why artists get out of bed every morning and do what they do. It's not what motivates them, not really."

"Then what does?" said Jason.

Claudia looked around with a faraway gaze and sighed.

"It's hard to explain," she said, "but you see, real art is about showing a part of yourself, something from very deep inside you that maybe even you didn't know was there. And that means making yourself very vulnerable, and that can be really scary. But you know, if you do it right, you can create something truly beautiful. Something that lasts."

She paused and looked down at her hands for a moment.

"Art and love," she said, "are a lot alike in that way."

Then Claudia looked up at him and smiled in an embarrassed way.

"Ugh," she groaned. "Did that sound as lame as I think it did?"

"Not coming from you," said Jason, laughing to put her at ease. Though such a tender association as the one she had just spoken might never have occurred to him, to Jason's ears it rang true. He understood very little about art, and he had come to doubt much of what he thought he knew of love, but it intrigued him that she could express herself so readily about both. He found that ability made her all the more attractive.

"Besides," he went on, "even though I might have a businessman's mind, I can still appreciate what you said about wanting to create something that lasts. I mean, isn't that something that just about everybody wants to do? It's just that different people go about it in different ways."

Claudia beamed at him.

"Are you suggesting that maybe art and business could mix after all?" she said, giving him that sideways glance that he found irresistible.

"Maybe," said Jason. "Could it hurt to give it a try?"

"I don't know," she said breezily. "It might be fun. But then again, we do seem to look at the world in different ways. Does that bother you?"

The lighthearted sound of her voice let him know that he was not to take the question seriously. Just the same, Jason shook his head and looked down at his hands, for suddenly the voices of doubt had returned to plague him. It was as if this moment of attraction to her had roused a chorus of them. Suddenly they were in full throat, reminding him of the past and warning him away from even the slightest notion that he might one day be able to find happiness with someone again.

"No," he said softly. "That doesn't bother me at all."

"Is there something that does?" said Claudia, her eyes now studying him with quiet intensity. When Jason did not reply right away, she reached out and touched his arm. "Is it about that long story you wouldn't tell me last night?" she asked gently. "Because you can tell it to me now if you like." Then, playfully, "This *is* our second date after all."

Jason looked back up and let his gaze meet hers, trying hard to hide the anxiety in his eyes, but knowing full well that he was failing.

"Maybe some other time," he said.

"Why not now?"

Jason took a breath and let it out slowly.

"Because I like you," he finally told her.

At that Claudia said nothing at first, but instead, quite unexpectedly, took his face in her hands and brought her lips to his, quieting the voices that sought to torment him.

"Well then," she whispered, "I guess we have more in common than we thought. What do you say we just leave the rest till later?"

With that she slipped her hand in his, pulled him to his feet, and led him back out the way they had come.

CHAPTER 25

Jason stood at the living room window and gazed out across the front lawn of the inn. It was three weeks later. February had given way to March, and the bitter cold to which he had come home had finally eased. Nearly all the snow had melted away by now, and here and there in the otherwise barren gardens the crocuses were pushing their way up through the soggy ground.

As he surveyed the scene, it struck Jason how altered the world outside suddenly seemed to him. He wondered if it was the absence of the snow and ice that made it appear so changed to his eye, or was it simply that he was looking at everything in a different way?

He supposed that he had Claudia to thank for that. As the days had gone by, and they had seen more and more of each other, the liking they shared for each other had begun to show signs of becoming something deeper. When he was with her, Jason felt a sense of contentment within that seemed to grow stronger by the day. At the same time, though, this feeling was tempered by one of great disquiet. Jason did not know what the future held for him, and he was still troubled by the past. And so he held back from her, trying to keep things from getting beyond his control. Just the same, he was finding it increasingly difficult to say good night to her whenever they were together.

"Are you planning to do some work for me today, or are you

just going to stare out that window all afternoon?" came Giulio's voice, shaking Jason from his thoughts.

Jason turned around and nodded to his father.

"Just taking a little break to admire the view from here," he replied with a smile.

Giulio walked over to his side and took a look outside for himself.

"You know, I think winter might finally be over," he said after a time. "It might try to take one or two more swipes at us, but that's all."

"I hope you're right," said Jason. "My blood is still too thin for this climate."

Giulio gave a little laugh; then he paused and cleared his throat, as if preparing himself to speak on a delicate subject.

"I, um, know we're living under the same roof," he began, "but lately I haven't seen much of you after work hours, and I've been wanting to talk to you."

"What about?"

"About you," said his father. "It's been two months now since you came home and you seem to be getting back on your feet a little."

"I'm getting there," said Jason.

"That's good," said Giulio. "But tell me, have you made any plans yet for the future—not that there's any hurry, mind you."

"None yet, Dad," Jason admitted. "Right now I'm just taking things day to day, if you know what I mean."

"And what do you think of this place?" said his father, gesturing about at the house. "Has working here been as bad as you thought it would be?"

Jason gave a shrug.

"I don't know," he said. "At first it was a little strange, but lately I've been starting to feel a little better about things."

"Things around here?"

"Things around everywhere," said Jason.

"Ah, a good woman will do that to you," said Giulio, glancing at him with a raised eyebrow.

"What makes you say that?" laughed a suddenly red-faced Jason.

"I have eyes," his father said. "So tell me, what's her name?"

Jason chuckled, for he knew there was no point in trying to bluff his father.

"Her name is Claudia," he said.

Giulio furrowed his brow for a moment before the name finally registered with him.

"Ah, would that be Miss Loren, the photographer?" he said brightly.

Jason simply nodded in reply.

Giulio patted him on the shoulder and gave him an approving nod.

"That's good, Jason," he said, sounding quite pleased. "She seemed like a very nice girl. I'm happy for you." Then, deadly serious, "But do you know what you're doing?"

Jason considered the question with equal seriousness.

"Not at all," he finally said with complete frankness.

Giulio gave a harrumph.

"Good," he chuckled. "Because when you think you know what you're doing, that's when you get in trouble."

With that he turned and started toward the dining room, but then stopped and looked over his shoulder.

"One of the lasagna ladies dropped off some peppers and sausage today," he said. "Can I count on you for dinner later on?"

Jason gave a sheepish grin and shook his head.

"Ah, you see," said his father, "it looks like you have made at least *some* plans after all."

Then, with an air of satisfaction, he went on his way to help Raymond set up the afternoon tea.

CHAPTER 26

Jason did indeed have plans for that night.

When he left the inn later that evening, he hurried home to shower and change. Before long he was on his way once more out the door, a curious Sundance following close at his heels until Jason unceremoniously shoved him back inside. Soon he was back in the pickup truck, driving across the city.

He was on his way to Claudia's of course. The two had made plans to have dinner together and perhaps catch a movie. Someplace casual was in order, and Jason had been thinking that it might be fun to take Claudia to the Post. When he climbed the back stairs to her apartment and finally arrived at her door, however, he discovered that there had been a change in the dining arrangements.

"What do you say we forget about going to a restaurant, and eat dinner right here tonight?" said Claudia to his surprise.

A quick whiff of the air told Jason that the matter had already been decided, for he caught the distinct aroma of garlic simmering in the kitchen. Apparently dinner had already been started.

"How could I say no?" he said.

Claudia stretched up and gave him a quick kiss.

"You can't," she said, pulling him inside. "Now go relax on

the couch and stay out of my way for a few minutes so I can get back to work."

Claudia's home was a small but cozy place. A single bedroom, bath, a modest living room, and even more modest kitchen. The decor was simple—a few paintings and strategically placed plants— but in an elegant way, for Claudia had the artist's eye for seeing that which was essential. While she went back to the kitchen to finish making dinner, Jason settled in on the couch and stretched out his legs.

"So what are we having?" he called to her. "Whatever it is, it smells good."

"I'm not too adventurous a cook just yet," replied Claudia, poking her head out of the kitchen, "so I'm just making some spaghetti with garlic and olive oil. I've got a salad and some garlic bread to go along with it. Do you think that will be enough?"

"Are you kidding? It sounds perfect."

"Good," said Claudia with a smile. "I'm just putting the spaghetti in the pot, so it shouldn't take too long."

With that she ducked back inside. A few moments later she brought a bottle of wine and an opener to the living room and put both on the coffee table in front of Jason.

"Here, you open that," she told him, "and I'll get some glasses. This way we can have a little sip while we wait for the pasta to cook."

While he was pulling the cork from the bottle, Jason happened to look in the corner of the room where Claudia kept an easel and her art supplies. On the easel stood a sketch pad opened to a drawing that immediately caught his eye. It was a rendering of the front of Bradley Mansion. As with her drawings at church, this one showed Claudia's eye for detail, particularly the little things one tended to overlook. The stonework below the windows, the urns that flanked the front steps, the lion's head door knocker. In one regard, however, the picture was not at all accurate, for she had embellished the front lawn by adding a fanciful fountain with a small statue of some graceful goddess at its center.

After Claudia returned and the wine was poured, Jason raised his glass to her.

"*Sante,*" said Claudia, clinking her glass against his as she settled onto the couch close beside him. She slipped off her shoes and curled her bare feet up onto the cushions.

"Actually, Italians say *salute*," Jason kidded her.

"We'll say *salute* when you cook for me," replied Claudia, leaning closer with a playful gleam in her eye.

Jason swallowed hard, for he was quite mesmerized by her gaze and distracted by the gentle curves of her body and the fresh scent of her hair. The urge to reach out and take her in his arms was almost more than he could resist, but he held back.

"Fair enough," he finally managed to say.

Jason took a sip of wine. It gave him a warm feeling inside, and he settled back, trying to relax a little.

"I like the drawing, by the way," he told her, nodding to the easel.

"Thank you," she said, modest as always. "It was just something quick I did using one of the outdoor shots I took the day we met."

"It came out great," said Jason. "But what's with the fountain?"

"Oh, that was just a little idea that came to me when I was playing around with the picture," she laughed. "As I was drawing, I kept thinking that there was something missing, but I couldn't think of what it was. Finally I decided to try the fountain in the front, and I liked the way it looked, so I left it there just for fun. I think it gives the house a sort of Italian country villa feel, if you know what I mean."

Jason took another sip of wine.

"A villa," he said, contemplating the picture. "That's an interesting idea."

"It's an interesting place," said Claudia.

She looked at him for a time before her expression suddenly changed and she gave a little sigh.

"What is it?" asked Jason.

Claudia hesitated for a moment.

"I was just thinking," she said at last, putting aside her wine-glass, "about your plans to move back to L.A. someday. I keep wondering why you would want to go back there and leave your family and such a nice place behind."

Jason gave a little sigh of his own.

"I know, I know, it's a long story," she huffed before he could reply. "But I'd really like to hear it someday. I think it might be good for you to tell it."

Jason fidgeted with his glass, letting the wine swirl around like the thoughts in his head.

"You will," he said. "I promise."

"In that case, I'm going to hold you to that," she said, eyeing him closely.

"I don't doubt you will," said Jason softly, unable to take his eyes away from her.

For a moment, Claudia said nothing. But then she smiled in a knowing way, reached out, and touched his face. She gently ran her fingers down his cheek and across his mouth before finally taking his face full in her hands. Jason melted at her touch and before he could even move she brought her mouth to his. She kissed him very softly at first, but then more deeply as she pulled herself onto him and pushed his shoulders back into the couch. There she stopped and looked down at him, letting her lovely hair fall about his face.

Jason sank back, helpless to resist her, and doubting that he even wanted to anymore, but still trying to hold back all the same.

Claudia reached out and caressed his face once more.

"I want to know you, Jason," she whispered. "I want to know

everything there is to know about you." She paused and brought her mouth to his ear. "How do you feel about that?" she breathed.

Jason gave a nervous laugh.

"Vulnerable," he tried to joke. "Just like an artist."

Claudia gave a soft laugh of her own and drew back from him for a moment.

"Well then," she told him, "if we play our cards right, maybe something beautiful will happen."

With that, she started to bring her mouth to his again. But just then, to Jason's relief, came the hissing of water boiling over onto the stove, and Claudia had to run to the kitchen to save the spaghetti.

CHAPTER 27

Just as Giulio had predicted, a few days later winter decided to take one last swipe at the region even though the calendar read that it was nearing the end of March and already officially spring. Early morning commuters that day found themselves confronted with roads covered in a slippery mixture of snow and sleet driven by a raging northeast wind. As the morning hours progressed and the temperature slowly rose, the snow and sleet gradually changed over into an icy wind-driven rain that blew sideways in great whipping sheets. All in all it was a wet, miserable day.

The fireplaces at Bradley Mansion were of course crackling early on. Breakfast was served, and by the late morning hours, after doing his part to help out, Jason was safely ensconced in his makeshift office in the closet on the third floor. Hanging on the wall in front of him was the sketch of the mansion that Claudia had drawn. Jason had been working on the marketing plan he had started for the inn, but at the moment he was taking a little break. He settled back in his chair and listened to the wind moaning through the rafters while he gazed at the sketch and thought about Claudia.

With each passing day, despite his hesitancy, Jason found his feelings for her deepening all the more. It was odd, but even though it had not been very long since they first met, it felt as though they had known each other their entire lives. It was a nice feeling, but one that also troubled Jason for the guilt from what had happened between him and Amanda weighed on him as heavily as ever, and he felt somehow undeserving of it. Then there was the matter of his plans to go back to Los Angeles one day. Claudia made the idea of staying where he was enticing at a time when a great part of him was still longing to leave.

Jason turned his gaze from the sketch of the inn and considered for a time the cramped surroundings in which he found himself. Choices, he knew, would sooner or later have to be made. For now, though, things in his life at least seemed to be sailing along on a more even keel. All he could do was wait and see what each new day brought.

When he came downstairs a little while later, Jason passed by the living room, where Mrs. Martinez was trying to explain to Raymond in her broken English some problem she was apparently having with the vacuum cleaner. As she spoke she kept gesturing back and forth between the plug and the outlet on the base of the wall.

"Yeah, yeah, I get it," Jason heard his brother saying impatiently. "The vacuum's not working right down here. What else is new? Try plugging it in someplace else." With that, Raymond gave a huff and went off to tend to some other business.

"What's with Ray today?" Jason asked Natalie later in the study.

"Who knows?" she said with a shrug. "He's been in a wicked mood lately."

"Something going on?" Jason wondered.

"I don't know," said Natalie. "I asked him the other day if there was something wrong, but he just said he had a lot of things on his mind."

Before they could discuss their brother further, they heard the slamming of the front door to the inn and a moment later the familiar figure of Carl, the mailman, appeared at the study door. Drenched from head to toe, the water dripping off his hat and rain slicker, he lingered out in the hall, holding up a bundle of mail he had just pulled from his sack.

"Good morning, Carl, you made it!" laughed Natalie, coming out from behind her desk.

"Hey, you know how it is," chuckled the mailman. "Not rain nor snow nor gloom of night can stop me, though it is trying its best today. It's a wild one out there."

"How are the roads, Carl?" Jason asked. "Any better than this morning?"

Carl gave a shrug.

"Eh, the snow is already all melted," he said. "But there's a lot of flooding in the streets, so you have to take it slow."

Natalie came over and eagerly snatched the bundle of mail from him.

"I hope there are no bills in here," she warned him.

"Ayyy," groaned Carl. "Everybody always blames the mailman."

"Who else are we going to blame?" said Natalie, retreating to her desk.

At that Carl gave another chuckle. Then he leaned in through the door and looked about the room with a hopeful gaze.

"Got time for a quick cup of coffee?" asked Natalie, as if on cue, as she sifted through the mail.

"Ooh, I would love just a sip," said Carl. "But then I have to run."

"I think we can arrange that," said Jason, already on his way to the kitchen.

Later, after Carl had gone, Jason stood at the window, watching the rain come down and the wind whip through the trees. Meantime, Natalie was busy behind him, sorting through the mail. Suddenly she gave a little coo of delight.

"What is it?" said Jason, turning from the window.

Natalie smiled and held up a neat little stack of checks that she had just found in the mail.

"Room deposits?" he said.

"A whole bunch," said his sister gleefully. "And a lot came in yesterday, too."

"That's great," said Jason, smiling, for his sister looked as though she had just won the lottery. "But why so much all of a sudden?"

"Well, there's the antiques show that's coming up at the convention center," explained Natalie. "And then there are lots of people coming for the flower show right after that. We always seem to get booked up for those things."

Jason came and sat on the edge of the desk and watched while she stamped the checks one by one, preparing them to be deposited at the bank.

"So, it was a good haul?" he said.

"Uff," grunted a relieved Natalie. "You have no idea how badly we needed this right now. There's a ton of bills to pay, not to mention one or two payroll checks, if you know what I mean. I've got to get this into the bank today."

The words were no sooner out of her mouth than the windows were suddenly buffeted by a tremendous gust of wind, the rain splattering against the panes. Natalie looked up and gave a shudder.

"God, it's brutal out there," she said. "I hate driving in weather like this."

With that she paused for a moment, as if trying to make up her mind about something, before turning to Jason with a pained expression.

"Um," she began hesitantly, her voice taking on a distinct pleading tone, "how would you feel about doing me a little favor?"

Jason folded his arms and gave her a skeptical look.

"Does it involve driving in weather like this?" he asked.

"It might," replied his sister. "That is, unless you feel like walking to the bank for me instead."

Jason had no intention of walking to the bank, but he had no objection to driving there to make the deposit for Natalie. If anything, though he didn't show it, he was inwardly pleased that she had asked him to do it. All the same, he could not help playing the imp.

"If I go, what's in it for me?" he asked with a mischievous smile.

"How about I put a good word in for you with the boss?" Natalie offered. "And maybe he'll give you a raise."

"Ha!" Jason laughed. "Good luck with that one."

Then he went to the closet to get his coat and hat.

The wind was still roaring for all it was worth later on when Jason pulled into the parking lot at the bank. It blew so hard against the side of the truck that it was all he could do just to push open his door. With the rain pelting him in the face, he tucked the deposit pouch into his coat pocket, pushed himself out into the wind, and hustled across the lot.

There was no one else waiting in line, so Jason was able to walk right up to the teller when he came through the lobby. She was a young woman with plain features, but a pleasant face. Her name tag read Trish. She smiled at Jason as he removed his hat and wiped the raindrops from his brow.

"How's it going out there?" she said.

"Wet and wild, Trish," laughed Jason.

"Still no letup, huh?"

Jason took a quick glance back over his shoulder to the door and shook his head.

"Not from what I can see," he told her. "It's blowing like crazy out there."

Trish smiled at him again and nodded to the deposit pouch.

"So, how can I help you today?" she said.

"Just making a deposit," said Jason. He unzipped the pouch, pulled out the checks and deposit slip Natalie had prepared, and handed them over.

Jason looked about absentmindedly as she got to work processing the deposit.

"I heard this weather might continue right through tomorrow," he heard one of the other tellers say.

"Sounds like it will be a good night to just stay inside and snuggle next to a fire," Trish mused in reply. Though she had spoken to the other teller, Jason got the distinct impression that she had said it for his benefit.

When she was done processing the deposit, Trish printed out the receipt and handed it over to Jason.

"There you are, all set," she told him with a smile. "Try to stay dry out there."

"I'll do my best," he told her.

With that Jason nodded a good-bye and headed back out through the lobby with the deposit receipt in hand. As he walked toward the doors, he reflected that Trish had indeed been right, it would be a good night to snuggle up by a fire. The thought of doing so with Claudia was happily playing in his mind when he stepped outside once more into the rain.

Jason had only taken a step or two when a ferocious blast of wind suddenly caught him by surprise. Instinctively he reached up to hold on to his hat, unwittingly letting go of the deposit receipt in the process. The slip of paper flew out of his hand like it had wings and landed several feet away on the sidewalk. Before he could reach down to grab it, another gust of wind carried it out onto the parking lot. With a curse, Jason chased after it, but soon gave up when it sailed far across the parking lot and lost itself somewhere with the rest of the litter beneath the cars.

Annoyed with himself, Jason stood there with his hands on his hips for a moment, scowling at the wind and rain. At last, though, he gave a sigh of resignation. There was nothing to be done, and at least he knew that the money was safely deposited in the bank. With that comforting thought in mind, he trudged off to the truck, his mood brightening once more as he thought of Claudia and finding a warm fire to snuggle by.

CHAPTER 28

It is amazing how much turmoil can result from the loss of a single slip of paper.

It would begin for Jason, and everyone for that matter, a few days later that following week when the checks Natalie had sent out to pay the inn's bills began to bounce. First it was the dairy to call early that afternoon, complaining that the check for their most recent invoice had been returned for insufficient funds. Soon after, it was the florist down the street from whom they often purchased arrangements to decorate the inn. Then came the hardware store and some of the other local businesses to whom she had sent payments.

A befuddled Natalie fielded the calls, appalled at what was happening. Naturally she assured all their vendors that it was simply an oversight and that new checks would be issued right away, but she was at a complete loss to explain the situation. By rights, there ought to have been more than enough money in their account to cover the checks she had written. Her bewilderment turned into outright alarm when Carl brought the mail a little while later and she found in it the overdraft notices from the bank. To her chagrin, not only had the checks to the vendors bounced, but so had most of the payroll checks. Desperate for answers, for everything seemed to be in order according to her check register, she picked up the telephone and called the bank.

As yet unaware of what was happening, Jason took his time getting back to the inn that afternoon. It had been a slow day, for there were few guests in the house, and he had stolen away just before noon to have lunch downtown with Claudia. To all appearances the peripatetic New England skies had seen fit to finally chase away winter once and for all, for the weather had suddenly turned delightfully warmer. Not wanting to waste the gift of such a beautiful early spring day inside, the two had sat on a park bench on Kennedy Plaza. There they watched the people passing by while they ate their lunch and basked in the warm sunshine. It was a very pleasant interlude and Jason drove back to Bradley Mansion in spirits as buoyant as they ever had been since he came home from California.

When he walked through the front door, there was no one to be seen, but Jason heard the low murmur of voices in the study. He strolled over and poked his head in. Inside he saw Raymond and Natalie hovering over the desk, gazing with troubled countenances at something on the computer monitor. Jason had no idea of what its cause might be, but there was an unmistakable feeling of tension in the air.

"Hey, guys," he said. "What's going on?"

At hearing his voice, Raymond straightened up and stood there with arms folded, glaring at Jason, while Natalie nervously shuffled around some papers on her desk.

"Come on in and sit down," said his brother in an ominous tone. "We've got a little problem here we need to talk to you about."

Jason felt his heart beat just a little faster, for he had heard those very same words before. Though it had been in a different place under very different circumstances, a nervous knot came to his stomach.

"Where's Dad?" he asked as he took a seat on the sofa.

"He's out, but he'll be back in a little while," said Raymond.

"That's why we wanted to talk to you now," added Natalie.

Jason looked back and forth between the two, trying with no luck to read their expressions.

"So what's the problem?" he asked.

"The problem," grumbled Raymond, "is that people have been playing basketball all over town with our checks today."

Jason shook his head in puzzlement.

"What are you talking about?" he said.

Natalie held up the insufficient funds notices she had just received in the mail that afternoon.

"Almost every single check that I've written this past week has bounced," she told him.

"That includes my paycheck and Nat's," added Raymond in a voice tinged with anger. "Funny, but yours happened to clear."

"I don't get it," said Jason. "What happened?"

"I just talked to the bank a little while ago," said Natalie. "They have no record of the deposit I gave you."

Jason sat up straight, for suddenly he began to understand where the conversation was going, and the nervous knot in his stomach grew tighter.

"But I made the deposit that day," he told them. "The money should be there."

"And where's the receipt?" asked Raymond.

Jason shifted uneasily.

"I lost it," he admitted, his cheeks reddening. "I dropped it when I came out of the bank and the wind took it. I already told Natalie that last week."

"Uh-huh," grunted Raymond in a cynical way. From the look on Natalie's face, Jason could see that she was no longer quite convinced of it either.

There was a long, terribly awkward silence.

"Jason, I hate to ask you this question," said Natalie very tentatively, "but is there anything you want to tell us?"

"About what?" he replied, growing defensive at the sight of the accusing looks in their eyes.

"About what happened to the money," snapped Raymond. "You know, some of us have families to support, and we need this place."

"What are you saying?" Jason shot back. "Are you telling me you think that I did something with the money?"

"Hey, we're in tough straits here right now," said Raymond angrily. "What are we supposed to think?"

Jason got to his feet and gaped at his brother and sister. He was filled with dismay and anger, as much of it directed at himself as at them, for he knew in his heart why fingers were pointing his way.

"I can't believe you would accuse me of this," he gasped.

"We need that money, Jason," insisted Raymond.

"Well, I don't have it!" Jason shouted back. "I put in the bank, just like I said!"

"Guys, please!" pleaded Natalie.

Just then Giulio walked through the door.

"Hey, what's with all the loud voices in here!" he exclaimed.

At the sight of their father, the three siblings fell silent. Giulio looked from one to the other, waiting for some explanation.

"Somebody want to tell me what's going on here?" he said tersely when none was forthcoming.

The silence continued.

"There's a problem with the bank, Dad," a nervous Natalie finally said. "There's money missing."

"And they think I took it," said Jason.

"What!" exclaimed his father. "That's ridiculous. How could you two even think such a thing?"

"Hey, I'm sorry," griped Raymond, "but you know, this is what happens when you have a history of committing fraud."

The remark stung Jason in his heart. Even Raymond himself

seemed to regret saying it the moment the words left his lips, for his shoulders suddenly slouched and he bowed his head.

"That's enough!" Giulio cried.

Jason looked at his brother and swallowed hard.

"I made one mistake," he said bitterly. "Just one. And now you're going to hold it over my head for the rest of my life?"

Raymond gave a sigh of frustration and ran his hand across his forehead.

"You know, Jason," his brother said wearily, "sometimes people get hurt when mistakes get made."

"You don't think I know that?" seethed Jason.

With that he turned angrily and walked quickly out of the room.

"Jason, come back!" Natalie called after him.

Giulio shook his head in consternation at his two older children and started out of the study after Jason. Just then, though, the front door swung open and in walked a middle-aged couple, the husband toting a pair of suitcases.

"Which way to check in?" said the man pleasantly.

Giulio took a breath and forced a smile to put on a good front, for that's what you do when you run a business.

"Right this way," he told them. "And welcome to Bradley Mansion."

CHAPTER 29

Jason stood at the kitchen sink and stared out the back window while he sipped a cup of coffee. It was early Sunday morning. He had intended to sleep much later, for he had been feeling tired to his very soul, but he had awoken from a terrible dream in which he had seen Amanda standing by the railing of a windswept bridge, holding an infant child.

"You want it"—she had sneered at him, holding the child out over of the edge—"come and get it."

Jason had shaken himself awake just at the awful moment when he was convinced that she was about to let the child go.

It was a miserable start to the day and his restless thoughts had driven him out of bed. The blowup with Raymond and Natalie over the missing deposit was now weighing heavily on his mind and he found he could not stop thinking about it. The day it happened, his father had covered the inn's expenses out of his own savings and instructed Natalie to prompt the bank to initiate an investigation into what had become of their missing deposit. The money had gone *somewhere* after all. The bank had told them that it would take at least a day or two to research it. The weekend had come, however, with no resolution, and so the whole matter remained in limbo.

Jason took his coffee and slouched into a chair at the table. It astonished him at how low he was feeling. He did not know which felt worse: being falsely accused of stealing from his family or knowing that it was own fault that his siblings would even have suspected him of doing such a thing in the first place. He heaved a sigh. Just when it had seemed like he had begun to step out of the shadow of his past, and the ponderous weight he had been carrying around inside had started to lighten, all at once it had come crashing down again. It pressed on him now as relentless as ever. How on earth, he wondered, would he ever be rid of it?

Just then the front door opened and Giulio brought Sundance in from their morning walk. The dog trotted into the kitchen, gave Jason a sniff, and promptly flopped down in the corner to rest. Giulio came in and nodded him a greeting.

"You're up bright and early for a Sunday," said his father.

"Early maybe," replied Jason. "Not so bright."

Giulio poured himself a cup of coffee and sat down next to him at the table.

"All the hoopla about the deposit still gnawing at you?" he said.

"It seems to be gnawing at everybody," said Jason.

"Eh, don't worry about it," grunted Giulio. "These things happen in families, especially family businesses. In the heat of the moment people always think and say stupid things that they don't really mean. It doesn't mean anything. Family is family at the end of the day. Trust me, your brother and sister don't really believe you did anything wrong."

"Why not?" sighed Jason. "If I was in their shoes, I probably would be thinking the same thing."

Giulio reached over and gave his son a gentle swat in the arm.

"You've got to get rid of that way of thinking about yourself," he said. "What's in the past is in the past. You have to bury it and move on."

"That's easier said than done."

"You're smart," said his father. "You'll find a way. But you're not going to find it by moping around here in the house. You need to get out for a while and clear your head."

"I know," said Jason. "I'm working on that."

"That mean you have plans for the day?"

Jason shook his head.

"Well, in that case, make some," said Giulio.

After his father had finished his coffee and gone off to Mass, Jason waited awhile before going to the telephone. Though he had been longing to see her, he had nonetheless been putting Claudia off since the confrontation with his brother and sister, for he wasn't at all ready to talk about what had happened and why. Just the night before, at the last minute, he had canceled their plans to have dinner together, using the vague excuse that he wasn't feeling well. Claudia had complained only a little, giving him the sense that she knew something else was wrong. Part of him wanted to put Claudia off a little longer to avoid having to talk about it. The greater part of him, though, was aching to see her, so he picked up the telephone and called her apartment to make their plans for the day.

"Hey there, stranger. Why do I get the feeling you've been trying to avoid me?" Claudia chided him later on after Jason picked her up at her apartment and the two were finally sitting in the truck. "You know a girl starts to worry when her boyfriend stands her up on a Saturday night."

"Sorry about that," Jason told her with a sigh. "I've had a few things going on. Please, don't take it personally. I just wouldn't have been very good company the past couple of days, so I was sparing you for your own good."

Claudia reached out and caressed his cheek for a moment.

"Sounds like you had a rough week," she said, gazing into his eyes as if she were trying to read his thoughts.

Jason shrugged and nodded.

"Anything we can do to make things better?" she asked, taking his hand.

"I don't know," he said, "but I was thinking maybe a change of scenery might help."

Claudia smiled. "In that case, let's go for a ride."

The two drove out of the city and ended up making their way to South County along Rhode Island's southern coast. It had been a long time since Jason was last there and he felt himself relax a little inside as he exited the highway and the ocean came into view. It helped that along the way Claudia kept the conversation light and breezy. After stopping for a late breakfast at a little diner in Narragansett, she suggested that it might be nice to take a walk along the shore, so Jason drove to the town beach and soon the two were walking down the steps out onto the sand.

It was a moody, overcast day, the ocean a cold green gray. A light, chilly breeze was rippling the water; nonetheless there were several intrepid surfers, all clad in dark neoprene suits, bobbing atop their boards out on the waves. The length of the beach itself was largely deserted, save for a handful of people strolling along here and there.

Claudia slipped her hand into Jason's and they started to walk the water's edge, keeping their distance from the gentle waves as they rolled up onto the shore. The two ambled down the beach until they came to the dunes on its north end, where they stopped and sat for a time on the sand. As they gazed out at the sea, Claudia entwined her arm around his and snuggled close to stay warm. Then she turned and kissed him softly on the cheek.

"So," she said gently, "when are you going to tell me what's wrong?"

Jason pursed his lips. Since he had met Claudia, he had hoped against reason that this moment would never come, but now that it was here, he could see no way of avoiding it any longer. He looked away down the beach where a surfer was struggling to paddle out past the breaking surf. For a moment, he wished that he too could be out on the waves, just floating carefree, for he could scarce remember how that felt.

"We had a problem at work this week," he finally said, turning back to her.

"What kind of problem?" she asked.

Jason gave a shrug, wondering how best to begin.

"Some money I deposited into the bank hasn't shown up in our account," he said.

"What happened?"

"I honestly don't know," he told her. "But things got a little crazy. Checks we had sent out started bouncing, and I ended up having this ridiculous argument with my brother and sister because they thought . . ."

He paused.

"Thought what?" asked Claudia.

"They thought maybe that I had taken it."

Claudia looked at him with a curious expression and shook her head.

"I don't understand," she said. "How could they even think you would do something like that?"

Jason did not reply right away, but instead looked down at his feet and kicked pensively at the sand.

"Is this about that long story of yours?" she said after a time.

Jason nodded.

"Well, maybe now would be a good time to tell it to me."

Jason felt the old fear gripping him again, the pressure of the boot against his chest, but there was no turning back, for it was time for her to know the truth about him. And so he told her everything, of his early days in Los Angeles, of what he and the others had done at Med-Device, and what happened between him and Amanda—and worst of all, the child.

Throughout it all, Claudia said not a word, but simply listened. When he was done, she remained silent, staring out across the bay. Her silence filled Jason with dread, and all he could do now was gaze with her, listening to the roar of the surf and the hissing of the water running back to the sea as he waited for her response.

At last Claudia looked back at him, her eyes searching his once more.

"Who are you really, Jason Mirabella?" she asked. "Who are you trying to be?"

Jason shook his head sadly.

"Honestly, I'm not sure yet," he told her. "I think that's what I've been trying to find out ever since I came home. All I know is that I'm not the same person I was."

Once more Claudia fell silent for a time before looking back at him with a half smile.

"Wow," she said with an ironic laugh. "I guess you really brought some heavy baggage with you when you came."

"It feels like I'm carrying it around every minute of the day," said Jason. "And the thing is, I know I deserve to carry it, especially when I think about the baby, knowing I was really the one responsible. How do I ever make up for that?"

"Have you told anyone besides me about this?" she asked.

"My father," said Jason. "But only about what happened at the company, nothing about Amanda."

"Why not?"

Jason gave an ironic laugh of his own.

"There are some things," he said, "that you just can't tell your father."

"Then maybe you should try telling someone else," said Claudia.

Jason stared at her.

"What do you mean?" he said.

"Jason, I don't know if this will help you because I don't understand all that much yet about everything that goes on when I go to church, but the one message I always seem to hear is that no matter what you might have done, the most important thing is that you go there and admit it, say you're sorry, and really mean it."

Jason shook his head and sighed.

"Saying you're sorry doesn't magically undo what's been done and make everything all right," he said.

"No, it doesn't," she told him. "But maybe what it does is give you a place to start over again."

Jason waited, for it seemed to him that Claudia wanted to say more. Instead, she released his arm and got to her feet. Jason stood as well and the two started back along the beach.

Later, Claudia barely spoke as they drove back to Providence. Jason let her keep her silence, for he himself was not sure of what to say. When they arrived at her apartment, she did not open her door to get out, but instead sat there staring pensively out the window.

"What are you thinking?" Jason asked.

Claudia turned and looked at him with saddened eyes.

"I'm thinking that maybe we shouldn't see each other for a while," she said softly.

Jason bowed his head, his heart full of dismay even though he had already resigned himself to the inevitability of this moment.

"Because of what I did?" he said.

"No," Claudia said to his surprise. "It's because of what you have to do."

"I don't understand," he said.

Claudia took his hands and held them tight.

"Jason," she told him tenderly, "I love you, and I think that you and I could have something really special together, but all along I've had this feeling that something has been holding you back from me—and now I think I know what is. Before you and I can have anything, you need to find a way to get over everything that has happened to you, and get rid of that baggage you say you've been carrying with you all the time."

"But the only time it feels any lighter is when I'm with you," he said miserably.

"Maybe, Jason, but it's still there all the same, and it's just going to keep coming between us until you find a way to deal with it. In your heart, I think you must know this too. Maybe that's really why you say you want to go back to California. You can't move forward because you keep looking back there."

Jason wanted to tell her that she was wrong, tell her that he had put everything behind him, but deep inside he knew otherwise.

"So where do we go from here?" he said.

"I guess we go back to where we were," said Claudia, her voice cracking.

"Alone?" sighed Jason.

Claudia's eyes were glistening with tears.

"I'm sorry," she told him, "but I just don't know what else to do. Good-bye, Jason."

Then she kissed him on the cheek, opened her door, and hurried inside to her apartment.

CHAPTER 30

Giulio Mirabella could not have asked for a quieter staff at Bradley Mansion the following day. With his three children still saying very little to one another beyond the absolutely necessary, there was certainly no difficulty enforcing his edict that calm and quiet were to be maintained at all times come what may.

No one, he was certain, truly believed in his heart that Jason had done anything underhanded, and he knew that Raymond and Natalie had offered him perfunctory apologies to that effect. Just the same, as he made his rounds of the inn that day, he found the crew of his little ship going about its business in a dour mood.

For his part, at the first opportunity, a sullen Jason took refuge in his little office where he made a halfhearted effort to do some work on the Web site he was creating for the inn. After a time, though, he gave up, for he found that he simply could not concentrate on it. He flipped the laptop shut and sat there, idly staring at the sketch of the inn Claudia had drawn for him. Thinking about the sketch made him think of her, and Jason tried to imagine where she might be at that moment and what she was doing. Then his thoughts turned to what she had told him the day before, about the baggage she said that he had brought home from California. He knew of course that she was right, that he had to find some way to rid himself of it, but when and how would he ever find the way to do it?

Jason was brooding over these things, searching for an answer, when he heard a soft knock on the door. He pushed it open and found Mrs. Martinez standing there next to her cleaning cart.

"Yes, what is it, Mrs. Martinez?" Jason asked with as much cordiality as he could muster at the moment. "Somebody looking for me?"

The housekeeper shook her head, and with a kinder expression than he had ever seen her give, beckoned for him to come out into the corridor. Curious as to what she was up to, Jason obeyed. To his surprise, Mrs. Martinez stepped past him into the closet and proceeded to tidy up things for him. She quickly organized the papers on his little desk into neat piles and ran a dust rag wherever she could about the place. Then she knelt down and gave the floor a quick sweep with a dustpan and brush before emptying the overflowing trash bin. Lastly she put the chair back in place, gave the whole area a quick blast from a can of air freshener, and beckoned for him to go back in if he liked.

Jason nodded and gave her an appreciative smile, for he knew that she had done it all just to cheer him up.

Mrs. Martinez gave a shrug and nodded kindly in return.

"Family, eh?" she said in her heavy accent. "Sometimes you want go like this."

Mrs. Martinez grimaced comically for effect and put her hands up as if she were choking someone.

Low as he was feeling, Jason could not help but give a little laugh.

"Yes," he told her. "Sometimes it really is like that."

Mrs. Martinez eyed him sharply.

"But love still there," she said, wagging a finger at him for emphasis. "You no forget."

With that she put everything back on her cleaning cart, and began to push it away down the corridor.

"Gracias, Señora," Jason called after.

"De nada," the woman called back, giving him a little wave over her shoulder.

Later that afternoon, as it was nearing the end of the day, Jason went downstairs and poked his head into the study. Inside, Natalie and his father were at the desk, looking over the latest occupancy numbers on the computer, but Raymond was nowhere to be seen. At looking up and seeing him there at the door, Natalie forced a sad smile and nodded him a greeting.

Jason nodded her one in return. Though he considered himself the aggrieved party in the argument with his brother and sister, he could not help feeling that somehow Natalie felt even worse about the whole thing than he did.

Jason turned to his father and gave him a questioning look.

"Anything?" he said.

"Nothing yet from the bank," said Giulio. "But don't worry, we'll hear something soon, I'm sure." His father gave him a gentle smile. "Why don't you head home for the night?"

"Yeah," said Jason with a shrug. "Maybe I will, if it's okay with you."

"Of course it is," said his father. "Got plans for the evening?"

Jason squirreled up the side of his mouth and shook his head.

"Nope, not really," he said, "other than maybe looking for someplace to dump some old baggage I've been looking to get rid of."

Before his sister or father could ask him to explain what he had meant, Jason grabbed his jacket and headed out the door.

Jason did not go home right away. Instead he drove aimlessly around the city, much as he had done that day after he first came home. This time, however, he was not trying to reacquaint himself with the place, but instead simply trying to lose himself for a while as he wound his way through the darkening streets. Inevitably—or at least so it seemed—he eventually found himself outside Claudia's apartment. He did not go to the door, but instead sat there in the truck, gazing forlornly up at her lighted window, hoping to catch a glimpse of her should she pass by.

After a long while, when she did not appear, Jason gave up and finally began to drive home. Along the way he thought about what Claudia had told him out on the beach, of how he needed to find a place to start over again. It sounded like a nice idea, but he had begun to doubt that such a place existed. Not long after, though, as he was nearing home, Jason passed by Blessed Sacrament and was surprised to see the parking lot filled and people ascending the stairs to the church's main entrance. His curiosity piqued, for he could not imagine what would be going on there on a weeknight, Jason pulled over and parked on the street.

He sat there for a time in the truck, just as he had done outside Claudia's apartment, restlessly watching the people walking in when he wasn't gazing at the church's stained-glass windows illuminated from the soft light within. Jason could not make up his mind as to whether he should go or stay. He wondered, though, if perhaps Claudia had been right after all, that he should try starting here if he ever wanted to move forward with his life again. Jason didn't know if this was the right time or the right place, but deep inside, for whatever reason, he suddenly needed to know why everyone had come that night, so he stepped out of the truck and crossed the street.

An elderly man and his wife were helping each other up the stairs to the entrance when Jason came to the bottom step. The husband teetered along with the help of a cane while the wife clutched his arm on one side and the handrail on the other. They were just drawing near to the heavy doors, so Jason hurried ahead and held one open for them.

"You're a scholar and a gentleman," said the silver-haired wife, beaming him a sweet, serene smile as the two passed him.

The husband smiled at him as well and doffed his cap in thanks. Then, as the two moved ahead of him and began to make their way inside, Jason overheard the wife saying, "Look at the people inside. I can't believe this week is Palm Sunday already."

"It comes fast," replied the husband.

That was when Jason realized that he had happened upon some sort of Lenten service that evening. Over the years, Jason had fallen into the habit of paying little or no attention to the season of Lent, so he was unsure of what the nature of the service would be, but now that he was here, he was all the more curious to know.

When he stepped inside, Jason took a seat far in the back in one of the row of pews that flanked the wall. Somehow he felt more comfortable there, just far enough away as it was from the rest of the congregation so that he could watch what was happening without anyone taking notice of him. Still not completely sure of why he had come, he listened to the soothing strains of the organ and waited for things to begin.

The service started with little fanfare. The priest walked in through the side door, soon followed by four others who went off and stationed themselves in various secluded corners within the church while he went to the front of the altar. There he invited the congregation to rise and began to recite the opening prayers, all of them calling on the Lord in different ways to help those in attendance find forgiveness and peace in whatever way they needed. It was then that it dawned on Jason that this was a Mass of reconciliation and that everyone there had come to make their confessions.

With the opening prayers completed, the priest invited all those who wished to confess to simply approach any one of the priests whenever they felt ready. Jason expected there to be at least some pause before anyone made a move, but to his surprise people immediately began to rise from the pews and walk straight up to the priest of their choice. Soon others followed, forming lines at a discreet distance from the confessors while the rest of the congregation sat and awaited their turns.

Jason watched them all, old and young, as they one by one fell in line to say their piece. Inside, a part of him wanted to get in line with them, but he held back, for suddenly he felt a great fear coming over him, a fear that the things he had done were beyond forgiveness. Jason had not gone to confession since before he made his confirmation, but back then it had been in the secret confines of the confessional. The thought of standing in full view in front of everyone paralyzed him until he looked about at the people around him and considered that he could not be the only one carrying around a heavy burden. They had all come there for a reason. Who could say, but some might have come for reasons worse than his own. The thought heartened Jason, for he realized that if they could find the courage to make a clean breast of things that night, then perhaps he could find it too.

Jason waited long into the service, when the lines to the priests began to dwindle, before very reluctantly getting to his feet and stepping out into the aisle. He looked anxiously about, wondering to which priest he should present himself. Up ahead, near the side altar, he saw a young man of his own age talking with head bowed to the eldest of the five priests hearing confessions. The priest, a thin but spry-looking man with white hair and a strong, but gentle-looking countenance, placed a comforting hand on the young man's shoulder while he listened.

Jason watched until the young man had finished and the priest sent him away with a blessing. There was no one else waiting in line, and at seeing Jason lingering timidly in the aisle, the priest gave him a reassuring nod and gestured for him to approach. Very slowly, for it felt as if he were dragging an anchor behind him, Jason walked toward him.

The priest smiled warmly as Jason drew near, putting him

only a little more at ease, for his heart was pounding within his chest.

"Hello," said the priest gently. "What's on your mind tonight?"

Jason swallowed hard and tried to look him squarely in the eye, but he found he could not do so. He took a deep breath and let it out. It didn't help. The back of his neck now hot with shame, he suddenly wanted for all the world to turn and run away, but then he felt the hand upon his shoulder.

"Just say it," the priest told him.

Jason breathed a heavy sigh and held his head up.

"Bless me, Father," he said at last, "for I have sinned."

CHAPTER 31

Jason sat in his office, staring as usual at Claudia's sketch of the inn while he tapped a pencil against his desk. It was early afternoon, and he had been thinking about the reconciliation Mass the night before. As much as he ruminated over it, he was still not sure of what he should make of the experience. None of his past had been magically undone, as he had known it would not, and as he glanced around at his surroundings he saw that his new place to start over again bore a marked resemblance to the old. Nothing in his life, so far as he could tell, had changed. Nonetheless, for some reason he did not quite understand, he was glad that he had chanced to pass by the church when he had, and he felt good about himself for having been able to go through with it when the time had come to face the priest. It had been good to get things off his chest in that way.

Jason had just tossed the pencil onto the desk and opened his laptop to spend a little time working on the inn's Web site—a project that seemed to keep getting pushed to the back burner—when he heard a knock on the door.

"Yes, Mrs. Martinez," he said, pushing the door open. "What is it this time?"

To Jason's surprise it was not the housekeeper he found outside the door, but his brother, Raymond. Wearing an expression that could be best described as contrite, Raymond stood there, shoulders slumped with his hands in his pockets. The two had barely spoken these past few days and there was a long awkward pause as the two considered each other.

"Hey," Jason finally said. "What's up?"

"Got a minute?" said his brother. "We, uh, need you downstairs."

"Yeah, sure," said Jason, flipping the laptop closed. He stood and came out of the closet. As he passed by, Raymond stuck his head in and gave the cramped space a quick inspection. He turned to Jason with a look of acute incredulity.

"How do you spend so much time holed up in here?"

Jason gave a shrug.

"It's not so bad," he told his brother. "After a while you get used to it."

Raymond made a dubious expression.

"To each his own, I guess."

"So, what's going on downstairs?" said Jason.

"Got a little problem we need to talk to you about," he answered.

Jason hesitated. "What did I do this time?"

"Nothing, don't worry," said Raymond. "We just need to ask you something."

Despite his brother's reassurance that he need not worry, Jason felt a bit on edge as the two descended the stairs. Natalie was sitting on the sofa when the two came into the study. At seeing Jason, she gave him a nervous smile.

"Hi, Nat," said Jason amiably, hoping to put her at ease. "What's the deal?"

"We have a little problem," she said.

"So Ray tells me. What is it? Something to do with the bank?"

"No," said Natalie. "We haven't heard from them yet."

"Then what?"

Raymond and Natalie exchanged glances, as if they were not sure as to which of them should go first. After an awkward pause, Raymond rubbed the back of his neck self-consciously and gave a little cough to clear his throat.

"The problem," he finally said, "is that Roger called in sick, so he can't work the watch tonight."

"So?" said Jason with a shrug. "Just have somebody else come in and work it."

"That's the other problem," said Natalie. "I've called everybody. No one can do it tonight."

"So that leaves it up to one of us," said Raymond, glancing back and forth between his sister and brother.

"I can't do it tonight," said Natalie. "Tommy and Jenna are both sick with really bad colds. And Dad, I know, has some kind of plans tonight with one of the lasagna ladies, not that we would want him to have to do it anyway."

Raymond scratched the back of his neck. "I'll do it if I have to," he said with a sigh, "but to tell you the truth, I was supposed to take Donna out to dinner tonight. It's kind of a special occasion."

There ensued a very long moment of silence between the three before Jason folded his arms and gave a little cough to clear his throat.

"Unless I'm miscounting here," he said with the hint of a smirk, "that leaves nobody else but me."

"That's kind of the same conclusion we came to," said Raymond gloomily. "I mean, it's gonna be easy. We've only got one room booked for the night. They're coming in from Maine. All you'd have to do is just show them to their room and go hang out for the rest of the night."

"So, what do you think?" said Natalie, cringing. "Do you think you could do it?"

Jason took his time in replying. His first instinct was to tell them to forget it, but then, perhaps owing to the lingering good feeling of having gone to confession the night before, he reconsidered. Jason knew that a lot of pride had to have been swallowed, particularly by Raymond, for them to ask of him this favor. And the more that he thought about, the more he realized that, over the years, one or the other of his siblings had probably stepped up and worked the watch many times without complaint for the good of the family. Despite the flare-up over the bank deposit, Jason understood that he owed a great deal to them, and that maybe it was time for him to step up and do his part for once.

"Tommy and Jenna," he said to Natalie, "are they going to be all right?"

"Oh yeah," she answered. "But you know how it is with little kids when they're sick and miserable. They just want their mommy with them."

"Then that's where you should be," he told her without hesitation.

Then Jason turned to Raymond and gave him an inquisitive nod.

"So, what's the big occasion?" he asked.

"It's our anniversary," said Raymond.

"Anniversary?" said Jason, puzzled. "But didn't you two get married in September?"

"It's the anniversary of the day we met," admitted Raymond, rolling his eyes. "Donna still likes to celebrate it."

Jason could not resist the temptation to needle his older brother.

"Why?" he deadpanned. "I would have thought it would be a day of mourning for her."

"Ayyy," cried Raymond in exasperation, throwing his hands up. "Just forget about it!"

Jason smiled and put up a hand to calm him down. "Relax, Ray. I'm just kidding."

Raymond's face lit up just a little.

"So, what are you saying, that you'll do it?" he asked hopefully.

"Eh, why not?" said Jason. "It's not like I've got anywhere else to go right now." He paused and shot them both an impish glance. "But just tell me one thing," he said. "Are you sure I'll be okay when they pay for the room when they check in? I haven't had much luck handling money lately, if you know what I mean."

"Don't worry, smarty," said Natalie with a playful huff. "They sent in a deposit days ago."

Jason grinned.

"In that case, I can't get into any more trouble, can I?" he said.

CHAPTER 32

Late that afternoon, Jason went home to collect his toiletry kit and a few other things for his overnight stay. While there he saw Giulio only in passing just as he was getting ready to go out for the evening. His father had seemed very pleased by the news that Jason would be working the watch that night.

"Ayyy, you know how many times I worked that shift when you kids were little," Giulio had told him, giving him a pat on the cheek. "It's good for you. Now no one can ever say that you haven't done your fair share. There's just a couple of things, though, that you have to remember. . . ."

At that Giulio had quickly recited a list of things for Jason to check on before turning in for the night. Among these were lights in various rooms that should be turned off, while certain others were to remain on all night in case guests were still up and about. The weather had started to warm, so he had to make sure no windows had been left open. And of course there were the doors to be locked. Lastly, he recommended a walk-through of the house just to check on things in general. Jason had assured his father that he would take care of it all, before finally managing to send him on his way.

When he returned to the inn a short while later, Jason found Raymond in the study, writing down some last-minute instructions for him.

"Hey, don't bother with that," Jason quipped. "Dad already gave me the whole spiel."

"Eh, it's easy to forget the little things," said Raymond with a grunt. "The most important thing is that you're not off wandering around when the guests show up. Their last name is Benton, by the way. They're driving in from Maine. They said that they probably wouldn't get here until around seven thirty or later, so you still have plenty of time to hang out and do whatever you want. Just keep an ear open for them."

"Anything else, boss?" said Jason with a grin.

"Can't think of anything," said Raymond, rubbing his chin thoughtfully in a way that reminded Jason of his father. "I guess that's about it. It should be a quiet night. You know my cell phone number, right?"

"Got it."

Raymond gave a shrug.

"Anything comes up, give me a call," he said. "We're going to be right down the street having dinner at Casserini's. Otherwise I'll see you in the morning."

With that Raymond started for the door, but then he hesitated for a moment.

"Hey," he said, giving Jason a nod. "I appreciate your doing this."

"Forget it," Jason told him. "It's my turn. Just go enjoy dinner."

"Thanks," said Raymond, turning to go.

"And have a happy anniversary," Jason called after him.

"Shaddup," replied his brother over his shoulder.

After Raymond had gone, Jason took his overnight bag and brought it to the tiny bedroom in the back where he would be sleeping that night. He dropped the bag on the bed and strolled back out to the living room. All was quiet and still there, save for the monotonous ticking of the clock on the mantel. Jason looked about the room as he listened to it. He had never known

Bradley Mansion to be anything but a tranquil place. Just the same, it gave him an odd, lonely feeling to suddenly find himself completely alone in it. It was not something that overly disquieted him, but Jason realized that he was looking forward very much to the Bentons' arrival.

As he was about to leave the room, Jason turned to the bookshelf, where he saw a photograph of his mother, Vera. He picked up the frame and held it to the light. In the picture, she was standing alone on the front step to the inn, smiling from ear to ear. Jason had seen that photograph of her countless times before, but for some reason just then the sight of his mother brought a smile to his own face. Imagining that she was somehow there, keeping him company while he waited, he gently placed the frame back on the shelf and left the room.

Back in the study, Jason passed the time at Natalie's computer, surfing the Web while he munched on a salami and capicol' sandwich he had made at home for his supper. As he ate, he found his thoughts drifting to Claudia, and he wondered what she was doing at that moment and if she was thinking at all of him. Though it had been just a few days, it seemed like a very long time since he had seen her, and it reinforced the sense of solitude he had felt since the moment Raymond left him there.

By the time seven thirty had come and long gone, and the Bentons had still not arrived, Jason's eyes were growing weary from reading on the computer monitor. With a sigh, he pushed away from the desk, turned on the little television Natalie kept in the corner, and flopped down on the sofa to see what there might be to watch. Lying back with the remote control in hand, he scanned the channels one by one, searching without success for something worthwhile. In the end he gave up and turned the television off.

It was then, just as he was letting himself relax into the cushions, that Jason heard from off in the distance the faint rumble of thunder. Across the room, the study window was open just a few inches, letting in the first hints of a breeze that nudged the curtains back and forth. A storm was definitely getting ready to roll in, but Jason could not yet tell how far away it might be. There came another low rumble. Jason found the sound of it somehow soothing, so he closed his eyes to listen to it and soon, without realizing it, dozed off into a light sleep.

A half hour later, the house exploded.

That at least is what the clap of thunder sounded like to Jason's drowsy mind. Jolted awake, he sat up straight, wondering what on earth had happened. Then he looked out the window just as the dark sky was illuminated by the brilliant white flash of lightning. The storm that had seemed so distant earlier had arrived while he slept.

Jason jumped up and began to move toward the window to watch the unfolding spectacle of the storm, only to be startled again, this time by the sound of the telephone ringing. He grabbed the cordless receiver from the desk and put it to his ear.

"Good morning, I mean evening, this is Bradley Mansion," he said, walking back to get a look out the window.

"Yes, hello," came the voice on the other end of the line. "This is Cyril Benton. My wife and I have a room booked for the night at your inn."

"Yes, Mr. Benton," said Jason pleasantly just as there was another crash of thunder and the rain began to fall outside, "we've been expecting you."

"I know," said Benton, "but I'm afraid we're not going to make it tonight. You see, our car broke down while we were driving through Massachusetts, so we'll be spending our night here unfortunately."

"I'm sorry to hear that, Mr. Benton," said Jason with sincerity.

"Yes, we were looking forward to staying at your inn," said Benton. "I know we gave the deposit for tonight, but I was wondering if it would be all right if we checked in tomorrow instead."

Jason almost had to laugh when he considered the empty house.

"I'm sure that won't be a problem, Mr. Benton," he told him. "I'll pencil you in right now and we'll see you tomorrow."

When he had finished taking the call and bid Mr. Benton a good night, Jason shut the study window and hurried out of the room to check on the rest of the house. By the time he was mounting the stairs for the second floor, the storm was roaring in its full fury, the lightning flashing almost nonstop, casting eerie moving shadows about the interior while the wind beat the rain against the side of the house.

Jason went from room to room, looking in each to make sure the windows were securely closed. He had just reached the end of the corridor and was about to ascend the stairs to the third floor when from outside there came a tremendous crack and ear-splitting boom like the firing of an enormous cannon. In that same instant a shower of sparks burst from the light fixture overhead, causing Jason to duck out of the way.

"What the—" Jason started to exclaim, but his voice was drowned out by another immense clap of thunder.

Startled out of his wits, he took a moment to realize that the house had been struck by lightning.

His heart pounding in his chest, Jason gazed worriedly at the light fixture, wondering what if anything he should do. Outside, the storm was still raging, and he heard another crack of thunder. Then Jason heard another sound, one that frightened him far more than the storm, coming from downstairs.

The smoke alarms.

His heart full of dread, Jason raced down the staircase to the first floor and stopped dead in his tracks at the entry to living room. There, to his horror, he saw tongues of fire climbing up the far wall. Desperately, he tried to reach for the fire extinguisher, but found his way to it already blocked by the fire. With no time to think, he grabbed a throw blanket from one of the couches and began to beat wildly at the flames, but quickly realized he was only making them spread faster. With astonishing speed, the fire reached the windows and the curtains caught flame.

It was in that terrible moment, when he realized that the blaze was already out of control, that Jason felt the sickening grip of panic take over, twisting his insides, squeezing the breath out of him. In his mind's eye he instantly saw the fire consuming the house, laying waste to everything his family had worked so hard to build.

Frantic to save it, he fled to the study telephone and called 9-1-1.

"You've got to come!" Jason screamed into the phone the moment the dispatcher picked up his call. "We've got a fire here!"

The dispatcher advised Jason to get out of the house immediately and wait outside for the fire department to arrive. Instead, Jason called his brother. With the cordless phone pressed against his ear, he ran back to the living room while the line rang. To his dismay, he saw that the fire was about to reach the bookcase. Without thinking, he lunged in and snatched away the photograph of his mother. Quickly he jumped back from the searing heat of the flames, and put his ear once more to the phone just as Raymond finally answered.

"Jason, is that you?" said his brother.

"Raymond, I'm in trouble!" Jason yelled in terror. Faced with the fire, he began to back out of the room. "You've got to come!"

Before he could say another word, Jason tripped and tumbled backward, striking his head on a side table on the way down. He rolled into the foyer and the world went black.

CHAPTER 33

Once when Jason was a small boy, he and two friends spent a winter's afternoon constructing an elaborate snow fort in the backyard. When it was completed they stockpiled an enormous mound of snowballs. Feeling quite confident in the fortifications he and his friends had built, Jason promptly challenged his brother and Raymond's own friends to a snowball fight.

It was of course a massacre by snowball fight standards. The older boys pelted the younger ones mercilessly until Jason's friends gave up and fled, bawling their eyes out. Jason tried to hold the fort a little longer, but when Raymond and his buddies began to gleefully kick in the sides, he himself fled, taking a snowball in the back of his head for his trouble. He ran to the front of the house, where he tried to hide in a little cave that he had dug out in the mound of snow on the corner of the driveway. No sooner had he jumped in than the top of the cave collapsed on him, trapping him in darkness. The weight of the snow pressed down so hard on him that Jason could scarcely breathe.

"Raymond, help me!" he cried in terror.

For a terrible moment, he thought that help would never come, but then he saw light breaking through the darkness and hands frantically pushing away the snow. Before he knew it, his brother had taken hold of him and pulled him out onto the driveway.

For a minute the two boys sat there trembling on the icy pavement, each afraid to speak of what might have happened, of how close they had come to tragedy.

"I'm sorry," Raymond finally said, still breathing hard from the fright and the effort of rescuing his brother. Then, in a pleading voice, "Please don't tell Mom and Dad. . . ."

Jason awoke, the memory of that long ago winter's day suddenly fresh in his mind. When he opened his eyes, he found himself looking into a very bright light. For a moment he thought he had died, and that this was the tunnel of light reaching into the great beyond, but then he realized that it was instead a man holding a small flashlight, shining it into one eye and then the other. With the man still hovering over him, Jason became aware of the sound of rushing air and wondered what it was until he understood that he was wearing an oxygen mask. As he became more fully awake, he saw that he was lying on a stretcher in an ambulance, being tended to by an emergency medical technician. The gentle sway of the vehicle told him that they were on the road, driving somewhere.

"Where am I?" were Jason's first worried words. "What happened to the house?"

The technician looked down at him and smiled.

"What happened is that you got very lucky," he said. "Where you're going is the hospital. I think you're fine, but we want to have a doc check you out just to be sure. You took a pretty good knock on the head."

"But how did I get here?" Jason wondered, suddenly cognizant of the throbbing pain emanating from the welt on the back of his head.

"Your brother," replied the technician. "He was already at the scene with you when we arrived. From what he told us, he got to the house and pulled you out onto the sidewalk just before the fire department got there. I'm sure he's following us right now. You'll see him once we get you to the ER."

Jason closed his eyes once more and tried to force a smile.

"That's my big brother," he murmured.

As the technician had predicted, Raymond was waiting with Donna outside the door when they rolled his stretcher into the emergency room. The two looked like nervous wrecks, worse than he felt.

"Jason, are you all right?" Raymond cried, hurrying alongside.

"You poor thing," added Donna, squeezing his hand.

"I'm fine," Jason assured them. Then, before he could say more, the EMTs pushed him through the doors into one of the treatment rooms, leaving Donna and Raymond to wait outside.

By the time the doctor had finished examining Jason, Giulio and Natalie had arrived at the hospital. The two rushed in with Raymond and Donna. Jason had never seen his father looking so shaken.

"My boy, my boy," he fretted. "Thank God, they say you're all right."

"Trust me, Dad, I'm fine," said Jason, "but how bad was the fire?"

"Who cares!" exclaimed his father. "The most important thing is that you're alive!"

"Really," added Natalie, coming to his side. "We'll worry about the house tomorrow." Her eyes welling up, she stroked his hair for a moment and took his hand. "Jason," she sighed, "I know this is not the time for this, but I'm so sorry."

"About what?"

"About everything that's happened with that stupid bank deposit," she said, tears rolling down her cheeks. "I know we're going to find out it was all a mistake. Please forgive me."

With red-rimmed eyes of his own, Raymond came to his other side.

"Forgive us both," he said. "I'm really sorry, too, Jason. I can't believe I said those things. You're my brother. I know you couldn't have done anything like that. I just got a little crazy that day."

"Stop it, you guys, will ya?" huffed Jason. "Especially you, Ray. I mean, come on, you just saved my life, pulling me out of there. I'm lucky to be alive."

Raymond brushed his eyes with the back of his hand and managed to give a little laugh. Then he leaned closer, so that the others wouldn't hear.

"That was really close," he whispered. "Let's not tell Dad too much about it."

CHAPTER 34

As lucky as he felt to be alive, Jason was dead to the world until he awoke the next morning. He slept late after coming home from the hospital, and Giulio, who left at first light for the inn, did not disturb him. When he finally opened his eyes, his body heavy with weariness, Jason lay in bed for a time, trying to piece together his recollections of the fire, particularly the last few moments before he had fallen backward and lost consciousness. The last thing he remembered was clutching the picture of his mother against his chest. The rest was a blur of confused thoughts, like something out of a strange dream, and he wondered for a time if it had all really happened. Then he passed his hand through his tousled hair. He felt a sharp jolt of pain when he touched the welt on the back of his head, evidence enough that he had not been dreaming after all.

His head still smarting, a wincing Jason sat up in bed and stretched out a hand for his laptop computer on the bedside table. By now Sundance, who had been sleeping out in the hall, had heard him stirring. The dog nudged the bedroom door open and wandered in to the side of the bed. There it rested its snout on the covers next to Jason and tried to get a look at just what his master was doing. Jason gave its ear a scratch and flipped open the computer.

When he was connected to the Internet, he navigated to the

online edition of the *Providence Journal* to see if he could find
any mention of the fire. There, in the local news section, he
found a brief, one-paragraph story under the headline FIRE DE-
PARTMENT CALLED TO INN. He read it eagerly, but to his disappointment the account of the incident provided few details
beyond the little that he already knew.

With a sigh, Jason went to close down the computer, but
then on a whim decided to check his e-mail. Other than spam,
he had not expected any messages at all, and so it came as a very
great surprise to see a message from Eddie. As chance would
have it, the message had come in just the night before at precisely the hour Jason had been lying unconscious, just outside
the reach of the flames engulfing the living room at Bradley
Mansion. It read simply:

> *Got something. Call me!*
> *E*

Stunned, Jason stared at the message. It was precisely the
news he had waited to hear throughout the long weeks since he
had first come home. And yet, perhaps because of the odd timing of its arrival, somehow he did not feel any sense of elation as
he might have expected. The glad tidings that there might finally be a new opportunity for him back in Los Angeles evoked
no feeling of relief in him, nor one of release for that matter. Instead, for reasons that he could not quite grasp, he felt somehow
let down in a strange way. As he continued to stare at the screen,
his thoughts a muddle, it suddenly occurred to him that he
could no longer make up his mind as to which things in his life
he should cling to and which ones he should let go. Fate, it
seemed, had abruptly dropped him at a crossroads, and which
direction he should take next was not at all clear to him.

Jason flopped back on the pillow and gazed up at the ceiling,
turning things over in his mind. He soon found himself rumi-

nating once more about the inn and the fire, and his thoughts turned to the picture of his mother he had snatched at the last moment from the flames. He had not seen it again since he had fallen and blacked out, and he worried for a time about what had become of it. Troubled at the thought that it might have been lost in the fire, he puzzled over its whereabouts until he finally rolled out of bed, put his feet on the floor, and with Sundance in tow wearily dragged himself downstairs to the kitchen.

As usual, the pot of coffee was waiting on the counter. Its aroma beckoned, but Jason went first to the telephone, hoping to learn just how extensive the damage from the fire had been. That there was no answer at the inn when he called did not overly concern him at first. Just the same, he tried Raymond's cell phone right away, but only reached his voice mail. Annoyed by his inability to reach anyone, Jason poured a cup of coffee and slid into a seat at the table. There he pensively tapped his fingers before swallowing a mouthful of the warm brew. Welcome as it was, it did little to dispel the feeling of unease growing in the pit of his stomach. Before long he gulped down the rest and hurried back upstairs to get himself dressed.

Later, as Jason drove to the inn, his heart in his mouth the whole way, he could only guess as to what he would find when he arrived. His mind conjured up the very worst scenarios, and he could not help imagining the place a pile of smoldering, scorched ruins. This image haunted him all along the way until the very moment he pulled up to the front of Bradley Mansion and beheld with great relief that the inn was still standing despite the near catastrophe. Out on the sidewalk stood Giulio assessing the exterior of the building with Raymond and another man Jason had never seen before. A hammer dangled from Raymond's hand; from the looks of things, he had just finished boarding up two of the living room windows. Jason stepped out of the car and went to join them. His father and brother smiled and nodded him a greeting as he drew near.

"Hey, what are you doing out of bed?" said Raymond, mussing up his brother's hair. "The doctor said you should be resting after the shot you took in the squash last night."

"Your brother's right," agreed Giulio.

"Eh," grunted Jason. "I'm fine." He paused and passed his gaze over the front of the inn. Save for the sheets of plywood covering the living room windows, and some torn-up sod on the front lawn where the firefighters had trod, there was little damage he could readily see. "How bad inside?" he wondered aloud.

"Ayyy, not so bad," said Giulio. "You can go see for yourself. Natalie's in the study right now. The firefighters got here pretty quick last night, so it didn't spread as far as it might have."

"Yeah, but what a friggin' mess they left," groused Raymond. "There's water and soot everywhere."

"Hey, don't complain," chuckled the other man. "It could have been worse."

"It could have been much worse," agreed Giulio with a solemn nod to the man. He turned and gestured to Jason.

"Vin, this is my son Jason, by the way," he said. "I don't think you two have met. Jason, this is Vin DiFrancesco, an old friend of mine. He works for the Department of Economic Development. He's one of the people to blame for all the development downtown that's giving us all *agita*."

DiFrancesco gave a good-natured laugh.

"Come on," he protested. "It hasn't been that bad. Besides, you have to admit that what helps the city will help you too sooner or later."

"Ayyy, that's what they always say," replied Giulio with a dismissive wave.

DiFrancesco laughed again. He was of the same age as his father, Jason guessed. Small in stature, he had bright, inquisitive eyes that lent him an air of intelligence. Like Giulio, he had that look about him of someone who had seen a thing or two in his time.

"Nice to meet you," said Jason as the two men shook hands.

"We haven't met before, but your father has told me a lot about you," said DiFrancesco.

Jason grinned.

"Well, I hope he didn't tell you *everything*," he said easily.

"Don't worry," chuckled the older man. "It was all good."

Jason turned to his father and gestured to the house. "So, what now, Dad?"

"What do you think?" grunted Giulio. "We clean up, and rewire the place—that's how the whole thing started, by the way—"

"I knew that wiring was bad news," grumbled Raymond, shaking his head.

"And then we fix the place up and reopen," his father went on. "Might take a little while. But I'm thinking maybe we'll have a big party when it's all done. How does that sound, Mr. Marketing?"

"A party to reopen the place sounds like a great idea," said Jason. "I'll try to work that into the plan."

Giulio gave DiFrancesco a nudge and nodded to Jason. "Did I tell you my son went to business school? He's got a good head for business, especially when it comes to marketing and PR and all that stuff."

"I think you might have mentioned it once or twice," his friend replied, giving Jason a wink.

"I bet he could show the guys in your department a thing or two," added Giulio for good measure.

Growing a bit red-faced by his father's thinly guised plug, Jason gave a nervous cough and nodded to the inn. "I think I'll head in and take a look around," he said.

"Sure, go have a look at things," said his father. "Just be careful. And be sure to stop by the study and talk to your sister. I think she has something to tell you."

"About what?"

"I'll leave that to her. Now go on," replied his father, shooing him off.

"I'll go with you," offered Raymond, and the two brothers headed up the walkway to the front door.

"I'm glad to see the place is still standing," said Jason as they went along. "I got worried before when I called and there was no answer. And then you didn't pick up your cell."

Raymond stopped on the front step and gave a laugh. "Sorry about that," he said. "I left it in the car. As for the phone inside, I think it got toasted last night. You must have dropped it somewhere in the living room. Natalie went out and bought a new one just a little while ago."

With that Raymond pushed open the door. Even before they had stepped inside, the acrid smell of smoke and soot assaulted Jason's nostrils, the first evidence that the largely unscarred exterior belied the condition of things inside. As they moved through the door and into the foyer, he at last got his first glimpse of the damage. Jason was aghast at what he saw. The living room had been all but destroyed, the lovely paneled walls, the ceiling, and floor all cracked and blackened from the flames. He gave a low whistle as he leaned in and regarded the charred remains of the furniture.

"Don't go in there," warned Raymond. "There's still stuff falling from the ceiling, and I'm not too sure about the floor. And watch your step, it's like a swamp in here. They really blasted everything with the hoses last night." He sighed and gave Jason a nudge. "Come on," he said, "let's go talk to Nat."

Natalie had the study windows wide open when Jason and Raymond walked in. At seeing her younger brother, she hurried out from behind her desk.

"Hey, there he is, all in one piece," she gushed, giving him a hug. "How does that head feel?"

"Like I went fifteen rounds with the champ," chuckled Jason, "but I'll get over it." He looked about the room. "Everything looks okay in here," he noted.

Natalie pulled away from him.

"Grazie a Dio," she said with a nod to the heavens. Then she waved her hand through the air as she retreated to her desk. "But uff, what a stench from that smoke! I've been trying to air the place out all morning, but it just seems to get worse."

"Eh, give it time," said Jason.

There ensued an odd moment of awkward silence in which Natalie exchanged glances with Raymond, who was now leaning against the doorjamb, the corner of his mouth curled up in a mildly pained expression. Puzzled, Jason looked at his brother, then back to his sister. Something was obviously going on, but exactly what he could not guess.

"So, what's up?" he asked Natalie. "Dad said you had something to tell me."

Natalie's cheeks reddened ever so slightly as she fidgeted with some papers on top of her desk before clearing her throat.

"Good news," she finally announced with a sheepish grin. "Guess who was the first to call this morning when I plugged the new phone in?"

"Dialing for Dollars?" ventured Jason.

"No, you idiot," grunted Raymond with an exasperated shake of his head. "It was the bank."

Jason gave the two a curious look. "The bank?" he said, at first not grasping the import of the call. "What did they want?"

"What do you think, silly?" exclaimed Natalie. "They found our money!"

It took a moment for the news to sink in, for in all the excitement of the past twenty-four hours, Jason had completely forgotten about the long-missing deposit.

"Ayyy, it's about time," he said with a laugh when it all finally dawned on him. "What happened to it?"

Natalie rolled her eyes.

"*Mannaggia,*" she said, throwing her hands up. "Some idiot transposed a figure when the deposit got processed and the money ended up in someone else's account. It's been there all this time and nobody knew it. Can you believe it?"

"I can believe it," muttered Raymond.

Jason folded his arms and struck a haughty pose. Then he looked at his two siblings and gave them a snide smile.

"Well then," he told them with an air of smug satisfaction, "unless I miss my guess, this officially takes me off the hook for any, let's say, suspicion of banking malfeasance?"

"Yeah, yeah, don't rub it in," groused Raymond.

"Why shouldn't I?" said Jason. "I think I've earned it."

"Come on," said Raymond with a mischievous grin. "You know we never *really* thought you took the money."

"Honest," Natalie chimed in sweetly, batting her eyes for emphasis.

"Ha!" scoffed Jason. "Nice try. You two had better smile when you say that. The way I look at it, you guys owe me."

"Eh, I don't know about that," said Raymond skeptically. "Don't forget, I did have to drag you out after you tried to burn the place down last night. I'm thinking that makes us all equal."

"You know, he might have a point there," opined Natalie.

"Yeah, right," said Jason with a good-natured grumble.

Jason did not know if it was a lingering effect of the knock on his head, a rush of magnanimity at having gone to confession just a few nights before, or perhaps simply his relief at finally having put the unpleasant matter behind him, but he was finding it difficult to hold any ill will against his brother and sister for what had happened between them because of the missing deposit.

"Well, I don't suppose I could really blame you guys for thinking what you did," he finally admitted. "I mean, all things considered, I probably would have done the same. And besides,

I was the knucklehead who lost the deposit slip in the first place. We could have cleared it all up in two minutes if I hadn't."

"That *was* a bonehead move," noted Raymond, giving him a half smile before hastily adding, "Not that I should have jumped to conclusions."

Raymond paused and gave a conciliatory shrug before reaching out to Jason with his fist clenched.

"So, what do you think?" he said, looking Jason straight in the eye. "We good?"

Jason paused for dramatic effect before reaching out to his brother.

"Yeah," he said, nodding in return as the two knocked knuckles. "I guess we are."

"Me too?" said a hopeful, misty-eyed Natalie, holding out her own fist.

"Yeah, you too, I guess," Jason told her as he knocked knuckles with her as well. Then for a moment, the three just stood there smiling.

"Gee," quipped Raymond, breaking the silence. "Isn't this just like a Kodak moment?"

They all laughed and, try as he might, Jason couldn't stop smiling, for it was the first time since he had come back to Rhode Island that he finally felt at home.

CHAPTER 35

"Jay Mirabella! What's the good word!"

As always, Eddie was his same ebullient self. Unable to resist his mounting curiosity any longer, Jason had borrowed his brother's cell phone and ascended the stairs to his cubbyhole of an office to call his friend. Though the flames from the fire had spared the upper floors, the pungent smell of smoke permeated the air even there. With no window to vent the little workspace, the odor was all the more unpleasant. Enduring it, however, was a small price to pay for the chance to speak in private.

Jason stretched out his legs into the hallway and leaned back in his chair.

"That's what I've been waiting to hear from you," he replied. "What's happening?"

Eddie laughed and spent the next few minutes catching him up on the latest goings-on out on the West Coast. Jason listened closely at first, but before long found his attention increasingly drawn to the wall behind his desk where Claudia's rendering of the inn still hung. Looking at it made him think of her. He wondered where she was and what she was doing and if she had heard about what had happened. Deep inside, he ached at the thought of her, so he tried all the harder to attend to his friend's voice.

Just the same, as he stared at the drawing while Eddie rambled on, his thoughts drifted from Claudia to the inn's future. He thought about the challenges ahead that his brother and sister and father would face in getting the place back in operation. True, the worst had not happened. The inn was still standing, but there was much work to be done and all hands would be needed to do it. That he was even contemplating not being there to help gave Jason a sharp pang of guilt, and he regretted having made the call. If, as he expected, Eddie had procured for him a tempting job opportunity, then he knew that he would soon be facing an unexpectedly difficult choice.

"So, anyway, back to business," Eddie was saying. "What did I tell you way back when, when you had all your little troubles? You just had to be patient because L.A.'s all about today, right?"

"That is what you said," Jason answered, trying hard to rekindle the enthusiasm in his voice. "So, what have you got?"

"A marketing spot came up at Mixed Media, one of our affiliates," Eddie told him. "It's not big, entry level basically, but if you want it, it's a foot back in the door and a chance to show 'em what you can do, if you know what I mean. I already talked to some people for you, so all you gotta do is fly out here next week, do the interview, and see if it works for you. If you like, great. You start the week after. If not, no harm done, right? So, what do you say?"

Torn as to what he should do, Jason hesitated for a moment before responding.

"Eddie, I'm not sure if I can do it," he finally said.

"*Commme* on," Eddie prodded him. "What do you mean, you're not sure? L.A.'s still your lady, man—and she wants you back!"

"I know, I know," sighed Jason. "It's just that it's not that easy."

"Why not?"

Jason gave another sigh. "It's my family's business—"

"That's right!" Eddie exclaimed before he could go any further. "I almost forgot. Your family's still running that motel in Providence, right?"

"It's a bed-and-breakfast!" laughed Jason. "Like I've told you a hundred times."

"Whatever," said Eddie. "But listen, that reminds me about something else I wanted to talk to you about."

"What's that?"

"I've got some people with a start-up production company looking into shooting a show in your town," Eddie replied.

"No kidding?" said Jason, intrigued. "What kind of show?"

"I dunno," said Eddie. "Some kind of crime show, I think. They're just getting their act together. Anyway, they want to send a crew out to Providence around the end of August to scope out the city. They'll need a place to stay, so I was thinking maybe you guys could put them up for a few nights if you had the space. They'll pay of course."

Jason inwardly groaned. In working on his marketing plan for the inn, this was just the kind of business that he had hoped to find ways to attract from time to time. He couldn't decide what to tell Eddie, so he went with the truth.

"That sounds great, Eddie," he told his friend, "but I gotta tell you that we had a little problem at the inn last night."

"What kind of problem?"

"A fire kind of problem," said Jason.

"Come on!" said Eddie. "Anybody hurt?"

"Nobody, thank God," replied Jason, rubbing the lump on his head. "I've only had a quick look around at things today, but I'm pretty sure we're gonna need to do some heavy-duty renovations, if you know what I mean. When did you say they'd be coming to town?"

"August, maybe September, I think," Eddie replied.

Jason rubbed his chin. "Honestly, I don't know how long it's gonna take to get the place back in shape. Till I know how things stand, I can't just bail on everybody."

"No problem," said Eddie. "I understand. You gotta do what you gotta do for your family. Tell you what, I'll sit on all this for a couple of days till you give me the word. Meantime, I'll send you the details on the job so you can think about it and we'll connect before the weekend. Deal?"

"Deal," said Jason. And then, with true sincerity he added, "Thanks, Eddie. It means a lot."

"Hey, no big," said Eddie. "What are friends for?"

Later, when Jason came back downstairs, he found the study empty. He went to the front door, looked out, and saw that Vin DiFrancesco had yet to leave. He and Giulio were still standing on the sidewalk. Natalie was with them, and the three were chatting away, gesturing now and then at the house while nearby on the front lawn Raymond was down on one knee, inspecting a piece of torn sod. Jason took a deep breath, and stepped out the door. By the time he reached the sidewalk, his brother had rejoined the conversation.

"So, how long do you think it will take to get the place back in shape?" Natalie was saying as he drew near.

"Ayy, not that long," mused Raymond. "Three, four months maybe, if the insurance comes through right away."

"Hey, that would be perfect," said Jason brightly.

The others turned and looked at him.

"What do you mean?" said Raymond.

Jason gave a cough to clear his throat.

"I just got a call from a friend of mine out in L.A.," he explained. "He's got a production company looking to come to Providence in August to scout out the city for some new TV show."

"Oooh, sounds exciting," cooed Natalie. "What's the show about?"

"I'm not sure," said Jason, "but he wanted to know if we could put them up here for a few nights while they're in town. If things work out like Ray says, I'm thinking maybe we'll be open right on time for them if we're lucky."

Vin DiFrancesco's eyes lit up.

"Excellent!" he exclaimed. "That's the kind of news I love to hear. Things like this are great for the state." He pulled a business card out of his wallet and handed it to Jason. "How about you give me a call when the details get worked out? I'd like to talk to these people, see what we can do for them. Maybe get some of their friends in showbiz to come and check out Rhode Island too, if you know what I mean."

"Sure thing," said Jason, tucking the card into his own wallet. "I'll let you know."

DiFrancesco smiled and gave Giulio a wink.

"You ever get tired of working for your father, give me a call," he told Jason. "We need all the bright young minds we can find."

"I'll keep it in mind."

"Good boy," said the older man. With that he said his good-byes to all and at last went on his way.

"He's a good man to know," said Giulio thoughtfully as he watched his friend go. "You'd be surprised, but for a little state, there are a lot of opportunities out there—and he knows where just about all of them are."

Just then a car with Maine license plates cruised slowly along the road before turning into the mansion's driveway. There it stopped and an elderly, but spry-looking couple stepped out of the car. The two exchanged puzzled looks as they gaped at the boarded windows.

"Who's that?" wondered Raymond aloud.

"I'm guessing that would be the Bentons," opined Jason.

"Oh boy," sighed Natalie. "I guess I'd better go and break the bad news to them."

"Make sure you let them know they can have their deposit back," Giulio called after her as she walked away.

"Yeah, hopefully there's plenty of money in the checking account now," chimed in Raymond, casting Jason a mischievous sideways glance before heading off to finish boarding up the windows on the side of the house.

Left to themselves, Jason and his father stood in silence for a few moments. At last Giulio turned and gave Jason a nod.

"I take it you've heard the good news," he said.

"About the bank? Yes, I heard," said Jason. "I'm glad that's over with."

"Me too," replied his father. "So, all's forgiven now, I hope?" Jason smiled and nodded his head.

"Yeah, I think we're all good now," he said with a chuckle.

Giulio gave a little laugh of his own and gestured to the house.

"Good, then," he said. "Come on, let's go in and talk."

"About what?" said Jason.

"About you," said his father, eyeing him closely. "Maybe I'm wrong, but I get the feeling your friend had something else to tell you besides that bit about the production company coming to town. I'd like to hear it."

With that he abruptly turned and started for the front door. Jason held back for a moment, the side of his mouth squirreled up in an expression of bemusement. How, he wondered, did his father always perceive these things, and why did it feel as if lately he was always going to confession?

CHAPTER 36

"So, what are you going to do?"

Giulio did not look directly at his son as he posed the question. Seated behind the study desk, he instead kept his gaze focused on the desktop where he had been fiddling with a small picture frame. The side of the frame had become dislodged and, while he waited for Jason's reply, he was trying to reattach it while taking great care not to damage the photograph inside. For his part, Jason had been sitting on the couch, his own gaze drawn away to the open window while he had recounted for Giulio his conversation with Eddie. Until now, he had paid little attention to what his father was doing. His face brightened when he finally paused to lean closer and take a look.

"Hey, that's Mom!" he exclaimed, avoiding for the moment making a response to his father's question.

"Yes," said Giulio, grinning with satisfaction as he snapped the side of the frame back into place. He looked over his handiwork for a moment before setting the frame on the corner of the desk. "You know, this has always been one of my favorite pictures of her. I'm grateful to you for rescuing her."

"I was afraid it had been lost in the fire," said Jason, relieved to see the photograph once more, but curious to know how it had managed to survive. "Where did you find it?"

"Your brother," replied Giulio. "He said you were still hold-

ing on to it for all you were worth when he dragged you away
from the flames last night. You held it so tight, the side of the
frame came loose when he tried to tug it out of your hands after
the ambulance came and they were putting you on the stretcher."
He paused and looked with affection at Jason. "You're a good
son," he told him.

"Thanks," said Jason, though he was not quite sure that his
father was right.

There was a long pause.

"So, you haven't answered my question," said Giulio after a
time. "What are you planning to do?"

Jason gave a shrug and sighed.

"Right now I'm not planning to do anything, Dad," he admitted. "I mean, I can't just go and leave you guys with this
mess. You're going to need all the help you can find to get the
place up and running again. So that means staying right here
and doing whatever I can to help until you do. Simple as that."

Giulio smiled and gave a grunt.

"Simple as that," he repeated to himself, as if he found the
notion somehow rather amusing. He looked at Jason and shook
his head. "That's very nice of you to offer," he said, "but you
can't stay here—at least not yet."

Jason could not quite believe his ears, for he had fully expected his father to be thrilled at learning of his intention to
stay.

"What do you mean?" he said. "I thought you would want
me to stick around and help out."

Giulio grunted another laugh.

"I would, Jason," he said. "Believe me, I would. Nothing
would please me more than to have you stay here at home—or
at least someplace a little closer to home than California."

"Then what's the problem?"

Giulio pushed himself away from the desk and came around

to the other side. There he sat next to Jason and put his hand on his shoulder.

"You can't hide here anymore, Jason," he said, looking him straight in the eye. "There's a big world out there, one that I know you've always wanted to be a part of. I don't know everything, but it seems to me that you've still got some unfinished business to take care of out there. Maybe it's got something to do with your career, getting back into business, and making a name for yourself again." Giulio paused and shrugged. "Or maybe it's about something else," he went on, "something that's got nothing at all to do with business. But whatever it is, you've got to go back and stare it down because I don't think you'll ever be truly happy again until you put it all to rest. Do you understand what I'm saying?"

Jason nodded, for though he had tried to tell himself otherwise, he understood even better than his father.

"Good," Giulio continued, "because all I want for you is to be happy. That's more important to me than anything else. And I don't care what is that you do to make a living, whether it's being some corporate bigwig or it's pumping gas. Sure, you made some mistakes the first time you went out West—some big ones. But you owned up to what you did, lived with the consequences, and took your medicine. Now you're ready to start all over again. In my eyes, that makes you a success already, so don't worry about anything. Just get out there and do it. Do it right, and don't look back until you're ready because this place will always be here for you if you decide that's what you want. *Capisc'*?"

Jason nodded again before giving his father a sideways glance.

"You know, Dad, it's just an interview," he told him. "I might not even get the job."

"Don't worry, you'll get the job," said Giulio without a hint of doubt in his voice.

Jason took a deep breath and let it out. Whatever his misgivings on the matter, it seemed like things had been decided for him.

"So, what do I do now?" he asked.

Giulio shrugged and threw his hands up in the air.

"What do you think," he said, giving his son a gentle swat on the arm. "You go home and start packing before I change my mind and try to make you stay."

Raymond came to the house the following Monday morning to give Jason a ride to the airport. Natalie arrived soon after to see her brother off. Knowing that it would not be long before it was time for him to go, she stepped quickly out of the car and hurried up the front walk, carrying with her a small paper bag. Once inside the house, she found her brothers and father assembled at the kitchen table, an excited Sundance scurrying about with tail wagging.

"Last night I printed out the marketing plan I've been working on," Jason was saying, a nervous twinge in his voice as he slid a file folder across the table to his father. "It's all in here, pretty much, though I would have liked to do more with it. And don't forget, just because I might be away, there's still lots of things I can do for you, like finishing the Web site and some of the PR stuff."

"Yes, yes, yes," huffed Giulio with a bemused smile. He gave the other two a wink. "I'll look it all over as soon as I get a chance. Just finish your coffee now and get out of here, will you please? I've got things to do today, you know."

At that, while Raymond looked on, Natalie reached into the paper bag she had brought and pulled out a small, gift-wrapped package. "We bought you a little going-away present," she said, handing it to Jason before he could get out of his chair.

"What's this?" said Jason, truly touched.

"Just open it," prodded Raymond.

Jason unwrapped the package and broke out into a smile; inside it was a brand-new BlackBerry. It was a thoughtful gift, and Jason gave his brother and sister a nod of appreciation.

"What is it?" said Giulio, leaning closer to get a look. "It looks like a little computer or something."

"It's a cell phone, Dad," said Jason. "A really nice one."

"Hey, you can't be a big-shot corporate exec walking around with just a go-phone," said Raymond, looking pleased that the gift had been well received.

"This is great, guys," said Jason. "But you really didn't have to do it."

Natalie reached out and gave his cheek a pinch.

"We wanted to," she said. "Now you have no excuse for not calling home more often."

"That's right," echoed Raymond. "We prepaid you for six months. After that, of course, you're on your own. If you can't find a job by then, it's your own fault."

"You're all heart," chuckled Jason. Then, barely above a whisper, for suddenly he found himself getting choked up, "Thanks, guys."

His own eyes welling up, Giulio slapped his hand down on the table and pushed his seat back. "Now," he declared, getting to his feet, "I think it's time for you to go!"

When his bags were finally stowed in the trunk of Raymond's car, Jason stood for a short time in silence, not quite sure of what to say.

"Good luck, Jason," said Natalie, giving him a hug before he had a chance to speak. "Don't forget us this time, okay?"

"I won't," Jason promised as she pulled away from him and wiped a tear from her eye.

"And don't forget who you are, or where you came from,"

said Giulio. "When things get tough, that's all you need to know." Then he took his son in a warm embrace and kissed him on the forehead before pushing him away to the car. In another moment he was buckled in his seat next to Raymond, and then they were off.

As they drove away, Jason looked back at his father and sister, and waved good-bye to them through the open window. Natalie and Giulio waved in return until the car turned the corner and drove out of sight. When it was gone, the two stood there watching for a time, as if they expected it to suddenly reappear. When it did not, Natalie laid her head against her father's shoulder.

"I miss him already," she said with a sniffle.

Giulio put his arm around his daughter and gave her a squeeze. "So do I," he sighed.

Then he turned and walked slowly back to the house.

CHAPTER 37

By the time Giulio arrived there, later that same morning, the Bradley Mansion Inn had become a beehive of activity. The cleanup crew had arrived on the scene, signaling that the initial phase of the restoration was under way. Gladdened by the distraction of the hubbub, feeling once again like the captain of his ship, Giulio ambled about the place, monitoring the operation and chatting with the workers until Raymond returned and took over for him. Relieved of his duties, he wandered back to the study, where he slid in behind the desk. Natalie had gone off to buy sandwiches for lunch, so for the time being he had the room to himself. Given a moment of relative quiet, he took the opportunity to look over the file folder Jason had given him. He opened it and took out the top page.

"Marketing and Public Relations Strategies for the Bradley Mansion Inn," he read aloud. Then, with a bemused harrumph, "Sounds like serious business."

Giulio flipped through the document, perusing with interest the in-depth analyses Jason had made of the inn, its operations, and its competition. He was of course impressed by Jason's work, the thoroughness and attention to detail, but he was not at all surprised by it. Giulio well knew what his son was capable of once he set his mind to a task. He read on, skimming the contents until he came to a summary Jason had written of specific recommendations for what they should do when the inn was finally ready to be reopened. The first item took him aback.

"Rename the inn?" he read aloud with curiosity, and more than a little incredulity. Such an idea had never before occurred to him, and he was not at all sure of its wisdom. The Bradley Mansion Inn had an established reputation; it was solid and dependable and reassuring. One didn't just toss all that aside. Then there were the logistics of a name change to think about, the bank accounts, the stationery, the bed-and-breakfast directories, not to mention the sign out front. The list was longer than he cared to imagine. No, no, it was not a good idea at all, he decided straightaway. But then, after reading on a little further, Giulio stopped for a moment to consider the name that Jason had suggested. He stared at it for a time before sitting back in his chair. Rubbing his chin, he gazed thoughtfully off into space and repeated it two or three times to himself.

"Hmm," he finally grunted, his face brightening. "I kind of like that. Has a nice ring to it. I wonder why none of us ever thought of it before."

Giulio gave a laugh, marveling at what a difference a simple thing like the change of a name could make in his thinking. For so long he had felt stymied, fretting about the inn's future, but not knowing what to do, the well of his imagination seemingly run dry. Now, suddenly, a thousand fresh ideas were sprouting in his mind. It was as if with the planting of one tiny seed, a forest of trees had grown and blossomed in a twinkling. Giulio well understood that the renaming of a rose would not make it smell any sweeter, but he also understood that it just might be the thing to make one look at it in a new way, a way that might make all the difference in the world to the inn's future prospects.

Giulio was happily reflecting on these things when his reveries were interrupted by a soft knock at the door. Coming back to himself, he looked to the doorway, expecting to find one of the cleanup workers. Instead he was surprised to see a young woman standing there, cautiously poking her head inside.

Giulio broke out into a great smile.

"Well, hello, Miss Loren," he said with a distinct air of pleasure. Jason had made no mention of her for some time, and he had assumed, not without regret, that she and his son had gone their separate ways. He got to his feet and made a polite bow. "Please come in."

"I hope I'm not bothering you," said Claudia meekly. "You obviously have a lot going on right now."

"You're not bothering me at all," Giulio assured her. He gestured to the couch. "Come, sit for a few minutes and tell me what brings you here today. I hope it's not to take more pictures of our inn. As you can see, we're not exactly looking our best at the moment."

"I was driving by and decided to stop when I saw the windows boarded up and all the workers coming and going," she explained. "What happened?"

Giulio gave a laugh.

"We had a little incident a few nights back," he told her. "A fire broke out in the living room and caused quite a mess on the rest of the first floor as you have no doubt observed."

"A fire," Claudia gasped. "I hope no one was hurt."

"Fortunately we had no guests in the house at the time," said Giulio, "but my son did take a bit of a knock on the head."

"Jason?" she said with a start. "Is he okay?"

"Oh yes, don't worry, he's fine," said Giulio. Then he furrowed his brow and gave a low grumble of irritation. "Obviously he didn't tell you about any of this himself."

Claudia shrugged, the side of her mouth curling into a half smile as she cast her gaze down at her hands.

"Actually, we haven't talked at all for a while," she admitted a bit gloomily.

"Why on earth not?" asked Giulio abruptly, the words escaping his lips before he had properly considered them. Once they had been given voice, he gave a nervous cough and fell silent, astonished by his own nosiness. Then again, she was a beautiful girl, and he could not help thinking his son something of a numbskull for letting her get away.

"Well, it's complicated," she said with another shrug. Then, looking away, "I think Jason was just going through a lot when I last saw him."

"Ah, you noticed," said Giulio.

"It was hard not to."

"I suppose not," agreed Giulio. Then, smiling warmly at her, "But you know, I think he has almost made his way through all of it—or at least the worst of it. I'm guessing that he has you to thank for that."

Claudia's cheeks flushed ever so slightly.

"I don't know about that," she said, barely above a whisper.

"I do," said Giulio.

Claudia took a deep breath and looked back out through the door.

"Is Jason here today?" she asked with hopeful eyes.

Giulio rubbed the back of his neck and gave another nervous cough.

"I'm afraid not," he told her.

"He *is* okay, isn't he?" she asked, her eyes showing concern.

"Oh yes, he's fit as a fiddle," Giulio answered gently. "But it's just that—well, you see, he went back to California just this morning."

Though she seemed to Giulio not all that surprised at hearing the news, the young woman nonetheless heaved a sigh and bit her lower lip. She seemed on the verge of tears, but then she pulled herself together and held her head up straight.

"I suppose that will be for the best for him," she said, gulping back her emotions.

Giulio gave a sigh on his own.

"I guess only time will tell," he said.

The two talked for just a little while longer, enough to make Giulio saddened that things had not worked out between Claudia and his son. Later, after he had walked Claudia out to her car and bid her good-bye, he stood at the edge of the lawn and watched her drive away. After so many years as an innkeeper, he had long ago become accustomed to people coming and going through his world, but this day had seen two good-byes that had affected him most deeply. He had felt sad—hopeful yes, but sad nonetheless—to see Jason go, not knowing when he would see his son again. And now he felt strangely sad once more at seeing Claudia go. There was, he reflected, nothing to be done for it. It was simply one of those things that came with the job of living one's life.

So, with that thought in mind, he strolled back to the front door. He stopped at the threshold and paused for a moment to look back over his shoulder. He listened to the chatter of the birds and breathed in the pleasant air. It had turned into a beautiful day, full of all the promise of early spring. It might be nice, he thought, to putter around outside and enjoy it for a while, but at the moment there was work inside to be done. And so, with a resolute grunt, he trained his eyes forward once more and clasped his hands behind his back.

"Steady as she goes," he commanded himself before stepping back on board.

CHAPTER 38

Jason sat down on the grass beneath a tree near the edge of the beach, looked out across the waves tumbling over the sand, and let out a sigh. It was Saturday morning, five days since his return to Los Angeles. He had stopped by that same spot for a few minutes every morning and afternoon, watching, waiting, but never quite certain as to exactly what he was doing there, or what he hoped to accomplish. Since his return, he had been filled with an odd sense of futility about things, a nagging feeling in the back of his mind that for too long he had gone about things all wrong, that despite whatever he might do, nothing could ever truly be put right again or at least made to feel the same as it once had.

This disquiet struck him as exceedingly odd, especially considering how well the week had gone to that point. Jason had been staying at Eddie's place. He had planned to check into a hotel when he first arrived, but his friend would hear none of it. It was a great reunion, and the two had gone out on the town that night to celebrate, revisiting some of Jason's old haunts. Eddie had arranged for Jason's interview to take place on Friday—he wanted the company to talk to Jason last—so they had spent the intervening nights doing much the same.

Jason had enjoyed himself well enough, but not nearly with the enthusiasm he once had. Something had changed, exactly what he could not quite decide, but for all his love of the city, he now felt somehow out of place. Perhaps it was because in all their comings and goings around town, he had encountered few familiar faces, and the people he did recognize seemed to have already forgotten him.

Come Friday, his interview at Mixed Media Productions could not have turned out better if it had been scripted. Jason had gone into his meeting with Ted Dorman, the company president, fully prepared to be put on the spot and made to explain the ignoble circumstances surrounding his departure from Med-Device Technologies. To his surprise, not to mention enormous relief, no questions whatsoever arose about those dark final days at his former employer. Eddie, he reasoned, had no doubt smoothed the path over for him. Or maybe his friend had been right all along, maybe L.A. really was all about today, and yesterday no longer mattered.

Whatever the case, the interview was a cakewalk. After a long, cordial discussion of the production company's operations and future plans, and its needs for someone with Jason's talents, Dorman had taken him for a little tour. Mixed Media's headquarters was a modest affair—a small reception area, several offices, a conference room—but Jason could feel the energy of the place. He could hear it in the voices coming from the offices as they passed, and see it in the faces of the men and women who worked there. They were young, fresh, eager faces, the faces of people who were excited about what they were doing and believed that they were part of something that was going to be big. Though it seemed from another life, Jason well remembered that feeling. He found their energy infectious, and he wondered if perhaps at long last he was back in his element.

This notion remained undiminished when Dorman stopped outside an open door and gestured for Jason to have a look at the office inside.

"This office would be yours if you came on board," said the company president with an almost apologetic smile.

Jason stepped inside. The rather tiny office was empty at the moment, save for a desk, personal computer, and chair. As he looked about the room, though, Jason had chuckled inwardly. As compact as it might have been, it was positively cavernous by comparison to his little closet on the third floor of the Bradley Mansion Inn. And though it did not offer much of a view, this little office had the distinct advantage of a window.

"As you can see, we're not very big yet," Dorman told him, "but we're growing."

Jason had only nodded and smiled.

Later, when the two had returned to Dorman's office, the talk turned to salary requirements, and Jason knew right away that he had made a favorable impression. When it became clear that Jason's expectations as to starting pay were in line with what the fledgling company could offer, Dorman did not beat around the bush.

"I'll be honest with you," he told Jason. "I've interviewed a lot of people this week, but I think you'd be a great fit here, and I'd love to have you come to work for us. What do you say?"

Jason was truly flattered by the offer, and very tempted to jump at it, but something told him to hold back, and so he had remained noncommital.

"I like what I've seen and what you've told me about the company," said Jason truthfully. "And I know I would do a good job for you. But just the same, I'd like to have a chance to think about it—if you wouldn't mind."

Though plainly disappointed that Jason had not replied yes, Dorman nonetheless smiled and nodded.

"Of course," he told him. "It's Friday. How about you take the weekend to mull it over and let me know your decision on Monday? Sound like a deal?"

"It does," said Jason, nodding in agreement.

At that Dorman got to this feet.

"Well, it's been a pleasure meeting you," he said as the two shook hands. Then, just before Jason turned to go, he added, "I hope you'll come on board with us. I think you could go a long way with us."

Now, as Jason sat by the beach and looked out over the water, those words kept swirling ceaselessly in his mind. It puzzled him as to why until it suddenly came to him how much they reminded him of that long ago conversation with Phil Langway back when Jason had come to Los Angeles for the very first time. His life, he reflected, seemed to have come full circle. He just wasn't sure if he was at the end of one circle, or the beginning of another.

Leaning back against the tree trunk, Jason let his gaze carry him far away to the horizon where a boat, its sails filled with the warm, gentle breeze, was skimming along the rim of the world. From his perspective it was little more than a speck in the distance, and it struck him as odd to imagine that someone was out there riding the great swell of the tides, perhaps staring back toward him, contemplating the shore as if from a star. In his life, Jason had lived on both coasts of the United States, often little more than a stone's throw from the sea, but seldom had he taken the time to truly contemplate the great expanses of water that surrounded it. Now, as the sailboat drifted farther and farther from sight, looking as if it were about to fall off the edge of the world, he was filled with an immense awe at how vast and deep and enigmatic was the ocean. It made him feel very small.

From somewhere nearby came the sound of laughter and Jason found his attention drawn to it. He turned and saw a group of teenagers laying their towels out on the sand. Before long the bare-chested boys were tossing around a ball while a radio blared and the bikini-clad girls, chattering nonstop among themselves, stretched out to soak up the brilliant sunshine. They were a happy, carefree lot, and Jason envied them for it. Somewhere along the line, it seemed like he had forgotten how to forget things and simply play. It was a trait he needed to rediscover, if only he knew where inside himself to look.

Jason turned away and gazed pensively at the sea for a time before picking up a pebble resting beside his leg. He turned it over in his fingers, its surface cool and smooth to the touch like a rosary bead, as his thoughts drifted to his plans for the weekend. Eddie had made plans for that night to hit the party circuit with his new girlfriend, insisting that Jason come along. Then on Sunday, Jason was invited to tag along with them to the house of some friends to, as his friend put it, "do Pasqua." Come Monday, he would accept the position at Mixed Media—how could he turn it down?—and start looking around for a new place of his own. Everything was falling back into place, and he had every right to be happy about it, but to his annoyance he found that this simply wasn't so. With a grunt of frustration, he gave the pebble a last look and flicked it away. Things, he told himself, would work themselves out. He would have to resign himself to finding happiness somewhere else along the way.

With that thought in mind, Jason decided it was time to leave. He was about to get to his feet when, off in the distance, something caught his eye. He put a hand up to shield his eyes from the sun and gazed down the beach. Far off he saw two figures jogging side by side along the shoreline in his direction. As they drew closer, he could plainly see that it was a man and woman. A jolt of nerves twisting his stomach, he swallowed hard and watched all the more intently. Soon the couple loped effortlessly into plain view and came to a stop down by the water's edge directly in his line of sight. Now there was no doubt.

The young woman, her long blond hair glistening in the sunlight, gave the man a kiss and hand in hand the two began to make their away across the beach, passing nearby to where Jason sat. She glanced his way just once as they passed and continued on her way, but then stopped short and looked back again. She tilted her head sideways, a look of curiosity coming over her face. Then suddenly her eyes widened and she gaped at him in obvious disbelief.

"Jason?" she gasped, barely above a whisper.

Slowly, as if encumbered by heavy chains, Jason got to his feet, dusted himself off, and nodded her a greeting.

"Hello, Amanda," he said.

CHAPTER 39

One Saturday night, back when the two had first become involved, Jason took Amanda to one of the more trendy—not to mention outrageously expensive—restaurants in town. It was a night that ought to have been instructive for him, but its lesson would go ignored, for he was already far beyond smitten with her. The price of keeping Amanda entertained was only a matter of the most remote consideration. Nothing, in his mind, was too good for her.

Amanda was, of course, as stunning as ever, motivation enough for Jason to throw plenty of money around to make certain that the service would be suitably fawning. The restaurant's staff was more than equal to the task, bowing graciously to her every whim, and it turned out to be a delightful evening. Amanda seemed well pleased with the performance. That she was happy was all in the world that mattered to Jason, and he had walked out of the restaurant in high spirits.

They would be short-lived.

When the car drove up to the entrance where they stood waiting, the valet jumped out from behind the wheel and rushed to the passenger's side to hold the door for Amanda. As she pulled her legs inside the car, the overeager valet started to push the door shut just a moment too soon, bumping her shin. It was not much of a blow at all, and clearly unintentional, but

Amanda let out a screech as if she had been mortally wounded. The valet apologized profusely, but it did no good. Before Jason could come to her aid, an irate Amanda laid into the valet, up-braiding him in the harshest and most unjustified way for his clumsiness. Despite Jason's efforts to mollify her, she ranted on at the poor young man until he finally managed to get her set-tled in the car and shut the door.

Blind to the notion that she might have overacted, but mor-tified nonetheless at her outburst, Jason turned apologetic eyes to the valet and offered him a twenty-dollar bill for his troubles.

The valet gave a shrug and waved it away.

"Forget it," he told Jason with a roll of eyes. "I'm just lucky I'm not the one that has to get in the car with her."

Now, as he stood at last before Amanda, the unpleasant mem-ory came fresh to Jason's mind. Oddly enough, he found himself at a loss for words, much as he had that long ago evening.

Indeed, what was there to say?

Jason had no clue as to where to begin. He of course no longer held any illusions about himself and Amanda. There was absolutely nothing left between them, not the faintest flicker of the tenderness they once shared. That had all vanished in the fires of that terrible day when he last saw her, and it seemed as if Jason's entire world had fallen apart forever. But none of that mattered now, for he had not gone there that morning in the hope of rekindling what had been lost. Something else had im-pelled him to go, something that for a long time he had not quite been able to get his head and heart around, but that he now saw clearly. Deep inside him there was a wound that still had not closed, one he had tried his best to ignore. But in the long months since they had parted ways, a voice in the back of Jason's mind had always told him that one day he would need to confront her again. Now he understood why: it was his only hope of ever finding a way to bind his broken spirit once and for all. He had tried often enough to imagine how such a scenario would play out, what he would say and do, how he would act, how *she* would react, but now that the moment had come and he was at last once again facing her, words failed him.

Not that many would be needed, he surmised as he stood there before her. Judging by the look on Amanda's face—one, if not of contempt, than something much akin to it—he was certain that she was about to storm off without giving him the time of day. Instead, to his surprise, her demeanor gradually softened into an expression of what seemed to Jason mild curiosity, though it was unquestionably tinged with disdain. She assessed him with a jaundiced eye before turning to her companion, a lean, well-muscled young man of Jason's age with skin as bronzed from the sun as her own.

"Why don't you go back to the car, Greg?" she told him. "I'll be there in just a minute."

Greg obviously did not find the situation to his liking, for he stood there with neck bulled and muscles tensed, regarding Jason with a look of suspicion and thinly veiled malice.

"Are you sure?" he grunted.

"Don't worry," said Amanda, giving him a gentle shove to send him on his way. "Everything's fine. Just wait for me at the car."

With great reluctance, Greg slowly walked off, but not before shooting Jason a menacing look. Jason stood his ground, watching impassively until the other man was out of earshot before turning back to face Amanda. Then he gave a little cough to clear his throat.

"He, um, seems like a nice guy," he offered awkwardly, hoping to break the ice just a little.

Her arms now folded, Amanda struck a haughty pose and looked down her nose at him.

"What are you doing here, Jason?" she said, eschewing any gesture to niceties. Then, after a moment's pause, "I thought you had gone away forever."

Jason slipped his hands into his pockets and gave a shrug.

"I thought so too," he replied. "It's just that—"

"I hope you haven't come here thinking that somehow you can get back together with me," she blurted before he could finish. "Because if you did, forget about it. I have nothing to say to you."

"No, it's nothing like that," said Jason, shaking his head. "I promise." He sat back down on the grass and gestured to the spot next to him. "Please, could we just talk for a minute? That's all I ask, and then I won't ever bother you again."

Amanda made no reply, but stood there assessing him with a wary gaze. Just then the breeze suddenly picked up, nudging across her face a few strands of her long, fine hair. With a practiced toss of her head, she casually flipped them aside. As she did so, Jason could not help but still admire her. She was as beautiful as ever, the blond hair and sleek jawline, her figure still slender and graceful like a statue. All the same, lovely as she was, Jason realized that hers was a beauty he no longer yearned to touch.

"Just one minute, and that's all," she finally told him.

Casting a glance in Greg's direction, she came closer and settled down beneath the tree, a discreet arm's length away from him. There she extended her legs and reached for her toes, easing herself forward until she had fully stretched out.

"So, how long have you been back in L.A.?" she asked with an air of indifference as she relaxed into the stretch and rested the side of her head against her knees.

Jason took a deep breath and looked away to the ocean as he let it out. For a few moments he scanned the horizon, hoping to once more spy the sailboat, but by now it was long gone from sight.

"I came for an interview," he said at last, looking only briefly her way before fixing his gaze once more on the sea. "Someone in the city offered me a job."

"A job?" she snickered. "Wow, that couldn't have been easy to pull off, especially for someone with your résumé."

Though he knew it was well deserved, the remark stung him, the wound inside twisting into a painful knot. Nonetheless he shrugged it off, not letting the hurt show on his face. This, he told himself, was something he had chosen to put himself through, and he would have to see it through to the end without complaint.

"Nothing comes easy these days," he said with another shrug. "But I guess, in a way, my résumé is why I came here."

Amanda straightened up and gave him a questioning look. "What do you mean?"

Jason let out a sigh and forced himself to look squarely in her eyes.

"Amanda, what I did was so wrong," he began. "What I did to you, what I did to your father and everybody at the company. And there's nothing I can do to erase it, nothing I can do to make up for it all. I ruined everything." He paused and shook his head glumly. "You know, for a long time I tried to convince myself that I had done it for you, but the truth is that I was just selfish and afraid, and I let myself get sucked right into the whole thing. It was all me, and there was just no excuse for it. Anyway, I'm never going to stop being sorry for it. I just wanted you to know that."

If what he had said moved her in any way, Amanda did not show it. Instead she looked at him and gave a dismissive laugh.

"Jason, get over it," she huffed. "Life goes on. After what you did, my father took the company's operations and merged it with one of his others. You and your friends cost him a lot of time and money and embarrassment, but he wasn't about to let some little bunch of peons ruin his plans and let it all go to waste. He moved on, so did all the people who worked for him—and so did I. You should do the same."

With that Amanda stood, adjusted her running clothes, and brushed her hands together as if ridding herself of him for the last time. Jason got to his feet as well.

"There's just one more thing," he hurried to say before letting her go.

Amanda eyes flashed impatience.

"What now?" she said, her voice dripping condescension.

Jason swallowed hard, for the time had come to face the worst of it. His eyes suddenly full of sorrow, his face no longer able to conceal the pain he had been carrying inside, he bowed his head.

"It's about the baby," he murmured, barely above a whisper. "I need to talk about it."

Amanda made no reply, but gave him a queer sort of look.

"The what?" she said.

"You know, the baby," said Jason a little louder for her benefit.

Amanda looked confused and taken aback.

"What are you talking about?" she said. Then all at once it dawned on her and she put her hand to her mouth to conceal a smile.

"Oh, that," she said in an offhanded way. She rolled her eyes and gave a shrug. "I don't know how to tell you this, Jason, but there was no baby."

"I know," Jason told her, heaving a heavy sigh. "I understand why you didn't want to keep it. It's just that—"

"No, Jason," Amanda cut him off, "you don't understand. What I'm telling you is that there was no baby at all, not then, not ever. Get it?"

Now it was Jason's turned to look confused. His mind whirling, he cocked his head to one side, as if he hadn't heard her properly.

"H-h-how do you," he stammered. "I mean . . . I don't understand. What are you trying to say?"

Amanda gave a groan of consternation and rolled her eyes again.

"Look," she told him. "You had been acting all weird and distant and distracted—and of course we all know why now, but I didn't then. I didn't know what was going on inside your head, and I just needed to know where I stood with you. I think I had a right to know. So I said what I said to find out, and I let you think what you wanted, and that's all there was to it."

Jason stared at her wide-eyed.

"Are you telling me you lied?" he gasped.

Amanda clicked her tongue in scorn.

"Oh, please," she said with a sneer. "Welcome to L.A. You thought I was pregnant and I wasn't. What's the big deal? Besides, what difference would it have made even if I had been?"

Jason could scarcely believe his ears. His jaw dropped open as he thought back on all the months he had tortured himself, all the guilt-ridden nights he had passed, anguishing for no reason over something that had never been. For a fleeting moment he was filled with outrage and bitterness at the thought that she could have purposely deceived him this way, but then suddenly both gave way to something miraculous, the power and wonder of it washing over him like a wave.

Release.

Jason looked away from her, his eyes roaming the great wide ocean as he realized what her revelation meant to him. He was free at last. That terrible, ponderous weight, the boot against his chest that had been squeezing every hope of joy out of him had finally lifted.

His eyes welling up, Jason turned back, his face beaming. "It makes all the difference in the world," he told her.

The sudden change in his countenance must have startled Amanda, for she quickly took a step back.

"Whatever," she said with a huff, backing slowly away. Then, without another word, she turned on her heel and hurried off to her car where Greg stood waiting.

Jason watched her go, his heart growing lighter with every step she took away from him. And when at last she reached the car, and Greg held open the door, all he could think of was how lucky he felt at not being the one who had to get in the car with her.

After the two finally drove out of sight, Jason leaned back against the tree and collapsed down to the ground. There he sat, holding his head in his hands, happy beyond words, but totally spent. It was if he had just awoken from a long, heart-pounding nightmare that he had feared would never end. To his amazement, dawn had come again. All the darkness that had overshadowed his life had finally been dispelled, and the light was pouring back in.

Tears rolling down his cheeks, Jason turned grateful eyes upward.

"Thank you," he whispered wearily, over and over again until the tears all had run their course and his eyes were once more dry and clear. Then he sat up straight and looked all about in wonder at the bright, beautiful world that surrounded him. Suddenly he felt like a giddy George Bailey, ready to go running through the streets of his beloved Bedford Falls. But Jason knew that Los Angeles was not Bedford Falls, and its streets were not his own. He realized just then that, for all his dreams and ambitions, they never had been. Amanda had spoken true about one thing, it really was time for him to move on, and for the first time since he could remember, he knew exactly what he wanted to do.

In a mad rush, Jason fumbled through his pockets until he managed to fish out the BlackBerry. In a flash he used it to connect to the Internet, his eyes glued to the little screen as he feverishly worked the buttons. Soon he had navigated to the proper Web site and found the information he was seeking.

His breath quickening, Jason gazed at the screen. There was a flight leaving early that afternoon. If he left right away, and the traffic wasn't too bad, he just might be able to get to the airport in time.

Jason sprang to his feet. It was time to go, but first he had a call to make. He dialed the number, put the phone to his ear, and waited until he heard his father's voice on the other end of the line.

"Dad, it's me," he said.

"Hey, Jason," his father replied happily. "I've been waiting for you to call. How are things going? Did everything turn out the way you hoped?"

"Yeah, Dad," Jason told him. "Everything turned out just great."

"So, what are you going to do?"

Jason stepped out from beneath the shadow of the tree, back into the warmth of the brilliant sunshine, and smiled.

"I'm coming home," he said.

CHAPTER 40

Roused from a sound sleep by the sudden jolt of the wheels touching down on the runway, Jason opened his eyes, straightened up, and looked out the window just as the plane came roaring to a stop. It was Sunday morning, and he was back in Providence.

From all around him came the metallic clicking of seat belts being unbuckled, and soon passengers were standing in the aisle, tugging their belongings from the overhead compartments. With a yawn, Jason wiped the sleep from his eyes and settled back once more in his seat as the plane taxied slowly to the gate. He was in no hurry to jump up, not because he wasn't happy to be back home, but simply because he had no luggage stored overhead to worry about. Slowed by the traffic on the expressway on his way to the airport the previous day, and delayed at the agency when he stopped to drop off his rental car, Jason had narrowly missed the early flight out of Los Angeles. With no other afternoon flights available, he had no choice but to wait around and take the red-eye later that night. In his haste to get to the airport, he had left all his luggage behind at Eddie's, trusting his friend to send it along whenever he got the chance. With time on his hands, Jason had briefly considered running back to retrieve his things, but instead decided to stay put in the airport. He did not want to take the risk of somehow missing the last flight. Besides, he had brought nothing with him to L.A. that could not be replaced.

When at last the plane pulled up to the gate, and the hatch was opened, Jason gave a quick stretch of his arms and rolled his stiff neck. He had stayed in California just long enough to adjust to Pacific time, and now the combined effects of the late flight and jet lag were already settling in on him. He yawned again and passed a hand through his tousled hair. He knew he was a sight, but what did he care? The long journey was over. Tired as he was, he still felt like he could climb Mount Everest, so he dragged himself to his feet and filed off the plane with the others.

When he stepped out into the surprisingly busy main terminal, Jason stopped and looked about, searching for either his father or brother. Giulio had assured him that someone would be there to meet him, and Jason fully expected to find either of the two waiting. Perhaps that's why he didn't notice the young woman standing nearby. Dressed all in white, she was looking his way with affectionate eyes, a mischievous smile illuminating her face.

"Do you need help, little boy?" she called to him. "Are you lost?"

His heart soaring at the sound of the familiar voice, a delighted Jason whirled around at once to face her.

"Claudia!" he exclaimed. He was grinning from ear to ear and there was nothing he could do to stop it. "What are you doing here?"

Claudia gave a little shrug and stepped close to him, her hands held demurely behind her back.

"Your father called me and said you might need a ride to Mass this morning," she said, gazing up into his eyes with such warmth that he could not have looked away even if he had wanted to. "It is Easter Sunday, you know."

"I'd almost forgot," said Jason.

Claudia looked to one side of him and then to the other.

"No baggage, I see," she said.

Jason gave a little shrug of his own.

"I'm traveling light these days," he told her.

"That's a good thing," said Claudia, stepping closer still so that Jason could breathe in the heavenly scent of her hair. She reached up and touched his face. "So, why did you come back?" she asked, caressing his cheek. "I heard you passed up a really nice job out there. What happened, was it the money?"

Jason shook his head and chuckled.

"Nope," he told her, leaning closer. "For once money had nothing to do with it."

At that Claudia clicked her tongue and draped her arms around his neck.

"You're not much of a businessman," she said just before their lips came together.

Later that afternoon, the two went to Natalie's house. At seeing him come through the front door, little Tommy and Jenna ran for their uncle Jason. Jason scooped the two toddlers up into his arms and carried them around as he introduced Claudia to the family. Then it was off to the dining room where a veritable feast awaited them all. Laid out on the table was an enormous antipasto platter layered with lettuce and tomatoes and piled with cheese and olives, roast peppers and artichokes, rolls of salami and prosciutto, and more. After this would come a ham and roasted leg of lamb and vegetables, not to mention a pan of lasagna and another of stuffed peppers Donna had baked. And if all that wasn't enough, afterward for dessert there would be Aunt Gracie's ricotta and rice pies, a loaf of sweet Easter bread, cookies and biscotti and other treats.

As they all gathered around the table, Raymond hastily went about, pouring the wine. When they were all seated, he tapped his fork against his glass to get everyone's attention.

"Listen up, everybody," he said. "I—I mean we—have a little announcement to make."

Donna was beaming now.

"Make it a very little one," joked Uncle Ernie. "We're all starving!"

"Ernie!" exclaimed Aunt Gracie, giving her husband an elbow in the ribs.

Raymond wasted no time, but got straight to the point.

"All I wanted to say is that pretty soon Tommy and Jenna are going to have a cousin," he told them.

There was a pause, for it took a moment for the meaning of the happy announcement to sink in. Then it was bedlam as they all realized that Donna was expecting, and it seemed like everyone was laughing and shouting for joy all at once. When the tumult finally settled down, Jason reached out and patted his brother on the shoulder.

"Nice going, big bro," he said.

Raymond could only smile in return.

Now it was Giulio's turn to speak. He stood and took his wineglass in hand.

"Well," he began, his face flush with joy. "It looks like this is a day of new beginnings. So here's to the newest member of the family, whatever his or her name is."

"Hear, hear!" said Natalie's husband, Michael, and the rest joined in.

"And who can say, maybe we'll be welcoming someone else to the family someday?" continued Giulio with a wink to Claudia.

"Don't listen to him," laughed Jason, squeezing her hand. "He'll just want you to come to work for him."

"I wouldn't mind," she said.

"Ah, and that brings me to one more new beginning," said his father. He gave Jason a sideways glance. "I've decided, at someone's suggestion, that when we reopen, we should rename the inn. How does the name *Villa Mirabella* sound to everyone?"

"Hey, I like it," said Raymond after a moment's consideration.

"Me too," added Natalie.

"Then that settles it," said Giulio, raising his glass once more. "To Villa Mirabella."

"To Villa Mirabella!" they all cried.

Then, when grace was said, and the chorus of "*salute*" and "*Buona Pasqua*" had subsided, they all settled down to eat.

Jason did not dig in right away, but instead looked happily at the faces gathered roundabout the table. His father, he reflected, had been right. He *had* been very lucky, and everything really had happened to him for a reason. At the touch of Claudia's shoulder against his, he realized that it had been a very good one. He saw now that everything was going to be all right, and always would be so long as he had life and love and family and friends to get him through. There was nothing for him to fear anymore, so he settled back and took a sip of wine, savoring with gladness the delicious warmth of it. He smiled and at long last, Jason Mirabella breathed easy.

VILLA MIRABELLA

PETER PEZZELLI

ABOUT THIS GUIDE

The suggested questions are included to
enhance your group's reading of Peter Pezzelli's
Villa Mirabella.

DISCUSSION QUESTIONS

1. Disgraced and discouraged, Jason swallows his pride and returns to Rhode Island. When he shows up at home, his father takes him in without question. Have you ever found yourself in Jason's position? Was your reception the same? Have you ever been in Giulio's position, welcoming a wayward child back into the fold? Why is it so hard to come home sometimes?

2. When Giulio tells them that Jason has returned, Ray and Natalie seem less than enthused by the news. Why is there an undercurrent of tension among the siblings? How do the dynamics of family, and of family businesses, influence the story?

3. Jason is surprised to discover that Ray is a talented woodworker, and that Natalie writes poetry. That he had never known these things about his brother and sister troubles him, and he laments to his father that he doesn't know people as well as he thought he did. Have you ever had a similar experience with someone in your own family? How did it make you feel?

4. Psychologists tell us that birth order can play an important role in personalities and family relationships. How does being the youngest child affect Jason's place in the family and his life choices? Are his decisions typical? What about Ray and Natalie?

5. Jason is tormented with guilt by his belief that Amanda has aborted their unborn child. Why does he react this way? Is his reaction one that most men would have today?

6. Because of his feelings of guilt, Jason holds back from Claudia, in effect disqualifying himself from her love, instead of moving forward with his life. Have you ever let negative feelings about your past hold you back from pursuing something or someone you love?

7. In the end, Jason learns that he has been deceived, that the terrible thing he thought about himself—and the one that caused him the most grief—was not really true. Ought he have displayed more anger at this revelation? How might you have reacted?

8. Giulio seems content to limit his romantic pursuits to occasional dinners with one of the "lasagna ladies." Why does he not seem interested in starting a deeper and more meaningful relationship with a woman?

9. Mrs. Martinez tells Jason that there is always love between us and our family members—even if sometimes we would like to strangle them! Have you found this to be so in your own family?

10. When we first encounter Jason, he is broke and broken, fearful, physically and emotionally exhausted, and spiritually drained. What phases does he go through in renewing himself?

11. Claudia tells Jason that asking for forgiveness doesn't magically make everything all right, but it gives one a place to start over again. Is this really so? If true, what implications does it have for our lives?